TO SLAY A DEMON

EMRY'S DEMONS

BOOK ONE

Gili Levy

TO A SLAY DEMON

Emry's Demons

Book One

Gili Levy

I am not what happened to me,
I am what I choose to become.

— Dr. Carl Jung

Dedication

To whoever is having a bad day, this book is for you.

Table of Contents

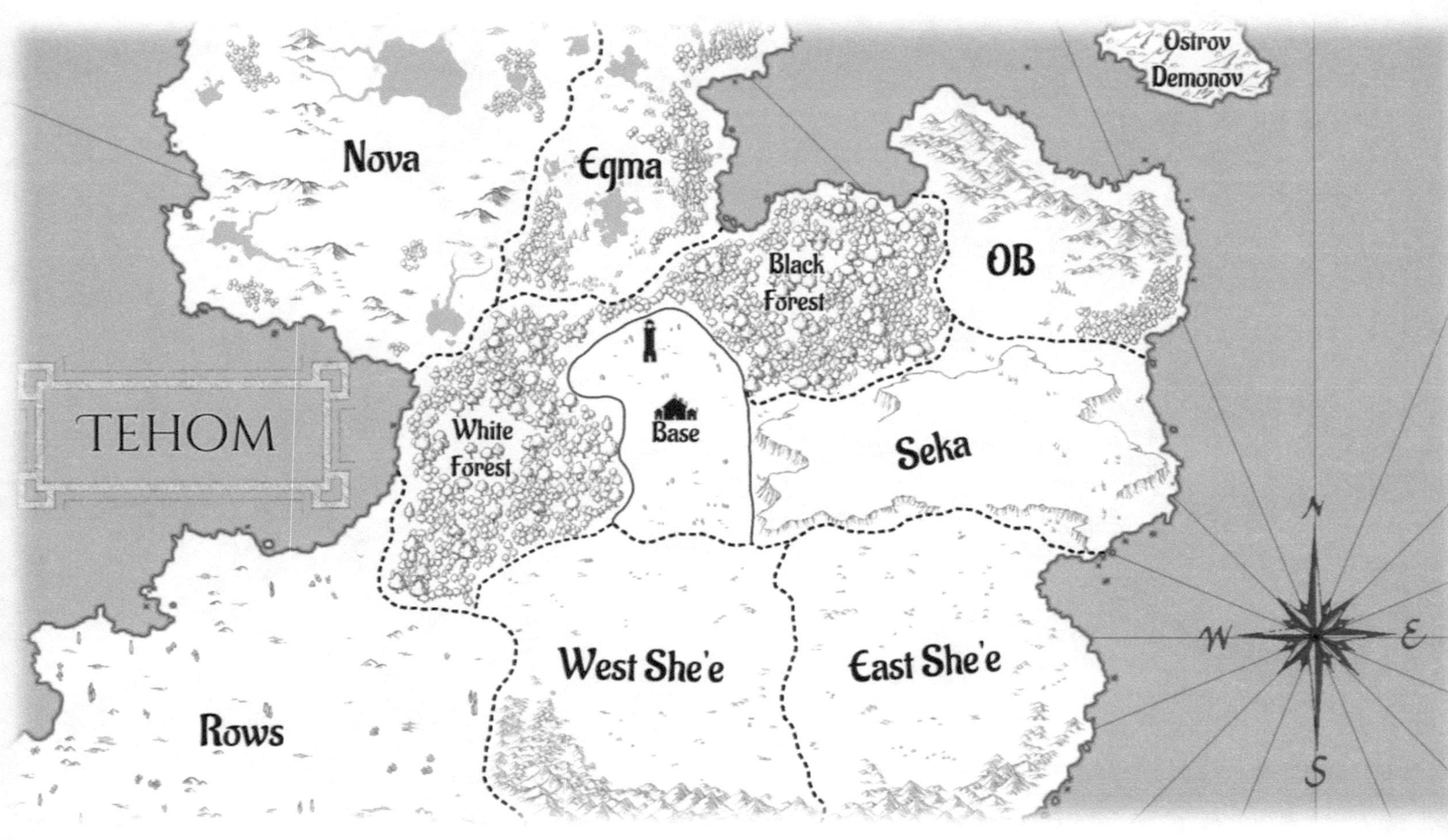

Ostrov Demonov
Nova
Egma
Black Forest
OB
TEHOM
White Forest
Base
Seka
Rows
West She'e
East She'e
N
E
S
W

Chapter 1

The Duels

Emry

This was the moment of truth, and Emry knew it. This was what she had been studying, training, and *fighting* for over the past few years.

And she was going to nail it.

She had to stand out from the masses. Ever since The Great War, children would join the army if there was nothing else waiting for them. Orphans, thieves, the starving, the unwanted—the army took them all to participate in the fight against demons. Some of these newly enlisted soldiers would be given a weapon and become slayers. They were paid well for risking their lives, that's for sure. Emry was downright poor, so enlisting at only twelve and leaving school behind was the only way to guarantee the survival of her parents and little sister. It had been nearly a decade since then. She was grown now. She was strong, and she was fearless.

That's what fighting did to a person. She and her squad had faced the cruelest of demons—the ugliest, the darkest. Now, many years later, it was *her* turn—and the turn of everyone who had enlisted at the same time. If they failed, the army would discharge them, and they would find themselves on the streets. If she failed, she and her family would be done for. Since the Slayer unit was the biggest in the army, their numbers would be cut drastically.

The soldiers were tested at the end of each quarter, giving them only two years to study and train between tests. Every eight years, closing a cycle, they were tested for leadership and for continuation in the army. The examinations for the Slayer unit included a timed, comprehensive knowledge exam and the

Duels. Emry had already finished the exam and knew she'd done well, but she wasn't sure it would be enough. Now, she was waiting on the smelly floor full of crumpled mattresses for her final combat, watching others fight their own. Winning one match wasn't even enough. They had to defeat enough of their comrades to truly stand out, or the army could still discharge them.

"Look." Shelly, another Slayer, pointed at the wall. "They're posting the knowledge scores."

Silence. A hush came over the room as three commanders entered carrying a sheet of paper with the ID numbers of the soldiers who'd passed the exam, ranked from first to last. Emry fisted her fingers. The weighted average of both the knowledge examination and the Duels would eventually determine the scores, so being rated first in the written test was important. She just had to be first. She had to be. She had been studying for that exam for years. *Years.* When her friends hung out, she would often stay alone and read.

The army was giving a prize for the soldier who ranked first overall in the combined categories. That soldier would be awarded a prestigious position and *a lot* of money. Money was all she could see, as she had been giving it everything she had.

Waiting for the results of the first test, her heart was pounding and her leg was irritably tapping on the floor. The commanders were taking their time, as if deliberately provoking everyone. Her big, green eyes stared at them impatiently.

She had to be first. She had to be first. She *had* to be first.

Her heart stopped as they attached the scores to the wall. Her ID *was* there, but it wasn't first. She could feel the rage inside of her—red, hot, angry violence spreading through her veins. She was rated second.

One of her teammates was patting her on the back as she took a deep breath. "It's a good score, Tiger."

"Thank you." Emry exhaled. "But it's not what I wanted."

She'd already been through eight combats by now, all of them against men, all of them she'd defeated. Each of her teammates was taken down in the Duels, but she stayed on. She was a beast, even if she didn't look like one. She knew that even though their own affairs with the army were over, her teammates were rooting for her. Finally, after years of hell by their hands, she became their star. Their tiger.

Each one of the six nations had its own symbol. An owl for Seka, a butterfly for Ob, a Chameleon for She'e. Born and raised in Rows, hers was one of the few Tiger families who survived The Great War. She hadn't had any choice but to enlist, especially after the Tigers betrayed humankind, sided with demons, and lost the war. Now, even years later, her family was still in constant danger. Not only from other people, but also from starvation. Someone had to get the money home, and the army was the only option. Her parents were too old to enlist, her sister too young. Regardless, Emry would never let her enlist, so there was no other option except for her. When she'd enlisted, she had been told that she was the only Tiger serving. Everyone called her Tiger, and it stuck. By now, only her family called her by her private name.

It was an insult. She knew it. But it was better than calling her a "demonizer"—a demon lover. In every bone in her body, she was a Slayer. Through the hard, dirty missions that they were assigned, Emry had proven it to them, and to herself. She was no demonizer, but she stayed a Tiger. And she knew she always would.

Standing tall with her arms folded, Emry waited, watching the others duel. The participants could fight to death, but it rarely went that far. She saw soldiers standing around, trying to guess who'd have the upper hand. She couldn't, for the life of her, understand how someone had managed to beat her in the knowledge test. She knew everything! *Everything*!

After a while, there was only one other soldier left; they were the last two standing. It was time.

Emry was going to fight once more for the top spot; she knew that she would not be brought down again. She would smash that soldier, whoever they were. She could already feel the animalistic urge to *hit*, to *hurt*, and then she saw who her opponent was. He was a tall guy—a *big* guy—all muscles beneath his smooth, tanned skin. He had black hair, a square jaw, and glinting ochre eyes.

Even Emry, a girl who almost never left the residence and rarely bothered to socialize, knew his name.

Damon Primrose.

His unique, magnetic eyes were happy in the triumph of victory, rounded by long, black eyelashes. Talking to a crowd of admirers surrounding him, he didn't look tense at all. He stood in the middle of them, cheerful, oblivious to how much the next moment was meaningful—not just for her, but for him as well.

"I can't believe you're up against him," one of her teammates said. "You know Primrose was in the elite group, right?"

"*Really?*" Emry narrowed her eyes.

"Yeah, and he didn't let anybody down. I've heard he killed more demons than all his teammates put together."

"Well, look at him," a girl said dreamingly. "God, I'd let him slay me if he wanted to."

Emry clenched her jaw. It seemed that this combat wouldn't be easy, but she didn't care. She hadn't been classified to the elite group of Slayers when she'd enlisted, but now things were different. *She* was different.

All the soldiers stepped back to the walls, clearing the middle area for the final duel. There was silence as Headley, the sixty-year-old unit commander, arrived. His tired yet strong blue eyes searched the crowd until he found what he was searching for, wordlessly summoning Emry and her rival to him.

They stepped in front of each other as Headley was talking, congratulating the ones who had won enough combats to continue their path in the army, offering goodbyes and gratitude to the ones who hadn't, and wishing them well.

Both Emry and Damon had made it, for sure. Neither would be kicked out. Now, it was just time to declare the winner, the best Slayer of their cycle, the one who would take the title and a pile of money. How many times had she dreamed of the moment Headley would raise her arm and declare her the winner? How many times had she dreamed of seeing the look in her family's eyes the moment she returned home with the cash?

Lost in thought, Emry suddenly noticed that her opponent was staring at her. He was frowning like he couldn't understand something. Good. Maybe he'd be baffled during their fight.

Up close, she could better appreciate his body. She'd seen a lot of muscular men, but most were wide where he was tall and broad. She couldn't see an inch of him, which wasn't smooth muscle. His body looked menacing, dangerous. If it wasn't for the smile that appeared on his face earlier, maybe she would have been more afraid to go up against him.

Maybe he just didn't get how someone like her had made it this far. Maybe he expected to face a man, not a girl with bright, ginger hair that was now tied up in a long ponytail. The moment he understood that she was looking back at him, his face relaxed, and then he smiled at her. She didn't smile back. Irritation started to swirl her stomach in reaction.

"So," Headley roared, "for the last time this cycle, Primrose, Tiger, are you ready?"

"Yes, sir!" they both responded in unison before looking at each other, ready to pounce.

"Duel!" Headley yelled and backed away.

Emry moved cautiously, her eyes watching her rival's every step. There was a wicked glint in his golden eyes. Was this amusing for him? Did he actually think he could take her down that easily?

When he took a step forwards, she made her move; a move she'd mastered over the years. The secret was in the speed of the rattling, unexpected hit. And she was always the fastest.

She raised her leg in one long lift, aiming for his throat. This usually left her opponents stunned on their knees, but he caught her leg before it could hit him.

What?

Emry felt his hand twisting her ankle and knew he was going to try to bring her down. She used his hand as an anchor to lift herself to the other side of him, her elbow pointed at his head.

Thwack! She hit him! She felt victorious, but at that exact moment, his knee met her arm and his other arm wrapped around the back of her other leg, bringing her down.

She tried to move, but he brought his leg over both of hers. How did he manage to push her legs to the ground with only one of his?

Damon's arm went to pin both of her arms the same way, like her punches did nothing to him, and she *knew* she was strong. He didn't even budge.

When all that was left for her to use was her head, he brought his other arm down, and with only two fingers, pushed her head back down. Her hair lost the tie holding it and spread on the mattress as Headley was counting next to them.

His body was almost pressed to hers. His eyes, now wild and animalistic, were staring down at her. But she couldn't even see his face. She couldn't see anything.

"Two! One!" Headley called. "Separate!"

Damon gently let go of her body and stood up, offering her his hand. Instead of taking it, she stood up on her own, dismissing him. All she could do was look down as Headley took both of their arms and lifted Damon's, declaring him the winner. Everyone cheered and clapped as her world shattered to pieces.

Humiliated, she stood there, knowing that she would never forget this moment. Nothing would ever be the same.

Emry felt everyone's eyes on her as she hurried across the hall and stormed out.

All this time that she'd spent was for nothing. All of her effort, for nothing. She was so angry she could have killed somebody. Why couldn't she kill *him?*

"Hey! Wait!"

She froze and turned around to see Damon Primrose trying to catch up to her. When he was only a step away, he stopped and smiled.

"This was a really good fight, the longest I've had," he said, offering her his hand again. "I just wanted to say good job." His deep voice had tenderness in it.

She stared at his hand, seething. "I don't want to shake your hand." Her tone was venomous. "I hate you. We're allowed to fight until one of us is dead, right?" She turned her back to him and pushed the door open. "You should have just killed me."

Chapter 2

Co-Leaders

Damon

"You should have just killed me."

Jenna shook her head, and her brown curls swayed. "I can't believe she said that to you. What a sore loser."

Damon sighed. His eyes scanned the forgotten, dusty corridor in the Intelligence building. "The thing is, she actually did really well, you know? She lasted longer than anyone else I've fought. Did she really think she could beat me?"

"Maybe she doesn't really know you." Jenna shifted her hazel eyes to look at him. "Have you seen her around?"

"No, never. I was very surprised when I saw her. She didn't look like a Slayer, but she still made it to runner-up."

"Really? What did she look like?"

"She looked..." Damon pondered. *Like she really wanted to kill me.* "She's a redhead, but there's something with her hair. It's really bright."

Jenna squinted her eyes. "What's her name?"

"Headley called her Tiger."

"I think I know who you're talking about. I helped to design a mission for her team last year when they hunted a demon in Seka. They talked about a girl who had to cover her hair because of its color."

"So what's her name?" Damon turned to look at her, and Jenna raised her brows.

"I don't know her private name since nobody uses it."

"She's a Tiger, which means that she's from Rows. It's a long way to get here from there."

"Yeah."

"If I had seen her wandering around, I would have thought she was Intelligence like you, you know?"

Jenna chuckled and playfully pulled at the sleeve of her purple uniform. "Too bad only Owls can be Intelligence. We also have to pass an interview and math tests before the army accepts us, unlike you Slayers."

"Yeah, we just have to risk our lives on missions. Not a big deal. Oh, and go through the Duels. That's real fun."

"Speaking of which, how was your victory party tonight? Sorry I couldn't come," she said, peeking up at him. "Did you score?"

He laughed and gazed at her. "Your mind is always in the gutter, huh?"

"*Yours* usually is."

"No, I had prior plans and stuff with someone who is really nice, but..."

He knew his best friend would be onto him eventually, but he didn't want to expose himself yet. Maybe he was making a big deal out of it for no reason at all, and he'd come back to his senses tomorrow. Still, he couldn't erase *her* accusing eyes from his mind. It made him feel uncomfortable. He didn't feel like celebrating at all.

"But?"

"I don't know. Must be tired."

"Interesting."

"What?"

"Just trying to remember when was the last time you were too tired for anything."

"Am I allowed to be tired? *Please*, Jenna?"

"Whatever." She rolled her eyes. "I'll keep an eye on you. You're getting your own team to lead soon. You need to be at your best."

He grinned. "It'll be great. I'm a fantastic role model, after all. Those lucky kids who get to be my soldiers will have a lot to learn from me."

Jenna put her face in her palm. "You caused so many problems in your former squad that you're lucky Headley didn't kick your ass. The only reason you're still here is because you're somehow good at everything without even trying."

"Yeah, huh? I bet you're jealous. I could have also been a better Intelligence officer than you."

"You wouldn't even make it to the interview, you podge."

* * *

The next day, Damon was waiting in front of Headley's office. The old man was supposed to arrive with his future co-leader, the partner with whom he would lead their new group of soldiers. He couldn't wait.

The army always assigned two leaders to each group of soldiers. The responsibility over novices—teaching them, training them—was too much for just one soldier. In missions, when leaders were responsible for their teams making it back to the base in one piece, it was crucial to have two instead of one.

When Headley walked in with *her* following, Damon's breath caught in his throat.

Emry's chin was pointed out proudly, and her high ponytail waved with each step. Once her green eyes landed on him, she stopped in her tracks. "*You.*"

If looks could kill... There was so much hate in her eyes that he wasn't sure how long he had before he'd burst into flames. He raised his arms in surrender.

Headley stood between them and sighed. "Primrose, Tiger, since you two made first and second place, you will be leading the new elite group enlisting this year. The day—"

"Wait," Emry interrupted, her eyes widening. "First *and* second place?"

Headley nodded tiredly. "You made it second at both examinations, and Primrose made it first at both of them."

As if she couldn't believe what she was hearing, she slowly turned to face him. "You're the one who beat me in the knowledge exam?"

At that moment, God alone knew why Damon wanted to say no, just so she wouldn't be so upset. But now he held her focus. For some reason, he wanted to keep on holding onto it.

"Guess I am." He flashed Emry a cocky grin. He saw her clenching her fists again and forced himself to shake it off. If she wanted to act out, then it was not his problem.

"Anyway, kids," Headley said. "I hope you're going to work well together, to be *professionals*, yeah? Primrose, I don't want to see you pulling any crap in front of your soldiers. Tiger, I'm counting on you."

Damon could see her shoulders relax a bit.

"What?" He pouted dramatically at his commander. "Seriously?"

Headley rolled his eyes. "You may be a monster when it comes to slaying demons, but I can't praise your behavior so far. You have to stop partying the way you do, stop talking back to your commanders, and start taking things seriously."

Damon rolled his eyes. "False accusations," he told his commander, who was absolutely right.

Even though Damon had a long history of disobeying him, he'd learned to fully appreciate the old man. He was probably in his sixties, but he never complained, never broke a sweat. He kept on training, exercising, and dieting; never letting himself go. He was a true leader, and Damon didn't have a single doubt when following him.

Headley sighed. "I want you two to sit together and review the info on your new soldiers, understood? I have their files with me. The novices are coming here tomorrow. Let me remind you that they're not just anybody, they're the most talented kids we found. I want you to bring out the greatness in them."

They both nodded as Headley handed Emry the files.

"How old are they?" she asked, her eyes scanning the files. Damon marveled at how soft her voice sounded—when it wasn't addressing him.

"Not too young." Headley scratched his light-gray hair. "I think the youngest is maybe fourteen."

She nodded. "Probably makes it easier."

"You two enlisted at twelve and thirteen, so you had plenty of experience by the time you were their age."

She peeked at him, probably surprised at the young age at which he'd enlisted. But then again, he was surprised to hear about her, too.

"Well then, nice job at the exams, both of you. Now go do your work." Headley slumped on the chair behind his desk and waved them off.

Damon opened the door, and she waited for him to move past it, but he held it for her to go first. She made a face at him but walked through anyway. When he closed it, she was already walking far ahead.

"Wait up!" he called, hurrying after her. She was fast, he noted, just like in their combat. That was the reason she'd survived that long.

"Why are you walking so fast?" he asked as he fell into step beside her.

Her tone was cold. "I don't enjoy wasting time."

"What a surprise." He sighed. "You're all business, aren't you? Just like the old man back there." He tossed a look back. "No wonder you get along so well."

The two of them stepped outside. This area of the base was mostly green, with some trees here and there, grass, and bushes. There was also sand at the gates, hinting at the desert, but inside, the ground was clear to walk on.

They sat at one of the bench tables, reading the files they had been given. Damon occasionally ogled at her between each new page.

Suddenly, Emry put down her stack of papers and her eyes snapped to him. "Okay, *what?*"

"You know," he started, holding back a laugh, "if we're going to be co-leaders, we're going to spend a lot of time together. Maybe you should stop hating me."

Emry blinked and crinkled her nose. "Fine. Whatever."

He could hear the softness that he'd envied earlier creeping into her voice again.

"Let's start over, shall we?" Grinning, he offered her his hand. *One more time*. "Damon Primrose."

She hesitated a bit before firmly gripping his hand in hers. Her handshake was strong, decisive. "Emry Tigridia, but you can call me Tiger."

Chapter 3

Her Name

Emry

"Well, it's nice to meet you, Emry." Despite his warm grin, Damon's eyes were wild, as if he was preparing himself for an adventure.

A weird feeling slithered down her spine, causing her to squirm where she sat. She'd been Tiger for so long that hearing his soothing voice speak her private name aloud felt far too intimate. Only her family called her Emry, and given the distance to Rows, she'd rarely seen them.

"Didn't you hear what I just said?" She scowled. "Everyone here calls me Tiger."

He shrugged, but Emry could see in his eyes that he liked the provocation. "I like your name better."

What was wrong with this guy?

"You know," she spat, "this is a part of my reputation. You might be a great Slayer, but so am I."

"Of course." He smiled.

She gritted her teeth but decided to let it go. She couldn't forbid him to call her by her name, and she wouldn't lower herself down to his childish level. "Whatever. We have six soldiers overall: three female, three male."

Damon stretched, flexing his biceps. "Who are they?"

Emry flipped through the pages. "We have one from Seka, one from West She'e, one from Ob, one from Nova, and two from Egma."

"Really? I'm from Egma." He grinned.

She stared at him for a moment to signal her disinterest in his interruptions. "Yeah," she said shortly, and continued to examine the pages.

Emry just didn't get him. He was so strong, so tough. She could feel it—she *had* felt it. So why was he all sunshine and humor? How could someone *that* threatening have such a calm demeanor?

"Can I see their faces?"

"What? Who?" Emry responded, snapping out of her thoughts.

"The recruits. Let me see their photos," he said, holding out his hand.

"Here." She handed over the new soldiers' portraits. "They all seem unscathed, it means that they don't have—"

"Look." He pointed at a curvy girl with soft, brown hair. "Ella has a scar, right next to her ear."

"What?" She took the picture from him.

The bruised tissue was faint and off to the far side of Ella's face. How did he catch it so easily?

"Now that we're leaders, we can make them tell us everything that's ever happened to them. We might get some interesting information."

"We can. It would probably be a good idea to know their backgrounds."

"Yeah?" Damon said with surprise. He obviously hadn't expected her to agree with anything he said.

"Sure."

"Great. What are their names?"

She fumbled with the papers. "Ella, Kalen, Anoki, Ahron, Riggs, and Lucy."

"Who's the fourteen-year-old?"

"Lucy."

"Hmm, a girl. They always have it rough when they're drafted at that age."

She lowered the files and stared at him incredulously.

Damon stared right back, his golden eyes pierced her gaze, and a hint of a smirk tugged at his lips. She had a feeling he was testing her on purpose. He was enjoying it, the bastard.

"You already know I started at twelve," Emry reminded him. "I coped better than most of the older boys."

"Really?" Damon cocked his head.

"Yes, *really*," she scoffed, exhaling loudly. "No one gave a shit about me being a girl, or about me being twelve. And they shouldn't have, because it didn't matter."

She wouldn't apologize for her harsh tone. That was who she was.

Emry cleared her throat. "Anyway, Kalen and Riggs are seventeen. The rest are sixteen."

Damon opened his mouth to speak, but stopped when he heard someone call his name.

"Damon! Hi." A tall, gorgeous brunette stepped next to him and linked her arm around one of his. "It was so much fun celebrating your championship last night! I knew you would win even before it started."

The girl's words sent a twinge of pain through Emry's heart.

"It sure was," Damon said with a smirk. "It's always like that when that crazy, old man is at the bar." Emry noticed how he ignored the jab made towards her.

The girl laughed as if he had said the funniest joke she'd ever heard, and Emry tried her best not to roll her eyes.

"I don't want to interrupt whatever this is." The brunette lazily waved her hand between Emry and Damon. "So, in short, I just wanted to ask—are you free tonight?"

Emry could swear she saw him grimace, but only for a brief moment. "Actually, no. We're changing residence today."

"Oh." She unlinked her arm from his. "Maybe next time?"

Emry let out a huff. Why was she still listening to this when there was work to be done?

"Maybe," he replied, straightening his posture.

The girl started her departure, giving Damon one last glance before she disappeared into the distance.

Damon's stare returned to Emry, studying her facial expression and posture.

"What?" she asked sharply.

"Nothing, nothing." He raised his hands in surrender. "Sorry about that."

She shifted herself away from him a bit. "You're pretty popular. I hope you enjoy it."

"I do enjoy it," he drawled. "Very much so. Does it bother you?"

"Why would it bother me?"

He shrugged, but didn't take his eyes off of her. "You could be popular too, if you wanted. I saw how your squad cheered for you before our fight."

"It was hell getting to that point with them, and popularity isn't important to me."

"Why?"

"I don't have time for this. We have more exams in two years. I didn't make it this time, but I need to study for the next one, and lead with you while I'm doing it."

"We have two years. Surely you won't be studying that entire time?"

The pain from earlier returned, stabbing deeper than before.

She looked at him again. "How long did *you* prepare for the competition you just *won*?"

"I studied for the knowledge part for a month."

A *month*.

She felt lost inside herself, as if she was bathing in her own anger, trapped in hell. She wanted to hit something, to *destroy* it.

Damn everything. Damn everyone. Damn her life.

"Hey, Emry?" he said gently.

She looked up, knowing her eyes would show the untamed emotion that she was feeling, but *his* eyes were gentle. Damon started to reach for her hand, but quickly decided against it. "I can tell those exams were important to you. You did so well, bested so many people... You're going to be the leader of the *elite* group. I'm sorry if you wanted the first place, but look at everything you've achieved."

She took a deep breath. "You've got nothing to be sorry for. You won fair and square." She rose to her feet. "It's *my* life, which is an utter joke. And the joke is always on *me*."

Chapter 4

Irreparable

Emry

Nothing could ever come easy. Everything, absolutely everything, had to be *so hard.* Emry tried so hard, she gave everything she had and it wasn't enough.

Would something, someday, be enough?

When she'd enlisted as a kid, she did it because her parents couldn't afford to feed her and her sister. But Emry had never expected to *like* it. She'd never expected to be a good soldier, one who earned respect from her colleagues, who worked hard enough to be worth listening to.

It wasn't like she had anywhere else to belong. She had been supporting her family for years, but she rarely actually saw them. She didn't like to think about it, and often just pushed it to the back of her mind, but Emry knew there was more than just physical distance between them.

Not many soldiers had a functional family, but the ones that did always received letters on weekends. She had a family, but they never sent her any letters. Maybe they didn't like the person she'd become as a soldier. Maybe she was too strong for them, too frightening. Whenever Emry visited, they always seemed like ghosts to her—distant, watching. Waiting for her to leave. She was an intruder. Unwanted. And so she'd just stopped visiting home. There was never such a place, anyway. Not for her.

As Emry was walking, she could still see Damon's concerned eyes as he tried to reach for her to comfort her. But after the way she treated him, why would he waste his time? Why show her compassion?

If she were him, she would have never, *ever* put her behavior towards him aside. Her pride wouldn't have allowed it.

Emry knew it wasn't Damon's fault that he was better than her. But the fact that he worked *so little* for what she had been dreaming about for years drove her crazy. If she really was that hopeless, what was the point with anything? The bitterness shouldn't have surprised her. She should have known that some people make it, and some people don't.

Damon

After his conversation with Emry, Damon had a long day of packing before starting guard duty at the eastern tower. Now that he was a squad leader, there were some lodging upgrades. He'd heard that his new residence was a quarter of a floor on the top story, with the other quarter belonging to Emry. The two would share a small bathroom, unlike their new recruits, who would be sleeping in the hall with a small communal bathroom.

Carrying his huge, black satchel on his back, he made his way up the stairs to the Slayers building. As he walked through the hall and up another set of stairs, Damon heard multiple voices chatting in the small corridor between the bedrooms.

"I'm sure you'd do great, Tiger. It's you, after all," a lanky guy said as he ran his fingers through his short, black hair. With his pale skin and almond-shaped eyes, it was clear he was from Nova. He wore blue fatigues, the color of the ICT—Information and Communications Technology unit.

"Thanks, I really appreciate it," Emry answered. "You guys have no idea what the last couple of days have been for me."

"That's because you're such a perfectionist," said a third person. "You did great, and we need to celebrate. How about tonight?"

Damon stepped inside the passageway, curious. Emry was visible from the open door to the right, sitting on the bed with a guy who looked a lot like the other Novan, but shorter and chubbier. When they noticed him, they stopped talking. Emry's green eyes studied him cautiously.

"Hi." Damon cocked his head. "Friends of Emry?"

"We don't call her that," the chubby one said as he awkwardly adjusted the collar of his uniform.

"Right," Damon grinned. "Too personal, huh?"

Unamused by his antics, Emry cut in. "These are my friends from ICT, Ian"—she gestured at the tall one—"and Glen." She gestured at the other. "They helped me move my things. Ian, Glen, this is—"

"Damon. I'll be co-leading with her."

"Yeah, we're well aware of who you are," Ian said, shifting his weight between his legs. "Your friends kicked us out when our squad tried to sit at the bar."

"Really?" Damon slung his bag over his shoulder again and raised an eyebrow. "Well, it *is* our spot."

Emry narrowed her eyes and stood up. "Seriously?"

"Tiger..." Glen pulled at her sleeve, hoping she wouldn't pick a fight.

"It is. And everyone knows it," Damon stated, walking to the left bedroom.

"I can't believe I'm going to lead a team with this guy," Emry mumbled.

Throwing his bag on the empty bed, he shouted, "Well you better believe it, because it's happening!"

She marched into his room, eyes blazing with anger. "Who the hell do you think you are?"

Ian and Glen lurked behind her. "Tiger, we need to—" Glen started.

"I know." She nodded at them. "Thank you for helping me. I'll see you guys tonight, yeah?"

They hesitated. "You sure you'll be okay?" Ian asked, his eyes moving to Damon.

Damon had to bite his tongue to keep himself from saying what he wanted to say to that guy. What came over him? He wasn't usually like this. He was decent; he was nice. It bothered him.

"Yeah, I got this," she assured them.

Damon snorted as they left, closing the door behind them. Finally, he was alone with her.

"What's your problem?" Emry snapped.

He took off his olive-green shirt to reveal a white undershirt. "I don't have one, but it seems like you do."

"I know. It's standing right in front of me." She crossed her arms. Her lips were pressed together.

He grabbed his bag and rummaged through it. "Well, I'm hitting the shower and going out, so you're going to have all that space for yourself, no problems in front of you."

She blushed with anger. "You were nice this morning. What is it? Some people don't deserve your kindness?"

He found the bar of soap he was looking for and turned to look at her. "I didn't pick that fight. It was your dorks who started it, Emry."

Again, Damon could see how unusual it was for her to be called by her name. It took her a moment to respond. "My *dorks*? You're unbelievably—Oh my God!" Emry quickly turned away upon noticing that he had continued to undress himself, pants first.

"Huh." He chuckled. "Most girls don't turn away at that part."

"I can't believe you're undressing in front of me! This is inappropriate!"

"Well, I'm going to hit the shower. We can keep fighting tomorrow if you'd like. We have some time before the kids come." He paused and walked to her, until his front was inches from her back. That close, he could see that divine color of her hair better, the bright strands dancing on her pale skin. "Unless you want to continue fighting right now. You'd have to join me, then, because I stink."

She jumped, surprised by how close his voice was to her, and he grinned. She almost turned, but then covered her eyes like a little kid. "Just leave!"

He laughed and passed her on his way out the door.

Emry

Emry stood at the entrance of the club and sighed. Why had she agreed to this? She wasn't much of a drinker and only went to parties if they were mandatory.

Anticipating the wild music that greeted her, the young Slayer entered the building and saw Damon celebrating with his gang. Despite him wearing black jeans and a black jacket, he stood out in the dark room. He looked toxic—dangerous even. Nevertheless, he was being swarmed by women. One was clinging to his arm, while another was pressing her chest firmly against him, trying to get his attention.

Suddenly, Emry felt a nudge in her side. "We ordered you a beer."

She turned to see her friend, Glen, standing at her side. "What? I can't hear you."

He raised his voice. "We ordered you a beer. Cherry, right?"

"God knows I only drink that junk." The two of them laughed in unison. "Can't have anything that isn't sweet."

Glen guided her to their table, where their friends were waiting. A while later, the music grew quiet and the old bartender, Colin, hit a huge drum that was attached to one of the back walls.

"Everybody, your attention, please!" Colin yelled, wrapping his arm around Damon's shoulder. They were both laughing hysterically. "Who here thought this lad was going to get first place?" Everyone cheered as Colin raised his glass. "To Primrose!"

"To Primrose!" the group roared back.

That was when Damon's haughty eyes found hers, and his smirk slowly morphed into curiosity.

What, exactly, was he looking at?

"Don't mind him, Tiger. I think they already celebrated for him last night. This was so unnecessary," Ian scoffed.

Trying to suppress the bitterness that threatened to climb up her chest again, Emry clutched her glass tighter. She had to get over it already. Life goes on, and second place was still noteworthy.

"You're right." She nodded confidently. "I'll get him next time."

When her friends finally decided to leave, they approached the bar to pay their bill.

"It's been taken care of." Colin motioned to the other side of the bar. "Primrose paid for your drinks."

Emry glanced at Damon from the corner of her eye, not wanting to fully look at him. She didn't know what to do with his gesture. Was he trying to mock her? Did he want something from her? This couldn't be good, and the last thing she wanted were mixed signals.

* * *

After escorting her friends to their residence, Emry made her way back to her own. The gray building stood tall next to a cliff, far from all the other housing units. For safety measures, a high fence was constructed around it, useless against those who were athletic enough to climb it.

She stretched her arms high up on the fence, closed her eyes and took a breath of the cool, fresh air. Yes, it was a bit chilly, but she preferred it that way. The soft wind on her skin and the darkness of the night reminded her that another day was finally over. That there was one less battle to fight. She devoted herself to the moment, but soon heard footsteps approaching.

"Emry."

She tensed and cautiously faced the figure in the shadows.

It looked as if the night that surrounded simply declared him king. The only feature that brightened the surrounding area was his striking golden eyes.

Damon.

Emry released her grip on the fence and crossed her arms. It seems the night had given her one more battle. "You paid for our drinks."

"That I did."

"Why?"

Damon walked closer until she was a whisper away. "Can't I do something nice for my co-leader without expecting anything in return?"

She shook her head. "Life doesn't work that way."

"According to who?"

"Me. *My* life doesn't work that way."

He studied her for a second. "I see."

Emry closed her eyes and took another breath. He was making her nervous. She didn't like it. The urge to run away was thrashing inside of her.

"In that case, there *is* something I want."

Of course. Her fists clenched, bracing herself for whatever he might ask. "What?"

He took another step towards her, and now his eyes blazed. "Say my name."

Emry blinked in surprise, taking a step back. "What?"

"You haven't said it, not even once. I've said yours multiple times. Say it."

She was still baffled, but it didn't seem to matter. "Why would you..." She paused. The look in his eyes was too much. Electricity filled the space between them. Something in the atmosphere had changed. Her heart was beating fast in her chest.

"Come on, *Tiger*." Damon cocked his head, amusement and fire dancing in his eyes. He was challenging her. "It's not even such a long name."

Emry closed her eyes, wanting nothing more than for this weird and unwelcome feeling to stop. "Fine, *Damon,* you're a piece of—"

"Yeah." He laughed. His eyes were gentle now, but she could still see the fire in them. "That works as well."

Chapter 5

The Kids

Damon

Damon had been lying in bed, reflecting on his behavior for hours. What was he thinking? It was as if common sense had left his brain the moment Emry was in his vicinity. Thoughts like this would get him nowhere, especially since she was his co-leader now.

Nothing was worth risking everything he had worked for. Damon knew he had to let that little distraction slide, but it could never happen again. He had to be professional. After all, she was just another lost soul inside this vicious organization.

Emry

Tying up her hair, Emry took a deep breath as she made sure everything was prepared for the long day ahead of her. After she had it mulled over instead of falling asleep, she came to the conclusion that Damon's behavior was probably typical of him. The rude, flirtatious antics he displayed were simply a part of his game, and it was stupid of her to worry. Still, some part of her couldn't get over the softness in his eyes she had seen the other night.

Emry walked out of the tiny washroom she shared with Damon, and into the corridor, where he was already waiting. He silently handed her a black belt and five different kinds of knives.

However, something felt different.

His eyes and posture were rigid as he looked down at her. Gone were the games. Now it was real. She looked into his eyes and saw the vigilance in his hard stare, the determination, and suddenly, for the first time, standing next to him felt right.

The pair walked to the hall to meet Headley. His tired, blue eyes acknowledged them as he gestured for them to walk with him to one of the gates. When they arrived at the sands outside, Damon stood to Headley's left, Emry to his right.

After a short while, they saw a bus park in front of them, raising a wave of dust. A group of adolescents emerged carrying trunks nearly as big as their owners. Some of them looked exhausted from the long trip as they lined up in front of their new commanding officers.

Riggs, tall, broad-shouldered seventeen-year-old, stood out with his ebony skin. If Emry hadn't known better, she would have thought he was older than her—his black hair, dark eyes, and a square face made him look very mature.

Next to him stood Kalen. His shaggy, blond hair veiled his blue eyes, and the way he slouched made him look shorter than he really was.

The last male and youngest male was Ahron. Unlike the others, he was as gaunt as a broomstick, and pale like the moon. Behind his glasses, his dark eyes quivered in fear; an unusual characteristic of a Slayer recruit.

Ella, who looked rather plain with her brown hair and tanned skin, had a glint of intelligence in her eyes. Her addition to the Slayer team was odd due to her being an Owl. She hadn't done well with the Intelligence unit's initiation process, and therefore was not accepted as Intelligence.

Anoki, straight from She'e, had dark skin and dark eyes. Her shiny, wavy hair fell like a waterfall down her back, but she looked shy and insecure.

Lucy, the youngest of them all, had short, auburn hair that reached her chin. She was much smaller compared to the others, but something about her wild grin told Emry that this girl was tougher than she looked.

Headley studied them swiftly before welcoming them. "Most of you are here because you probably didn't have the best life," he stated, his voice loud and clear. "That, or you're stupid."

"If you think the army is going to be a nice place to escape from your troubles, you're both wrong and right. It *is* an escape, but let me assure you"—his stare turned menacing—"nice, it is not. You've been chosen to be Slayers. You're going to be at risk *all* the time, not only in fights, but also here at the base. In the next few months, you're going to study about demons and train to get stronger. You're going to have to stand watch and perform duties on your own. No one is responsible for you here but yourselves and your leaders." He gestured at Emry and Damon, who still stood with their arms crossed behind their backs. "Here, you are soldiers. There is no free will, just hierarchy and commands. You are going to listen to your leaders. They are the best Slayers we've got, and you're going to do what they say."

He paused for a moment, studying them again. "We chose the six of you as the top candidates, each for a different reason. If you have a problem, if you have a complaint, if you have an emergency, if you're happy, if you're sad, anything—you speak to your leaders. If needed, they'll talk to me. Understood?"

"Yes, sir!" they shouted. Though it sounded more like a squeak from some of them.

"Good." He gestured to his left. "This is Damon Primrose, winner of the Duels this cycle. Out of all the Slayers, he's defeated the most demons."

Emry felt her blood freeze when she glanced at Damon, at his hard body, his hard eyes. She already knew that he slayed the most demons out of his group, but out of all the Slayers?

"Tiger." Headley introduced her with a gesture to his right. "Second place at the Duels this cycle. Now, listen carefully. You want to be strong soldiers? You can train. You want to be smart soldiers? You can study. You want to stay alive? You listen to her."

Emry felt her pride being mended. He was right. If there was one thing she excelled at, it was staying alive. Whether she had to survive against demons or people, it didn't matter.

"Alright." Headley rubbed his palms together. "I've already had private conversations with each of you." He passed his stare between them. "The beginning is not going to be as tough as the next few years, but it is going to be hard. I wish you all the best here in the army, and in this unit specifically."

With that, he made his leave.

Emry and Damon exchanged a quick glance before they drifted closer, closing the gap Headley had created.

"We're going to our residence," Emry said, emulating Headley's tone. "You're going to be sleeping in your sleeping bags, so you should unfold them at night and fix them in the morning. You should be thankful that the other groups have to sleep outside in tents."

Damon proceeded. "You'll be sharing toilets and showers. Don't leave any of your belongings unattended. If you need anything, you take it with you at the moment. If we spot anything there, we will confiscate it. No bars of soap, no towels."

"Are all of you set? Anything to say before we go?" Emry asked. When no one answered, she nodded. "Good. Let's go."

The group made their way to the building and up the stairs until they reached the top floor. Once there, the kids unpacked their belongings, each claiming a spot in the main hall.

"I'm giving the first lecture. You'll give the next, right?" Damon asked.

Emry looked at him, surprised that he didn't remember. "No, you said you'd do the second."

Damon scrunched his face in uncertainty. "Well, shit." He studied the teens, who were still unpacking and sharing stories about their families. "Can we switch? I'll owe you."

She frowned at him. "Got someplace to go?"

"Actually, yes."

What, for the love of God, was more important than giving a lecture to his soldiers on their first day in the army? Whatever it was, she didn't care. She actually wanted some time without him to observe the recruits on her own. Still, this was highly irresponsible of him.

"I'll just do both," she said.

"You're sure?" He relaxed. "I swear I'll make it up to you."

"Yeah, just go."

Damon nodded and came closer to her, but his eyes were still watching the kids. "If anything goes wrong, or you need something, I'll be at Intelligence Hall. Okay?"

"It's just the first talk. Everything will be fine."

"Alright. I'll be back after lunch," he said, hurrying out.

She took a deep breath and cleared her throat. "We're leaving in two minutes, so prepare yourselves. We're having our first class."

* * *

The feud between demons and humans had a long and bloody history. The demons claimed that Lilith, their ancestor, predated Eve, the humans' ancestor. They believed that Earth belonged to demons and that humans should die because they were never supposed to exist.

Instead of accepting a peace offering of sharing the land, the demons attacked time and time again. No amount of pleading from the humans did any good. When the demons started sending their own children to die—when they started to kill themselves for the sake of killing humans—the humans stopped begging for forgiveness over a feud they did not start. They fought back.

The demons had always been stronger, but internal conflict and anger allowed them to be divided and weakened. And so it went, decade after decade. This was something every soldier knew before coming into the army.

* * *

"As I've explained, we usually don't face the Belaya, demons who possess a human figure. We rarely face the monstrous type, the Chernaya. They're clever and will try to exploit your weaknesses. Tomorrow, we'll talk more about the three kinds of demons and their levels. I'm dismissing you early so that you may get your uniforms and weapons. Do you—yes, Kalen?"

All eyes turned to him. "Is the army really going to trust us with weapons?"

"That's the army, genius," murmured Ella.

"That's so dangerous," mumbled Ahron.

"What if someone goes insane and starts attacking people?" Lucy asked, a smile stretching across her thin lips.

Emry laughed a little. It was weird, but they *were* just kids. She had to be a little gentle with them. "Do you guys know how old I was the first time I held a knife?" She raised a brow. "Twelve. I was alone with two older girls and a bunch of guys. And guess what? I was not in the elite group like you are. What you guys are going to go through is much nicer because there's no need to break your spirit first. You're already disciplined."

"But—" Anoki started, but Emry had raised a hand to silence her.

"You are going to carry weapons," Emry continued. "And yes, someone might lose their mind and use it against you. Wouldn't be the first time. Any more questions before I let you go? It's *your* time. Use it wisely, especially if you want to make it for lunch." Emry wasn't surprised when no one spoke up. "Alright." She nodded. "You're dismissed."

They ran out of the cabin, leaving her behind. They were good kids, and she was glad that Damon wasn't present. Spending time alone with them made her feel more relaxed—something she could never feel around him.

Now that Emry had decided to let her new recruits go early, she had some spare time. She slowly walked outside of the cabin, which was a rare change from her usual pace of always being in a rush. When she passed by Intelligence Hall, cheers and laughter seeped from inside—a clear sign that their exams were over, and those that had passed were celebrating.

"Let's go, Intelligence!" a man's voice—*Damon's* voice—shouted.

Frowning, Emry made her way inside, curious as to what business he could possibly have in this department. Among the sea of purple uniforms, Emry spotted Damon sitting with a short, curly-haired girl. The medal around her neck shone almost as bright as her brown eyes when she smiled up at him. She didn't look like the girls that were usually surrounding him. She was rather plain, her face a little mousy. It surprised Emry, but it made sense—he had ditched her to support his girlfriend.

Chapter 6

Obstacles

Emry

Later in the Mess Hall, Emry waited anxiously to see if all of her new soldiers, and Damon, had made it there on time. What could he have been doing instead of eating lunch? Surely he still couldn't be with—

"Tiger, you need to eat," Glen said, shaking his head at her untouched sandwich. He was always the gentle, caring one of their trio. "Come on, they'll make it."

With a sigh, she took a bite from her chocolate spread sandwich. There were decent, hot meals served, but she had to get her dose of sugar. Emry chewed as her eyes scanned the room.

Just then, Damon strode into the dining room with a group of Intelligence. The mousy girl was on his shoulders as they celebrated her win with shouting and songs of morale, accompanied by the clapping of soldiers who were already sitting and eating.

"The Intelligence department had tests today, huh?" Glen sighed and took a napkin. "I'm so scared of ours."

"You said it's next week, right?" Emry asked absentmindedly.

"Yeah. It would have been better if it was tomorrow so we'd be done with it, but *no*," Ian said sarcastically. "Let us wait so we suffer slowly. The tension is killing us."

"I'm sure you'll do great." Emry tried to cheer them on, but it came out weak. "Unlike me."

Ian rolled his eyes dramatically, and the three of them laughed as he threw one of his potato cubes at her.

"Can you move over?" a deep voice suddenly asked. "I need to speak to my co-leader."

They looked up to see Damon gazing at them, and with a huff, Glen moved over a few spaces to allow Damon to take his spot.

"How did the classes go?" he asked quietly.

Emry looked down, hating herself for being affected by their proximity. "It went fine. They're smart, a bit overwhelmed, but they understood everything."

"Did you teach them about the different kinds of demons?"

"We started talking about it, but we didn't finish."

"Alright. I can continue talking about it after lunch."

Emry shook her head. "I gave them the rest of the day off to familiarize themselves with the base and each other. I figured it would help them relax a little, give them time to reflect on their decision to join the army, and ease into their new life. If they have second thoughts, it's better to know now than later."

Damon looked at her thoughtfully. "Sure." He moved away from her a little so he could fully observe her. His eyes, darker than their usual shade, were amused. "They'll be fine, Emry."

She shrugged.

"Alright then." He glanced at his friends' table. "That means we have some free time to ourselves."

"Yeah," she huffed. "You can go and celebrate your girlfriend's victory."

His eyes snapped to hers. "What?"

"You don't have to prete—"

A loud noise interrupted their conversation, and everyone switched their focus to the source.

Damon

The army was cruel to anyone who was different. Damon was very much aware of that, though he didn't think his new recruits would learn it so fast. Anoki stood next to the food line, her small mouth slightly open, gaping at her tray of food strewn across the floor. In front of her stood a thin, brown-haired guy with a venomous look in his blue eyes.

"People coming from West She'e don't deserve to eat food," he growled. "You can use magic to feed yourself, right? This is an abomination. You—"

The guy didn't get to finish his sentence. Emry's punch went straight to his face, knocking him to the ground. He yelped, and she kicked him in the stomach.

Damon raised a brow in surprise. One second she was right next to him, the next she wasn't. *How did she do it?* Shaking the thought, he rushed over to hold her back as she cursed at the guy.

"Calm down," he whispered in her ear.

"Hey! What's going on here?" yelled another soldier who was running towards them. "That's one of my soldiers! Did you beat him up? What the hell is the matter with you? Think you have the right because you guys are Slayers?"

The entire room went silent, waiting for a response to his accusation. Damon released Emry and walked up to the angry unit leader.

"Your soldier messed with ours, knocked her tray out of her hands," he said quietly. "Maybe he wouldn't have gotten his ass kicked if you'd have taught him not to run his prejudiced mouth. This time, my co-leader took care of it. Next time, *I'll* take care of it. I'll beat him senseless *and* make sure he's expelled. Understood?"

He knew the message was clear when the guy took a step back and. There was fear in his eyes, but also respect. He knew that Damon was being fair with him.

"Won't happen again."

Damon knew that the guy who attacked Anoki wasn't the only racist the army had to offer. Most of the people here were homeless kids or prisoners who'd been given another chance. They carried their prejudices and superstitions they'd learned from the streets or jail with them. He could only imagine the kind of hell that Emry herself had to go through being a Tiger. Not everyone was elite, but it didn't mean they had the right to behave like that to others. Facing Anoki, he placed a hand on her shoulder and gripped it tightly.

"You okay?"

She nodded, pressing her lips together to stop herself from crying. It was only her first day, and she must have been exhausted, but it was better not to show any weaknesses. The army didn't protect them from feuds among soldiers; they had to survive their company themselves.

After a few minutes, Emry approached them with a new plate full of food, but Anoki waved it away.

"No, thanks," Anoki choked. "I *can't.*"

Emry shook her head and shoved the plate into her hands. "Sit down and eat. You'll need energy for training."

"Emry's right. We'll escort you to your friends so you can sit with them." Damon's eyes were softened as he spoke.

Anoki's eyes darted around the room. "I... I think they're still at the armory."

"Then I'll sit with you," Emry said, signaling to her friends in blue. "Come on."

Damon couldn't remember when he'd last seen a leader care so much about their soldiers. Usually, novices were just thrown into the water and learned how to swim. That, or they'd sink. Just by looking at Emry, he was certain she wouldn't let any one of their soldiers drown.

Emry

That night, their small group filled the hall that had belonged to just Emry and Damon a few hours ago. Damon passed between them, handing out the schedules that Emry had made for them. "You have fifteen minutes to study your schedules, brush your teeth, and prepare for bed," Emry announced.

The kids groaned in unison, but didn't budge.

"Anyone who isn't in bed before lights out will have the honor of cleaning the commodes for a week," Damon added, prompting the teens to clamber to their feet in a mad dash to not be the last person in the bathroom. Only one of them remained in the hall, seemingly unphased by the threat.

"Anoki, aren't you going?" Emry asked as the shy girl finished making her sleeping bag on the floor.

"No, I already brushed my teeth. I didn't want to wait until the last minute."

"I see... Then could you help me with something outside?"

"Sure. I'll get my shoes."

"We'll be back soon, Damon."

The young girl hesitated, as if waiting for his approval. He looked at the two of them with bewilderment, and nodded. It was strange that Emry had called him by his family name, but he passed it off as her being professional in front of their new recruit.

Anoki gathered her shoes and followed Emry down the stairs, into the night.

"How do you feel about what happened today?" Emry asked, gesturing for the girl to sit on the stairs.

Anoki laughed bitterly as she sat down. "Awful."

"That guy was a dumbass," Emry said with a nod. "And he won't be the only one you'll encounter here."

Anoki's dark eyes stared at her, suggesting that the young girl had already been through worse.

"He wasn't the first. People are *mean*," she said, looking down at her hands. "Those outside of West She'e think they're better because of their different traditions and religions. I practically ran away from West She'e, but I hate it when people judge me for being born there."

Emry nodded and turned her face towards the night sky.

"People try to look for weaknesses in others, and use them when they feel threatened or bad about themselves. But weakness doesn't cancel out strength. I'm a Tiger, I should know."

"I've heard about The Great War," Anoki said, looking wide-eyed at her commanding officer. "I was just a toddler when it happened."

"It left my family with nothing. When I enlisted, a little after the war was over, do you know what they called me? Tiger. But not in the manner you hear it now. It was people's way of humiliating me, the demonizer. They didn't want to say my name. Said that I didn't deserve to have one. That I didn't deserve to have human rights since my people sided with demons."

Anoki shivered at the gentle wind that caressed them, scattering their hair. Emry closed her eyes for a few seconds and relished the breeze.

"Even before I got into the army, I used to see my mother and father getting beaten up, but they eventually learned to hide, be quiet, and stay alert. When I enlisted, I learned that sleeping was dangerous. I always had a knife with me in bed because I was scared someone would attack me. They did, if you're curious. So I learned how to break a nose, how to make them bleed… Nothing fatal, of course. I didn't want to cause too many problems." She exhaled. "I learned how to hear steps, how to *feel* steps. There's no surprising me—not anymore."

There was a long silence between them. "I can't believe you survived it. That *someone* survived it," Anoki whispered.

"I'm sure you have your own stories, too." Emry stared into Anoki's eyes. "If you want to make it here, you'll have to stay strong. Laugh at their stupid remarks, laugh at their racism. It's their sad story to tell, not yours. You are much better than that."

Anoki took a deep breath. "Thank you, Tiger. I… needed this."

"Of course. Now, go back to the hall. We have a long day planned for you all tomorrow."

Anoki left, and Emry closed her eyes as the wind blew again. She didn't mind talking about her past if she had to make a point, but it wasn't easy. She told Anoki only a tiny piece of what she'd been through, and apparently it was enough to make the girl feel better. Right now, it was all Emry really cared about.

When she opened her eyes and stood up, she nearly tripped over her own legs when she saw Damon's dark silhouette. He was leaning against the gray building, arms crossed. His stare was aimed at the ground in front of her feet.

How long had he been standing there? How much did he hear?

"That was a powerful talk." His voice was rough. He pushed himself off the wall and sauntered towards her. "It's good that you talked to her."

She didn't know what to say. He wasn't supposed to hear any of it. "How long were you standing there?"

"Enough to hear a bit of what you've been through. I'm sure you went easy on her with the details."

"So you were eavesdropping."

He smiled gently, looking sincere. "I came out after making sure the others were in bed. You were in the middle of talking, so I waited. I didn't mean to listen, of course."

"*Of course*," she said, sliding her hands into her pockets.

"You know... if I'd been on your team, I wouldn't have let any of those nasty things happen." His eyes were so gentle it made her heart flutter.

Emry swallowed hard. "Thanks... Damon." She shoved her hands deeper into her pockets, still unsure of what to say. Just saying his name felt strange, changing the air between them, empowering his presence. "I managed on my own, though. I didn't need anyone to rescue me."

He nodded. "Now you're the only one left of that team. Out of all of them, you're the one who made it."

It didn't click until he said that. She looked down at the grass to hide her smile because, hell, he was right.

Chapter 7

Night Snack

Emry

Tossing and turning in bed always felt like a nightmare. Not because it was terrifying, but because it was a waste of time. It made Emry feel like she had this weakness that separated her from everybody else. Sleep felt impossible, and no matter how hard she tried, it eluded her. She thought she'd slept better before enlisting, but it was hard to recall. Whenever she'd dozed off, she'd be easily roused soon after, leaving her frustrated and ragged. Running on less than five hours a night was taking a toll on her, but there was nothing she could do about it.

Emry sat up and stared at the wall of her tiny, dark room. Her stomach growled as she pushed her blanket aside, rose to her feet, and made her way to the door. Peeking out, Emry saw that the door across from hers was closed, with no noise coming from it. Damon was probably sleeping like every other damn person at two in the morning. Continuing on, she made her way through the hall, being careful not to wake the kids as she crept across the wooden floors.

Stepping into the kitchen, she felt the cool tiles under her feet—something she'd always loved about it. The room was void of decorations, but it had the essentials: cupboards, a sink, a stove, a fridge, and a table.

Emry opened a cabinet and retrieved a small bag. She breathed a sigh of relief, thankful that no one else had restlessly wandered here. She didn't like to unfold her little bag of supplies when people were around. It was humiliating, how little it contained. She hadn't bought food for so long, and now she was left with nearly nothing.

"Doesn't seem like much."

Startled, she turned around and scowled at Damon, who was standing at the entrance. Wasn't he sleeping? Of all people to see her like this...

Shame. That was all she could feel in every cell of her body. It was coursing through her, burning her cheeks. She wished the ground would open up and swallow her whole. Emry resented this feeling. She hated it when others saw that she had nothing. And around him, it felt even worse.

She had to get it together. She would try to steal some food tomorrow from breakfast and sneak it to the Slayers building. It was forbidden, but Emry had done it a couple of times before. She could do it again. She took a deep breath, closed her bag, and put it back before making her way to the kitchen doorway.

"Wait."

Emry faced Damon to see two big sandwiches in his hands.

"I've made extra," Damon said. "Want to share?"

The young Slayer stood there stunned for a moment, but caught herself.

"Thank you, but I don't need your charity." Her voice was harsh. She cleared her throat and turned to leave again, but was stopped short.

"Alright," he conceded with a shrug. "I'll just throw one away. It's such a shame. I just can't eat both of them by myself."

"Seriously? That's a straight-up lie."

"Maybe," he admitted. "But I'll still throw one away, so it's better you have it instead, no?"

Was he for real? That monstrous sandwich was worth way too much to be thrown away. It was a fundamental rule for her to not throw away food.

She hesitantly joined him at the table. "This is really unnecessary," she murmured, taking the sandwich.

Emry didn't know how to feel about the fact that he was actually willing to throw food away just to get her to take it.

"Relax. You're just helping out a friend," Damon said jovially.

They ate quietly. She had to admit to herself that she was thankful he was being persistent. That sandwich had tomatoes, lettuce, barbeque sauce, chicken... Things she rarely bought.

Feeling a pinch at her heart, she realized she was also thankful for his kindness. It baffled her, made her embarrassed, a little suspicious, a little curious, but it also felt *good*. And it was terrifying. She didn't even dare to *think* about their conversation from last night. The fire in his amber eyes as he'd looked at her... Maybe she had hallucinated it.

"It's good to see you eating healthy for a change," he said as he finished his sandwich.

Emry wrinkled her nose. "What do you mean?"

"You always eat sugary shit."

"How..." Emry began, too shocked to deny it. "How the hell do you know that?"

"That cherry thing you had in the club." He wrinkled his nose in disgust. "And your lunch today—I mean, come on. That little chocolate spread sandwich was your food?"

He sounded so scornful that she laughed.

"And also," he continued, but she could feel that he was turning a bit apprehensive. "Your bag."

He was right. Even in her bag, the only things she had left were a few pieces of bread and jam. Pretty unhealthy for a soldier.

"You don't miss a thing, do you?" Emry ventured.

"Not as a rule."

She cleared her throat. "So, I guess that's you returning the favor you asked of me today?"

"What?" Damon asked, eyes wide. "No. Don't worry about that. I'll make it up to you, I promise. I just really had to go today, and I totally forgot." He smiled apologetically. "Never happens."

She shrugged. "It's good that you remembered in time, so your girlfriend wouldn't be mad at you for being a no-show."

"Right. My *girlfriend.*" He entwined his fingers on the table, eyeing her. "Do you usually do that?"

"Do what?" She raised her eyes to meet his.

"Make assumptions."

Why did that irritate her?

"I do, like everybody else. Of course, I can't be right all the time, like *you,*" she huffed, but it only made him smile smugly.

"Of course," he repeated.

They fell into silence, with her nibbling on what was left of her sandwich.

"She's not my girlfriend," he blurted out, his voice gentle and factual.

"Then who is she?"

"My best friend—my ally."

Emry tilted her head. Whoever that girl was, she meant a lot to him.

"Some people say guys and girls can't be friends," she said, not meeting his eyes. She had no idea why she said that.

"Really?" he replied in disbelief. "That's funny, coming from you."

"What do you mean?"

"Well, you do have your own pair of fans."

She blew out a breath. "They're just my friends, not my *fans.* Who's the one making assumptions now?"

Damon shrugged, but his eyes didn't leave hers. "Maybe. But I don't think I'm wrong."

She snorted. "Yeah, we've already established that you're always right."

He laughed. "You know my friend you mentioned? I think you'd like her."

"Do you think *she'd* like *me?*"

"Why wouldn't she?"

"Well..." She paused, caught off-guard as he watched her intently. "First, I don't think I'm very likable. And second... Now that we're co-leaders, I'm going to be around you. A lot. Would she really be fine with that?"

Emry's heart began to beat faster as she felt heat spreading down her cheeks at mentioning how close they were going to get.

"Hmm..." He pondered for a moment, but she caught the way his eyes traced the redness on her face before he averted them. "You just keep convincing me you make bad assumptions, because now you just made another two."

"You're kidding, right?" She scowled.

Damon's smile was predatory. "I'm serious."

"Do *you* find me likable?"

"Not just me." He looked unsatisfied somehow.

She was curious now. "What's that supposed to mean?"

Emry saw him tuck his tongue inside of his cheek, as if he was contemplating whether to say or not to speak up.

"Some of my friends were talking about you at the club. Turns out you spoke to someone on kitchen duty or something, and they recognized you at our duel. They were very impressed with you."

"Huh." She knitted her brow. "That's good to know."

For some reason, he wrinkled his nose. "Sure."

"What?"

"Those friends." He shook his head. "You're too good for them. They're not really the best people."

She was too good for someone? The Tiger? That was a first. She waited for him to keep talking, but he didn't.

"And what does that have to say about you?"

"That I can get along with many kinds of people?"

She rolled her eyes. It was weird, having a good time with him at this hour of night. Another wave of gratitude washed over her. "Thank you for the sandwich," she said quietly. "I'll pay you back for that."

"It's just a sandwich. Besides, I got what I wanted in the end."

"What?"

"Your company."

She bit her lip, but quickly rolled her eyes afterwards so he wouldn't see how his stupid quips affected her. "So you're back to your lines?"

Damon got to his feet as well. "As I said before, I'm just saying what's on my mind. It's very liberating."

Suddenly, Emry felt exposed. He was leaning against the table, watching her, and she realized it was the first time he'd ever seen her in civilian clothing. She was wearing pink shorts and a white shirt. He was subtle, but he wasn't self-conscious enough to even try to hide the fact that he was staring.

She couldn't stand it. Emry looked out the window, into the dark night outside. She sighed as he glanced at the clock.

"Four already," he said.

"Great."

"How about I have the morning with them?"

"What?" She turned to look at him.

He shrugged. "We need to wake them up in about three hours. I'll do it. I'll also take them to breakfast after practice. You can sleep in, if you want."

She looked down. "But... *why?*"

He smirked. "I want some alone time with them, just like you had today. I wouldn't want you to become their favorite, now would I? Headley already talked you up enough."

She snorted. "Yeah, right. I bet you're already their favorite."

He laughed. "I really don't think so. If I were them, *you* would be my favorite."

"You just can't stop that, can you?"

He titled his head, looking serious all of a sudden. "It looks like I've got no filter around you."

She took a deep breath, holding her feelings at bay. "Goodnight, Damon."

He glanced at the window, deep in thought. "Goodnight, Emry."

Chapter 8

First Practice

Damon

After their little meeting in the shared kitchen, Damon didn't bother trying to sleep. What was the purpose? He had to get up soon, anyway. It wasn't the first night he'd gone without sleep. Visions, screaming faces... They all haunted him almost every single night.

He was glad he'd found *her* in the kitchen. The misery on Emry's face when he'd caught her staring at her supplies tugged at his heart. He didn't know if she would accept his help, but she did, and he was more grateful than he should have been.

There was sadness inside of her, he understood. Something painful, and not entirely whole. She was so cautious, smart, and hardworking... It felt like she'd never let herself take too many breaks. It seemed, sometimes, that she still viewed herself as the underdog. In some ways, she wasn't mistaken.

He tore himself from the little window, opened his bedroom door, and walked into the hall.

"Hey!" he half-whispered, not wanting to wake Emry up. "Get up. Now!"

The older ones got up quickly, but he could see Ahron and Lucy struggling.

"It's so early..." Lucy murmured, her short, red hair scattered around her face.

Ahron sighed and tossed aside his blanket.

"*Now,*" Damon repeated to Lucy, his voice hard. "You want to go home this weekend, right? Don't give me a reason to make you stay and do extra duties."

Lucy opened her eyes at once. "I'm awake. I'm awake."

Damon stretched as he scanned the room. "You've got ten minutes to pack your sleeping bags and get ready for practice. We'll train outside."

"What?" Anoki started, a bit frightened.

"You better move, not talk." He indicated with his chin. "Come on. Nine minutes and thirty seconds."

Damon was sure he heard her curse under her breath. He suppressed a smile. "You know what, do it quietly and I'll give you an extra minute."

* * *

"Can't... go... on..." Ella panted, her bangs glued to her forehead by large beads of sweat.

"Come on, weaklings," Damon yelled as he did one-armed pushups. "All you do is complain!"

Ahron, Anoki, and Ella were struggling to breathe, so he eventually let them rest. Lucy didn't waver, she just kept quiet and did what she had to do. She even seemed to enjoy it.

"You three," Damon said to the rest, "the one who stays last gets to go home Thursday morning instead of late that evening."

He saw their eyes pop open, and he smiled to himself as determination drove them beyond what they thought they were capable of. Lucy stopped first and sprawled on the ground.

He called to her, and she raised her head from her knees to peek at him. He nodded in appreciation. "Good job."

She nodded back and put her head back between her knees. Now, it was between Kalen and Riggs. Damon and the rest watched as the two competed.

"Who do you guys think will win?" he asked them.

Ella tilted her head. "Riggs."

Damon laughed. "So sure?"

She shrugged. "He seems stronger."

Damon nodded. The girl was not wrong. "Anyone else?"

Anoki just stared. "How do *you* keep going?"

"And with one hand," said Lucy, astounded.

"I've been a Slayer for a long time now. You'll get there too."

"No, we will not," Ahron suddenly said, causing Damon to raise an eyebrow. Ahron's cheeks turned red, and he looked down. "I'm sorry, I didn't mean—"

"No, continue," Damon insisted. "What do you think, Ahron?"

"Well, we're not built like you. And even if we were, what you're doing with such ease is just... inhuman."

Damon laughed, sweat rolling down his back. "If I can do it, you can do it. Don't think like that, kid. It's not the way to go if you want to be successful around here."

Ahron nodded quietly, just as Kalen crumpled to the ground, Riggs right after him.

"Aaaaand, we have a winner!" Lucy shouted.

"Told you," Ella teased with satisfaction, earning eyerolls from Anoki and Ahron.

"I think you're the real winner, Damon," Lucy said.

Out of the corner of his eye, he could see Emry coming their way. Seeing her made his pulse jump. He was about to give up and fall to the ground, but he urged himself to go on a little longer.

"I hope so, champ," he whispered.

Curious, Lucy turned to see what he was looking at. When she looked back at him with a frown, he just offered a grin.

Emry

"I see you're all sweaty." Emry observed them more closely. Her soldiers were practically groaning and scowling on the hard ground. "How do you guys feel?"

"Like we're about to die," Kalen grunted.

"Perfect." Emry watched the kids wipe sweat and dirt from their faces.

Meanwhile, Damon was shirtless, doing one-armed pushups. Every muscle he had was glinting with sweat in the sun, rippling and tensing, but he raised his eyes to her with ease and grinned. He was so wildly beautiful that she wouldn't have been sure he was real had he not been doing push-ups right before her eyes.

"Morning, you," he said. "Did you manage to get any sleep at all?"

She shook her head, and in one swift move, he jumped up to his feet, standing in front of her in all of his glory. She had to resist taking a step back for how embarrassed that actually made her feel.

"You're feeling okay?" he asked her quietly, even though *he* was the one who had woken up early.

"Yeah, I'm fine," she answered, hesitantly studying his face. "How was practice?"

"Good. Riggs is going home early on Thursday."

"Already? You're awarding them too fast."

"And they think *I'm* the bad cop." Damon returned his focus to their squad. "We still have a few minutes left for practice, and Emry here doesn't want me to let you guys rest." He winked at them as she turned to him in shock. "Go back to the building and bring the weapons that you chose from the armory yesterday."

When the kids were out of sight, she elbowed him, but he didn't even flinch. "Seriously?"

Amused, he stared back at her. "Did I lie?"

She pursed her lips and crossed her arms, feeling like a little kid. Damn it. Why did he have a comeback for every little thing she said?

Their ungainly soldiers were soon back with their weapons.

"I see you all have a knife," Damon announced, exchanging a swift glance with Emry. "We will practice holding it after lunch break. After that, you'll have class. Right now"—He bent down and pulled his own knife from the belt that was lying on the ground—"I'll show you basic moves."

He looked at Emry and ran his hand above the metal, and Emry could see the kids shiver in dread. "Do you trust me?"

She knew what he wanted. Emry took a breath and turned, waiting. His huge arm went around her and brought her closer, so her back was snug to his front, causing her stupid heart to beat fast at their proximity.

"This spot,"—Damon pressed the knife against her lower stomach—"is the demons' weak spot. That's where you want to cut a Belaya," he said as his arm curled under both of Emry's arms and went up, essentially paralyzing them. His head dropped to her neck, and she felt the knife now pressed to the other side of her stomach. "A quick slash from here"—he pressed the knife harder—"to here"—he pressed the knife to the other side—"is the best move you can make to neutralize a demon."

They stayed like that for a moment, his lips almost touching her neck. She felt her heart still racing, though she stubbornly tried to calm it down. Damon finally released her arms and went to her waist instead, and she felt the knife press to her neck. His fingers spread across her waist as if he was trying to touch as much of her as possible. It was a stupid thought, but when she heard his voice deepened, she wasn't so sure.

"If you can't reach the belly, you should try for the neck. Cut here." He indicated with the knife at the side of Emry's neck. "And not here." He pulled the blade so the tip was facing the front of her neck. "Because that won't do the same damage. They have thick muscles in their throats, the bastards, so you should try to hit the side. Got it?"

"Yes, sir!" they said in unison.

Emry could see Ahron shiver as his dark almond eyes focused on the knife.

"Good," Damon said, releasing his co-leader. "Now go have a shower. You've got twenty minutes—"

"Fifteen." Emry cleared her throat, finding her voice.

"Fifteen to get to the dining room for lunch. Understood?"

Their confirmation wasn't enthusiastic.

"There are more showers on the second floor. Use them," Emry suggested. "Go!"

The recruits ran towards the building with Damon watching. "I'm going to hit the shower as well."

"Of course," she said matter-of-factly. "I can take them to the Mess Hall. Take your time."

But he didn't move. Not until she raised her eyes to look at him. Then he smiled, as if he was waiting for her just to do that. "I'll be there on time."

Chapter 9

The Trooper

Emry

"Do you all know how to locate your city's train station to come back here next week?" Emry asked them, *again.*

The unit had reassembled in the Slayers building after Thursday's dinner. The week had passed quickly. Except for morning practices, they spent most of their time studying. Emry knew that it was for the best, but she was also waiting impatiently for them to be ready for the tough stuff. Their soldiers had come to realize that *she* was the tough leader. If Damon gave them ten minutes to get up in the mornings, she gave them seven. She was surprised to hear them complaining and comparing her to him. And there she thought she was being generous.

"Remember the protocol. Send us a message when you get home," Damon added.

He handed out a Toki to everyone. It was a small, black machine with one red and one green button. Each team had its own set, so if one of the soldiers pressed green, only their group members would see a green light pop up on their Toki's screens. Since Riggs had already left, Damon and Emry needed to see five green lights after the kids departed to know that everyone was safely back at home. The red button was for emergencies. Emry had no idea how the machine worked. To her it was just another device created by magic that they took from demons.

"If one of you forgets, there will be consequences," Damon said, meeting each of their eyes one by one. "Don't give us a reason to give you more kitchen duties next week."

They all grumbled.

"Alright," Emry said, silencing them. "You're free to go. If there's something going on at home that we need to know about, make sure to tell us before you go. Damon and I are always available for you, remember that."

She wished she could overlook how he almost automatically stepped a little closer to her.

The kids went to pack, but Lucy stepped forwards. "I'm leaving my house today. I'll be renting a place close to the border Egma has with Nova."

"Good luck to you." Damon grinned, his eyes warm and enthusiastic. "Are you excited?"

She smiled back at him. "I really just want to get it over with. It was important for me to know that we actually get to spend weekends at home, so I could fix this up."

"That's how it starts," Emry clarified. "After a few months, when Damon and I decide it's time, you guys will stay some weekends."

"Are you guys staying weekends as well?" Lucy asked.

"We have to stay every two weeks," Damon answered.

Emry shrugged. "I'm staying every week."

They both turned to look at her and she realized that they were waiting for an explanation. "You know I live in Rows. It usually takes me almost two days to get home. Besides, when you're older than twenty, you can go on solo missions during the weekend. It usually pays off."

Damon took a step even closer to her. "You're taking up missions?"

"Almost every week."

He fell quiet—*dead quiet*—and for some reason, she didn't want to look him in the eye. *Stupid.*

Lucy cleared her throat. "Damon, you don't take missions like Tiger does?"

He shook his head. "Not often. Usually, those missions are very dangerous, Luce. That's why I'm a little surprised here." His eyes were judgmental and somber.

Emry raised her chin. "Nothing to be surprised about. I'm a soldier, I'm a Slayer. This is what we do."

Lucy looked at her admiringly. "You are so strong, Tiger."

Emry smiled at her. I felt good to be regarded with anything other than scrutiny.

"You'll get there," she assured the girl. "By the way, I have a sister your age. Well, not quite. She's a bit younger than you."

Lucy grinned. "Do I remind you of her?"

"Not really, but that's okay. She wouldn't make it in the army. You will."

Smiling from ear to ear, Lucy went back to her bag to pack her stuff.

"You never said anything about having a sister," Damon said. "I assume she's not going to enlist."

"No. She's going to school, where she belongs." Suddenly feeling suffocated from so much, she changed the subject. "Are you going home this weekend?"

He thought for a moment and then shook his head. "No, I've got some paperwork to do."

"Oh, alright," she acknowledged uncomfortably. It meant that they were going to have the entire place to themselves, again. She felt lucky that her friends were also staying to study for their final exams. She wished with all of her heart that they would be successful enough so both of them would get to stay in the army. The three of them were just a bunch of nerds and nobodies, even among the soldiers. They were her friends, and some days, it was all that mattered.

"Do you have any plans?"

"Plans?"

"Tonight," Damon whispered. "Do you have any plans tonight?"

His eyes were intense as he waited for her answer.

Feeling puzzled, she shook her head. "I was thinking of helping my friends study, but—"

"Great." He grinned like a child. "Because I still owe you, and I want to finally make it up to you."

"You don't have to—"

"No," he insisted. "I promised you. I haven't forgotten."

"You really shouldn't—"

"I think we're ready," Ella interrupted. The others had already lined up with their bags. "Hey, Limbs." She raised an eyebrow at Ahron, who was struggling to carry his bag. "Can't you stand up straight?"

Ahron blushed and tried to stammer out a reply. "I—"

"Shut up," Lucy grumbled. "You think you're tougher? We can meet on the streets and I'll beat the hell out of you."

"I would very much like to watch that." Damon chuckled, and Emry smacked him. "Ouch!"

"You're all horrible." Anoki put her head in her palm. "Just a bunch of bullies."

"Well, sorry we're not good enough for you, Princess," Ella scoffed.

"Anoki's right." Kalen straightened his posture. It was clear that he didn't want to fight, but his eyes were decisive. "Just stop arguing."

"Look at us. I can't believe we're actually doing it." Ahron shook his head. "How are we going to survive this?"

"Because the only other option is to be left with nothing," Emry answered firmly, and they all fell silent. "Now, if you guys are done wasting time, we'll walk you to the gate."

Damon

Even if their soldiers were a pain in the ass sometimes, it was still hard to part with them for the weekend. Damon had grown attached to their bickering.

They complained so damn much and were at each other's throat so often that he wondered if the problem was personally them or their situation.

He could see it wasn't easy for Emry to say goodbye. either. They both felt the same devotion to help their soldiers survive. They'd be fine, though, those kids. They knew what they were doing, and they had sass.

"Hmm..." Emry chewed on her lip, looking a bit insecure. "I'm going to Headley's office. I need to stop by to collect some files."

"Alright. I'll go train and shower. I'll see you at the hall later?"

Her green eyes widened. "You're going to train? Now? We've been up since five in the morning."

Damon grinned. He'd never wanted to impress anybody before, but with her, he wouldn't miss an opportunity to try. "Yeah, but we only had a short class today, so I didn't have a chance to train at all." He took a step closer to her, examining her face.

He knew she usually had difficulty falling asleep. She had always looked so exhausted to him in the mornings. He had tried to take over the morning training, but she wouldn't let him. Of course, she wouldn't. She was so stubborn, but she looked uncertain now.

"Are you tired?" he eventually asked. He had an urge to tuck her long, ginger hair behind her ear.

She shook her head. "No, but—"

"I'll see you later, then," he said quickly, leaving before she could ask what he was up to.

Emry

When Emry returned to the Slayers building, she found Damon in his room. His wet hair dripped onto his olive-green shirt as he vigorously dried it with a towel. Emry watched him for a moment, but was caught off-guard when he spun around, staring right at her. She cleared her throat and tried to think about something to say—*anything*—but nothing came.

However, he put a big smile on his face, and just like that, the uneasiness lessened. "Good! You're back." He tossed the towel to the floor and flashed her a big smile, easing the tension that she felt. "Still not tired?"

"Not really. I'd probably stay up even if I were."

Damon laughed. "You and I aren't very lucky when it comes to resting." He closed the door after him. "Come on."

"Where are we going?" she asked as they stepped onto the grass outside. The sky was already dark, and only their footsteps could be heard.

"To a place I've got a feeling you'll really like."

She scowled. "You're not taking me to the club, right?"

He threw his head back with laughter. "Don't be silly. I said a place I think you'd *like*."

"How do you know I don't like the club?"

He snorted. He was in a good mood, she noted.

"First, I don't see you there often. Second, that night after the finals, you didn't seem comfortable."

"How would you know? I sat far from you." She frowned. Had he been scoping her out?

He shrugged. "Even from a distance, I saw you squirming in your seat."

So he had.

"We're here," he announced.

In front of them was the Trooper—a supermarket bigger than any store in Rows, and probably one of the biggest in the country. The best thing about it was that it was open twenty-four seven and located right in the middle of the base.

Emry loved the Trooper. She loved the wide selection of items, the smell of freshly baked bread... things that she'd never really experienced as a child. Still, these things were too expensive, and she usually just snuck food out of the dining room.

They entered and were instantly greeted by colorful shelves, workers running around, and endless aisles.

Damon pulled out a cart. "You ready? I thought it might be nice to do some shopping while the kids are away and we have some free time."

Mixed feelings rushed through her. Bewilderment and shock that he was actually spending his Thursday night with her for this.

"No." She backed away from him, already feeling her cheeks heat up. "I told you, I don't take charity."

He pulled the cart aside and looked directly at her. His intense eyes were stormy. "That's splendid, because I won't give you charity. I owe you, remember? I want to make it up to you."

"This isn't the same. You're giving more than you took."

"What you did for me meant a lot. If you won't let me make it up to you, then I guess we'll have a problem."

"Are you serious right now?"

"Dead serious."

"Can you actually compare me replacing you in a lecture and you buying shit for me?"

"I absolutely can. I had money, but I really needed time, and I didn't have any. You gave me some. It's only fair."

Irritated, she crossed her arms, feeling tired all of a sudden. "Fine, whatever. If you want to trade your money for my time, so be it."

"Great." Damon moved cheerfully, pushing the cart alongside her. "Get whatever you want."

Emry looked up at him as he went down the first aisle. She knew he knew she was staring.

"What?" he eventually asked.

"This is extremely unnecessary. You're unbelievable, you know that?"

One corner of his lips lifted. "You said that to me once."

She averted her gaze. "Then it's probably true."

Chapter 10

Legitimacy

Emry

After a bit, it seemed as though Damon had made peace with her uncooperative attitude; he just kept pulling stuff he liked for himself.

"Okay, I figured you'd be as stubborn as a mule," he said knowingly to her sour face. "But let's see you being like that *here*."

He pulled the cart to the snacks and candy section and Emry felt her willpower dissolve. Sweets were her absolute weakness.

"Come on." With a triumphant smirk, he gestured at shelves filled with packed cakes, cream-filled candies, and other sugary goodness. "This must be heaven for you."

Emry swallowed. "Why are you being like this?"

He shrugged. "I'm only making it up to you, but you make it so difficult."

She stubbornly held her ground, and he sighed.

"Still grumpy?" he asked. "Alright. Let's see... What would you like to have..."

Emry couldn't help but quickly glance at a big package of assorted chocolates. Hazelnut, caramel, raspberry, peanut butter... She had been eyeing that package ever since the Trooper started selling it.

"Ah-ha! I have an idea." Damon marched towards the shelf.

"Damon—" she started, but then she saw him hesitate.

"Hmm... There's a chocolate package and there's a vanilla package..." He deliberated a moment before picking up the correct one. "Oh right, you always prefer chocolate."

She couldn't believe her ears. "How do you know that?"

"During breakfast, you always take chocolate pudding, never vanilla." He shook his head and snuck another package into the cart. "Just so you don't run out of it too soon."

Emry was speechless. When had someone paid that much attention to her before? Maybe this was how Damon behaved with everybody. She remembered catching a glimpse of how observant he really was when he'd noticed the scar next to Ella's ear the other day.

"I think we're cool, right?" He examined their cart. "I just grabbed you everything I usually get myself, because you like making both of our lives so much harder."

"I could say the same about you."

"Lighten up. Is there anything else you need?

Emry examined the items in the cart. It was so full that she dreaded the thought of the cashier announcing the total. Some part of her wanted to just leave, right then and there. It was more than she could afford for months, maybe even a year.

She shook her head. "No. That's more than enough."

* * *

After they paid for everything, they made their way back to their residence. As the two soldiers put away their groceries, Emry's stomach growled in protest of their adventure.

"Are you hungry?" Damon asked.

It was almost midnight, but she was ravenous. The second that she hesitated was long enough to spur him into action. He was already slicing vegetables, bread, and meat. Seeing his inhumanly precise movements with the knife reminded Emry of the demonstration Damon did for the kids. Her heart fluttered thinking about his hands traversing her body. No doubt he was an excellent Slayer. Even standing next to him right now felt dangerous somehow.

Damon finished quickly, and they sat down across from each other, eating in silence just like they had the other night. She didn't really have anything to say, but she felt his amber eyes on her, studying her every move. In the end, she just stared back at him.

"You're staring."

One of his lips moved up into a smile. "You're funny when you're eating."

She scowled. "What?"

"Yeah." He chuckled bitterly. "I already told you that I don't have a filter, especially around you. You'll just have to get used to it."

"Fine," she relented.

Emry looked down at her food and suddenly felt bad. They were having fun, and he was trying to do a nice thing for her, so why was it so hard to accept it?

"Umm," she said, trying to start a new conversation. "What do you think about the week we just had?"

"It was awesome. I now understand why these recruits were chosen for the elite group; they're all clever bastards."

She couldn't help but laugh. "Yeah, right? Seems like you have a bond with each of them, especially Lucy."

Damon smiled. "She's got what it takes to be a great leader, no doubt."

"She's so brave and focused."

"Definitely. You know they adore you, right?"

"What?"

"They do. And it doesn't matter how tough you are with them, they know how much you care. I've noticed how you've grown close to Anoki."

Emry averted her gaze. "I think she just needs someone who gets what she's going through, you know?"

For some reason, he looked mesmerized. "I do."

"I never had anyone to lean on when I was young, so it feels good to be that person for someone else. It means a lot to me."

He looked at her intently. "Your leaders probably didn't understand you."

"No, they didn't. They were actually very apprehensive of me, and they were confused. I was just a kid, but I was a Tiger." The old resentment surfaced inside of her. "They didn't know if they could trust me."

"I see." Damon shoved his plate aside and clasped his hands together. "You didn't deserve to go through that."

She shrugged, but his words touched her. "No one does. The world isn't fair, but that's how things go."

"Yeah, huh." He chuckled. She thought she'd imagined it, but she saw a brief bitterness in his eyes again. "Are you done?"

"Yes."

"Let's go to sleep. It's late."

"Okay."

They washed the dishes and went to the empty hall.

"It's going to be so weird tomorrow, now that they're not here," she mused.

"Try to rest this weekend while they're gone. Before you know it, they'll be back, complaining their asses off."

Emry nodded, but she knew she wouldn't really rest. She always found things to do, and tomorrow she'd need to get up early for a mission.

"Will *you* take it easy this weekend?"

He smirked at her. "I'm usually pretty wild on the weekends."

She rolled her eyes. "I'm *shocked*. Really."

His laugh filled the space. "Try to sleep, Emry."

"Right back at you."

Damon

Blood, blood, blood.

Dripping down the walls, spreading across the floor.

On his hands, tingeing his clothes.

Coating his throat, burning hot with the taste of metal. Choking him. Burning him.

Damon's upper body shot up like a gunshot, his heart slamming against his chest. Desperate to slow his breathing, he hung his head and closed his eyes. The scenes from his nightmare slowly dissolved, but he could still feel the panic and taste the blood on his tongue. His body felt cold and clammy with sweat. He had to get up.

It was nine in the morning, and Emry was probably still sleeping. She had to be—they'd both gone to bed fairly late last night. Damon tossed the blanket aside and went to the bathroom for a shower. He closed his eyes as the water hit his head and back, then raised his face to meet the stream, letting the warm liquid cascade down his chest.

With all the tasks he had to complete that day, Damon's thoughts wandered. Headley didn't give him a lot of free time, plus he had a watch at noon. He definitely wouldn't make it on time to the big dinner they held every Friday night.

Once dressed, Damon headed out. A wave of cheering and laughter washed over him as he reached the bottom floor of their building.

"Primrose, my man!" a fellow Slayer greeted.

Damon's lips twitched in a smile as he stared at the incoming group of Slayers with smudges of blood on their clothes.

"How was your mission?" he asked, patting the guy's shoulder.

He had a bleeding scratch on his cheek, but other than that, he was fine.

"Awesome. We were in the White Forest."

Damon's eyes widened. "That's dangerous."

"It's big money, bro."

"Not enough."

"Actually, you might be right. We barely made it out, and only thanks to that ginger."

Damon felt his blood freeze. "Ginger? You mean my co-leader?"

The guy blinked. "She's your co-leader?"

A second later, Emry walked by with bloody wounds all over her body, and a deeper cut under her ribs. Her clothes were shredded, and out of the others that accompanied her, she definitely looked the worst. Regardless, there was still a cheerful light in her eyes as she laughed with the others. Emry was radiant, enchanting, even.

Damon had never seen her ever that happy. Still, it wasn't enough to stop the drumming in his head as she walked past his friend, ignorant to his presence. He was pissed.

"Dude?"

"Yes, she is," Damon hissed, marching after her.

When he reached their quarters, Emry faced him, and her eyes lit up.

"Hi," she simply said, a little cautious. A pale shoulder blade peeked from her torn uniform.

"What were you thinking?" His voice came out low and rough.

Her eyes turned hard. "What?"

"Taking a mission in the White Forest?"

She shook off her fatigue shirt and tossed it aside, revealing a black shirt that hadn't fared much better. Her now-exposed arms matched her brutalized shoulder, but it didn't seem like she cared as she strode towards him.

"The missions I take are my fucking business, not yours." The look in her eyes screamed at him to back off.

He couldn't.

"What about the kids? You want them to have only one leader? Or worse— get kicked out because their irresponsible leader got herself killed on a mission she *volunteered* for?"

"I was not the only participant—"

"None of them are leaders and all of them are adrenaline junkies who have nothing to lose except the money they burn gambling every Friday night." His eyes blazed.

Emry stayed silent, and Damon could almost hear her thinking. She *had* to know he was right.

At last, venom colored her eyes as she said, "It's my right to take missions. You can blame the rules that allow it, but that's how things are. So again, the missions I take are *my* fucking business." She slammed the door in his face.

Damon's anger surprised him. He took a deep breath. Had he overstepped? Yes.

He wasn't supposed to care that much, didn't have the legitimacy to care that much. But she could have died, and their unit could have fallen apart, so screw legitimacy.

Chapter 11

Poison

Damon

"I panicked, Jenna," Damon groaned. "I just panicked. She scared the shit out of me, so I yelled at her."

Jenna put her face in her hands. "Of course you did."

They were sitting inside a tiny cell on the top of a little tower, looking down on one of the gates. Sure, she wasn't supposed to be in there with him while he was on watch, but she was on the floor. If someone were to pass by, they'd only be able to see *his* head through the open window.

"She could have died, Jen. Just how stupid can she be to take a mission like that?"

Jenna could hear the anger and dissatisfaction in his voice.

"It's her choice, Damon," she said, lifting her chin. Damon knew, he just knew she was going to say something insightful like she always did. "They went to the White Forest, you say? She was probably paid well. Maybe she needs the money."

"You think she needs it so much that she'd risk her life when she doesn't have to?"

Jenna shrugged and leaned against the wall. "Either way,"—she sent him a piercing stare—"It's not any of your business, and you usually wouldn't care."

Damon turned his gaze to the window. "You're right." His eyes were losing focus, mimicking his blurry mind.

"We've been friends for years now, but I've never seen you like this."

He laughed heartily. "Yeah? I don't know why. Maybe the years around here have finally made me lose it"

She burst out laughing, but the glint in her eyes told him she wasn't buying any crap. "I'm going to get dressed for dinner, uniform and all. You still have some time to spend here."

He sighed. "Yeah, three hours of joy."

"Too much time alone with your brain, huh?"

"Smartass."

"They're paying me to be that."

* * *

After Damon's shift ended, he made his way to the dining room decorated for Friday night's formal dinner. The dining room was full of babble, joy, and jokes. The tables were wrapped with white tablecloths and topped with clean dinnerware laid out at each seat. Unlike Damon who was wearing his green fatigues with his knife set at his hip, other soldiers were in their dress uniforms.

He took a plate and started to fill it with food from the serving counter, but something felt wrong.

"The cooks made the spicy chicken in the marinade you like. What's up with you?" Jenna said as she approached him.

"Where's Emry?"

"Tiger's not here."

Damon's eyes searched for the table where the ICT soldiers were sitting.

"I figured you'd want to ask them where she was, so I already did." Jenna took a small chunk of bread from one of the breadbaskets.

His attention snapped to his friend. "And?"

"They said she went to bed early because she was tired after the mission."

Damon pondered that for a moment, then for another. He put his plate down on the counter. "I'm going to check on her."

Jenna didn't look surprised. "And your food?"

He shrugged. "I'll come back for it. I just want to make sure everything's alright with her. I have a bad feeling."

He rushed outside, earning a few curious stares. Usually, Damon Primrose wouldn't miss Friday's dinner for anything.

When he knocked on Emry's door, it took her a moment to reply. When Damon entered, he saw her sitting on her bed, head hanging low between her knees, as she was panting.

"What's going on?" He hurried to her.

"I don't know." She swallowed. "I don't... I just don't feel well."

"Damn it! I'm taking you to the infirmary. Can you walk? Do you want me to carry you?"

That made her shoot him a look, even in pain. "Don't be ridiculous."

Emry stood up, but she was breathing hard and shaking. He put his arm around her, but she only managed two steps before nearly collapsing to the floor.

He sighed and lifted her into his arms. "You know what? I don't think I'm being ridiculous."

"Whatever," she mumbled into his shirt before going quiet.

When he glanced down, he saw that she'd passed out. He carried her to the infirmary, where medical soldiers in pink uniforms examined her.

"No doubt she was poisoned," the doctor said. "She was in the White Forest today, right?"

Damon nodded. "Yes."

"Some of the demons there have highly poisonous claws. She's got a lot of scratches."

"Makes sense. Is she going to be okay?" Damon worriedly ran his hand through his hair. "She was fine when she returned."

"Why didn't she come here sooner?"

Because she's a headstrong idiot, thought Damon. "I guess she didn't think she needed to."

Holding a syringe, the doctor injected a clear liquid into Emry's arm. "This is a fast-acting antidote. I predict she'll develop a fever soon, so she'll need plenty of rest. Bring her here again if she gets worse."

"Anything else I should know?"

The doctor looked at him strangely. "You're her co-leader, right?"

"Yes."

"Just keep an eye on her, make sure she rests. She shouldn't partake in any training for the next few days. Can you carry her to the Slayers' building on your own, or do you need help?"

It was a ridiculous question, and they both knew it. The doctor was just being polite. He'd already taken her lean figure in his arms. "I'll be fine. Did anyone bring food for you and the medics?"

The doctor smiled at him. "Yes, thank you for asking."

* * *

When Emry woke in her bed, she was confused and sluggish.

"You got poisoned during the mission today," he told her, stretching his arms. "I took you to the infirmary, and they gave you an antidote."

She sat up and took a moment to comprehend what was said. "Fine. Thanks for helping me, I guess."

"Of course." The room felt awkward, but he couldn't leave yet. "Listen, about today…"

She opened her tired eyes to look at him. "What?"

"I shouldn't have yelled at you. You're right, the missions you take are none of my business." He turned and walked to the door.

That was it. He'd done what he had to do as her co-leader, and now it was time to go.

"Damon."

He stopped in his tracks.

"My family owns a store in Rows. After The Great War, only a few Tiger families stayed there, everyone else escaped. These families are our only buyers since everyone else boycotts our store." They were both silent for a minute before she continued. "These missions pay well, and I need money. I'm providing for my family. I'm the one making sure they have food on the table."

Damon sat beside her on the bed. "You can't provide for them if you're dead." He looked into her eyes. Her hair was scattered around her face, and it took everything for him not to brush it back.

Emry sighed and looked up at him, her eyes unusually warm and tired. He wanted to tuck her in, just so she could have some rest. It baffled him, scared him. He didn't *have* to worry about her now.

"I believed I could make it, and look at that—I'm alive, and I got the cash."

He pressed his lips together, trying to choose his words carefully. "What if you didn't make it?"

"But I did."

"But what if you didn't?" Damon's voice started to get louder. He tried to remind himself that he didn't want to fight with her again, but something in her—in that apathy to her own life—just drove him crazy.

"Then I'd be dead." Emry closed her eyes peacefully.

He exhaled loudly.

"Maybe it wouldn't be so bad, either."

"Emry—"

"I'm used to that," she whispered. "I've been doing this for a long time now. I get the money home. That's what keeps me alive." She tried to suppress a yawn, and he realized she was too tired to understand his mood. "That's why I was being like that to you when you won the Duels. I was preparing for it for years, Damon. *Years.* And I was the best on my team. No one could beat me. I was going to be the winner and get the money and the honor. I studied hard, aced my tests, didn't let myself hang out and had fun with the rest. I only saw that one goal, only to be beaten by one person and get second place." She closed her eyes and rubbed them with her fists. "I wanted to kill you back then. Hell, I was pissed *you* didn't kill *me*."

Damon remained quiet, processing the information. She was never that honest with him. His hands reached for her and rotated her body so she would look at him.

"Take the money," he whispered. "I don't need it. I don't need the prizes. I don't need anything. Take it all—it's yours."

Even now, she had that pissed off look in her green eyes that managed to frustrate him every single time. "No."

"Why not?"

She shrugged, and she winced in pain.

"Damn it," he said, pressing the back of his hand to her forehead. "Lie here and rest. I'm going to make you tea. Have you eaten anything?"

"I'm not hungry."

"So I'm going to fix you something to eat as well."

"You never listen," she scoffed.

"I *always* listen."

"Aren't you leaving?"

"I need to, but I'm kind of scared to leave you alone," he admitted.

She closed her eyes. "I'm just going to sleep. I'll be fine."

Chapter 12

Different

Emry

Emry tossed and turned in bed. Damon hadn't left long ago, but now that she was alone, she could feel every muscle and bone in her body aching. It was such bad timing, but she didn't regret the mission. The White Forest was dangerous enough that a visit was worth good money. Eventually, her body would heal.

When Emry opened her eyes, she saw an unfamiliar girl reading at the desk in the corner. Long, brown curls drooped over her face as her brown eyes stayed locked on Emry. After a few seconds, it clicked—that was Damon's best friend.

"I'm Jenna. You've probably seen me around. Damon asked me to watch over you while he's out."

Emry struggled to rise up. "Seriously?"

Jenna looked amused. "Yes."

"That's stupid and unnecessary."

"It's also thoughtful and caring."

The room fell silent. Eventually, Jenna returned to her reading.

"Why did you agree to do this, anyway? Don't you have better things to do than keep an eye on a stranger?" Emry asked irritably.

"I'm doing them now."

She realized that something about Jenna stood out to her. It wasn't just the cleverness in her eyes; it was her aura. It had nobleness, logic, and a cold expertise. The matter-of-fact way she turned whenever Emry spoke made it hard to be angry. Emry didn't want to argue with her, but she couldn't help herself.

"You're not supposed to be here."

"Do you want me to go?"

"No, I just stated that you're not supposed to be here."

She sighed. "And yet, here I am. Are we going somewhere with this?"

"You break rules for him?"

"He's my friend. It's what we do."

"I'm not surprised that he made you come here."

"I know, right?" the girl murmured, her eyes darting to her notes. "That bastard is so enthusiastic about any rule that he can break."

That made Emry laugh. And it hurt.

A hint of a smile lightened Jenna's face. "How are you feeling?" Emry took a deep breath. "I've been better."

"I figured."

Emry glanced at her. "You have a response to everything, don't you? No wonder you two are friends."

That made Jenna smile again, and Emry wanted to smack herself for feeling proud of it.

"Awesome. You're awake," Damon said from the doorway. In his hands was a tray of food and drinks.

Emry nodded and felt herself blush. He had helped her when she was weak, and now he was smiling as if it was taken for granted. She wasn't used to that, and didn't know how to respond. "I'm just so tired."

"I know." His amber eyes were tender. "I brought food."

"What do you have there?" Jenna asked, trying to peek at the tray.

"Just food from dinner. I got you and me some chicken." He winked. "Sweet!"

"And for you." He put a plate before Emry on a pillow. "A little of everything."

Emry stared. She hadn't eaten all day, but she didn't want to now.

"I—"

"Just a few bites," he insisted, taking a seat next to Jenna. "How is she?"

"She isn't the best sleeper, is she?"

"No." His brows furrowed, and he looked at Jenna for an explanation.

"She tossed and turned a lot in pain."

Emry didn't know how to feel about those two talking about her in her own room.

Damon eyed Emry for a moment. "I should have grabbed pain killers from the infirmary when I left. I'd better go get them."

Why was the way he was looking at her so intolerable?

"That's enough." She put her fork down. "I can go get my own painkillers. I don't need you guys. Just go do whatever the hell you need to do, and leave me alone."

Damon crossed his arms. "Em—"

Jenna shot Damon a look that silenced his protest. "Alright, Tiger. Go and get your painkillers." She gestured at the door.

Emry put the tray down and threw the blanket aside. Every movement made her hot and achy, but she knew she couldn't rely on them. Showing weakness was not an option, and nothing ever was free—especially not kindness.

After managing to sit up, Emry slowly managed to stand. They watched as she made one move and then another before collapsing into Damon's waiting arms.

"Damn it," she mumbled, trying to push him away.

"Go," Jenna told Damon. "I'll stay here."

With a stiff nod, Damon left.

"So this is how it goes? He does everything you tell him?" Emry snapped, cheeks tainted red with shame. She reached for the bed.

"Actually, it was *his* idea to get painkillers," Jenna said, without looking up from her notes.

"Whatever. Why did you agree to be here, anyway?"

"You already asked, and I answered—he's my friend."

"Yeah, but it's a big favor for a *friend*."

Jenna turned to look directly at Emry, her eyes shining with amusement. "What are you getting at, Tiger?"

Emry felt her heart pound in her chest. Maybe it was the fever, but she decided to ask. "Aren't you and Damon together?"

"Why would you think that? What behavior did we display to give you that impression?"

"I don't know." Emry rolled onto her side and her eyes met Jenna's. "You just seem really close."

It took a moment before Jenna responded. "We're just friends."

Why was it so hard to believe her?

Jenna sighed, and her expression grew kinder, lost the amusement. "He's my best friend in the whole world, and I'd do anything for him, but I'm not attracted to him."

How could someone *not* be attracted to him?

"You seem surprised."

Emry felt ashamed. What was she thinking? She was being inappropriate. It must have been that poison swirling her mind.

"You're right. It's none of my business."

"It isn't, but I sense that you're not comfortable."

"It doesn't matter how I feel."

"Do you want to feel better, though?"

"What?"

"There's a better chance that I'd be into you than him."

"Huh?" Emry scrunched her face in confusion.

"I'm a lesbian, you idiot."

Emry felt like the most ridiculous person in the world. "Oh."

Jenna examined her. "The chances are dwindling, though. Don't get me wrong, you're a knockout, but you're also an imbecile."

"Shut up," Emry growled. "How was I supposed to guess that you like women?"

"It's not just that. You're being rude to people who try to help you. That thing with the painkillers. What was that about? If he volunteers to get them for you, let him."

If Emry could move, that girl would be dead right now. Unfortunately, she was bedridden. "I don't need anyone. The minute you rely on people, you become weak."

"When I first met Damon, all I did was rely on him."

"How?"

"When we were first drafted, he was a Slayer in the elite unit, and I was Intelligence. One night, a bunch of Slayers—not from his group—broke into my residence for fun and read my diary. They learned that I was a lesbian, and didn't like that. When I got to the building, they were waiting for me. They jumped me, tore my bag... Damon happened to be passing by, and he beat them all bloody."

Emry's ears were ringing, and she could see his figure before her eyes. *If I'd been on your former team, I wouldn't have let any of those nasty things happen.*

"Ever since, he's never left my side. At first, it was because he was scared for me. You know how it is—no gay person is well-received here."

Emry nodded. She was well aware that anyone who was different was an immediate target.

"But then," Jenna continued, "we just bonded over our similarities. I'll always owe him for standing up for me. I was a short, clumsy nerd, and he was already a popular Slayer from the elite group, but none of it ever really mattered to him. He was the first person here to see me for me."

Emry looked at the ceiling, replaying his kind gestures towards her in her head. "Was he like that to a lot of people?"

Jenna looked at her with a penetrating stare. "Yeah, he was. It's one of the reasons people like him so much."

"Huh."

She should have known. The feeling of disappointment, the bungling feeling in her heart felt, worse now. Jenna was right, she *was* a fucking idiot.

"It's different with you, though," Jenna stated, shattering her mind to pieces.

"*What?*"

Before she could answer, Damon burst inside holding a small bottle of painkillers. Emry wasn't sure if the ridiculous amount of relief that she felt was because of the painkillers or him, but she also wished that he'd come just a few minutes later.

He sighed disappointedly when he saw the full plate next to her bed. "Come on."

"Just give me the damn pills." She tried to reach for them, but he backed away.

"These are pretty strong. The doc said you should be very careful with them."

"Fine."

"You have to eat first."

They had a staring battle for a moment, but Emry angrily relented. She took the plate and slowly started to dig in.

"Must everything be so hard with her?" Jenna asked with a raised brow.

"You've got no idea. Only a week now and I'm already losing my mind."

"You two are sickeningly condescending," Emry mumbled with a mouthful of food. "You think you're so smart, don't you?"

"We *are* smart," said Jenna.

"And we *are* condescending," Damon said, elbowing her, and they burst into laughter.

Emry's face grew hotter, and she soon realized that their boisterous laughter was growing quieter.

"She's passing out," she heard Jenna's voice say from somewhere far away.

Emry thought she heard Damon curse. She felt herself leaning against his abdomen, his arm under her lulling head. He cradled her and put her to bed.

Emry closed her eyes, feeling herself drifting off, but she could still hear them talking.

"I'll wake up in a few hours to check on her. She's still burning up."

"Don't exhaust yourself too much, Damon."

"I won't."

"I told her how we met, by the way."

"You did?" Emry could hear relief in his voice.

Jenna chuckled. "You're glad I told her I prefer women, aren't you?"

She could not make out what he answered back, as the voices turned into silence.

Chapter 13

Education

Damon

Damon had spent most of his weekend taking care of Emry. She was barely conscious on Saturday, but on Sunday, she looked a bit better.

When Monday arrived, Damon stood alone at the gate, waiting for their squad. Once they arrived, they all gathered into a half-circle around him, looking exhausted from their travels and confused to see him alone.

"I hope the first weekend as an enlisted citizen went well. Are you all ready for this week?" Damon said.

"Where's Tiger?" Kalen asked, baffled.

All his soldiers were frowning at him. *Great*, Damon thought.

He glared back at them. "Thank you for being thrilled to see me, shitheads. Emry's sick."

They grumbled in disappointment. It was understandable, though. Emry had always been the one to help them with paperwork and other things that would bore him. They knew they could depend on her for anything.

"I'm not happy about it either, but we're going to let her rest for a few days," he informed.

"What happened?" Ella asked, adjusting her brown hair into a neat ponytail.

Damon rubbed his palms together. "You've all had a long journey. Let's get you settled, then we'll talk. When we enter the house, be as quiet as possible so that you don't wake her. Understood?"

"Yes, sir," they replied unenthusiastically.

Back in the hall, the group sat on the cold floor around Damon.

"Emry was poisoned by a demon during a mission on Friday. She was given some medicine, and the doctor ordered her to rest for a few days."

The room stayed quiet for a moment.

"I knew it! One dangerous mission and that's it," Ahron whined.

"Of course. That's the military," Anoki gently pointed out as she brushed her black tresses from her face. "We have to get used to it."

"Why are you even here if you're that afraid?" Riggs asked.

Ahron looked down and scratched his knee. "I have nowhere else to go."

"Did your parents kick you out?" Lucy asked sympathetically. "Mine kicked me out, but they had their reasons."

"No, I kicked *myself* out," Ahron responded.

"What do you mean?" Kalen asked.

"My house wasn't the best place for a kid," he explained, adjusting his glasses on his nose. "I had to find somewhere else to live to get a better education."

"Education? *Here?*" Ella scoffed incredulously.

Ahron just shrugged in response.

"Why did they put you in the Slayer Unit of all things?" Riggs wondered aloud.

"Do you think Ahron doesn't belong in our little group?" Damon interrupted, his brow raised.

Riggs rubbed the back of his neck and avoided Damon's eyes. "Well, he's afraid of weapons, of dying..."

Damon chuckled. "We all are. It doesn't mean shit."

"It doesn't?" Lucy asked.

"It doesn't."

"So what *does* matter?" Anoki asked, her eyes shining with curiosity.

"What matters," Damon said in a much more serious tone, "is your ability to learn."

"How is my ability to learn going to help me against demons?" Kalen asked. *Stupid question,* Damon thought.

"Learning will help you focus on your weaknesses and strengths. You'll learn to counter-attack, memorize your enemy's movements, and analyze positioning." Damon shook his head in disappointment. "You think you're safe just because you're big and tall? That's how soldiers fall."

Lucy broke the prolonged silence that followed. "Tiger isn't so big, and she's one of the best."

"The point is, if you want to be successful at anything, you must have the ability to learn." Damon looked directly at Ahron. "And I expect that from all of you."

They nodded in unison.

"Alright, take an hour to rest. After that, we'll practice."

"Damn it. I thought we were supposed to have classes on Monday, not practice," Ella whispered to Riggs.

"You were supposed to," Damon said, making her jump. "But Emry was supposed to lead those classes, and since she's out, there's been a change of plans. Oh, and don't bother whispering. I hear everything. If you were whispering around Emry, she'd punish you. Rest assured."

"Ah," Ahron muttered uneasily. "Why don't *you* teach us, then?"

"That's a good question." Damon grinned. "I'd just rather have practice."

Ella frowned at everything Damon said, but waited until he left the hall to protest. "If Tiger heard that he's doing practice instead of class, *he'd* be punished!"

"You have one strike left!" They all jumped at Damon's voice from the stairs outside the hall.

* * *

By the time evening rolled around, they were covered in sweat and mud.

"Let me see how Emry is doing," Damon told them in the hall. "I have no idea why, especially now, but maybe she'll want to see you guys. Stay here."

He walked to her door and gently knocked. "Emry?"

It took a moment before she answered. "Come in."

He found her sitting on her bed, still pale and weak. Maybe it was because she was tired, but her green eyes welcomed him with tenderness. They lacked the fight and the coldness they usually held.

Damon's breathing hitched when he saw her. "There's a bunch of troublemakers out there wanting to say hello." He pointed outside.

Her eyes lit up. She almost rolled out of bed, but then peeked at herself under the blanket and cursed. "I need to change first. Can you…" Emry pointed her finger, making swirling motion.

He blew out a breath and turned around. Different images of her passed through his mind, and with each one, he froze. He couldn't do that, he couldn't yearn for that. Damon could never get what he wanted, because that would destroy everything he worked so hard to build. Everything *she* worked so hard to build.

He thought he was over this little infatuation with her. He'd carried her, taken care of her, but he thought it was only for the sake of friendship, group unity, and leadership. Regardless, as he heard the rustling of her clothes behind him, he found himself stupidly, desperately *wanting* her.

Emry

"Alright," Emry said, latching the button on her pants.

Damon faced her as soon as she spoke. The first thing she noticed was how dark his eyes were. Usually, they had a special hue, like molten gold. Right now, they were dark, frustrated, and staring right into hers. In an instant, Emry felt herself tense. She couldn't help but be trapped by his stare.

The atmosphere changed. Emry could feel her mouth go dry, and her heart beating fast against her chest cavity. She knew that feeling. *That* was the feeling she had every time she was in danger, but somehow, it was different now.

Damon cleared his throat, and the spell was broken. She took a deep breath and relished in his mud-covered body and ruffled hair. Oddly, the thick, sticky mud only complimented him.

He smirked and opened her door, gesturing for her to leave first. She frowned, but did it anyway.

Cheers erupted from their recruits, leaving her feeling self-conscious.

"Hey there," she said as she took a seat against the wall and closed her eyes for a moment.

"Did you really get poisoned?" Anoki asked, her dark brows creased with worry.

"No," Ella said sarcastically. "Damon probably lied to us just for the fun of it."

"Shut up," Anoki spat.

"You shut up," Ella retorted eloquently.

"Hey!" Damon raised a brow. "Knock it off."

They both fell silent, and Emry shook her head fondly. "How was your first weekend out?"

"Mine was okay. I finally got my little apartment fixed," Lucy bragged.

Emry nodded at her. "I'm glad to hear it."

Riggs drew closer to Emry. "How are you feeling?"

"I'm fine. I feel a lot better than I did on Friday. I think I'm going to be back with you guys tomorrow."

Ahron looked worried. "But you're struggling to move."

Emry smiled reassuringly. "I'll be fine." Then she finally took a proper look at all of them. "Wait, how did you get so dirty during class?"

"We didn't have class," Kalen blurted out.

"What do you mean you *didn't have class*?" The volume of Emry's voice had increased significantly.

"Told you," Ella whispered.

"Umm..." Ahron said uncomfortably. "We had practice instead."

Emry glared at Damon, and a guilty look washed over his face.

"Great team spirit you got there," he sneered. "I should punish all of you for being tactless morons."

Emry closed her eyes, trying to calm the rage inside of her, but ultimately decided not to yell at him in front of the teens. However, after their soldiers went to sleep, Emry followed Damon to his room, closing the door behind them.

"We need to talk," she barked.

He turned to her as if he knew what was going to happen. "What?" His tone was rock hard.

She came closer. "You seriously chose practice over class today? What the hell were you thinking?"

"I did. So what?"

"You shouldn't have. Why do you think they have a schedule?"

He shrugged and turned away.

"Don't walk away from me!"

He faced her again and crossed his arms. "I didn't feel like doing class, okay? Why do you have to be so obsessive about every goddamn thing?"

"Obsessive?"

"You heard me."

If she could have burned him right then, she would've. "Well," she said quietly, "being obsessive is what's kept me alive. There's a reason they're supposed to have more classes than practices at the beginning. What will happen next year when they face a demon and can't tell a Golubaya and Belaya apart?"

"If they die next year, that's not going to be the reason. Maybe the reason would be you being so uptight about everything."

Emry couldn't believe what she was hearing. "Screw you, Damon! If you keep doing shit like this, Headley will hear about it!" She stomped off to her room and slammed the door.

Damon's bitter cackle and parting words came clear through the walls. "Be my guest."

Chapter 14

Morons

Emry

Emry spent the next morning in the ICT building, helping her friends study. She reluctantly left the morning classes to Damon, but it was clear that she was still livid at the situation. Nevertheless, Glen and Ian were more important.

"Just be calm, alright? You'll do great," she encouraged them.

This was it for Ian and Glen, and she could feel their excitement and apprehension. These were her best friends, and they were on the verge of panic.

"Right," Glen said, clutching a paper bag. "Great." He held the bag up to his mouth and took a deep breath.

"And the odds are in your favor," Emry added. "The two of you have been fixing everything around here. You've got this."

"That's right." Ian blew out a breath and paced around the room. "That's right. Right?"

"Right," Emry said confidently. "You'd better. I don't have any real friends around here except for you guys."

Ian halted in his tracks. "What about Primrose? I thought you were starting to get along."

"Called me 'obsessive' last night."

They both stared at her. Glen froze with his paper bag half-full of air.

Emry shrugged. "It's fine. I don't give a shit."

"That jerk thinks he's such a big shot," Ian declared.

"Are you okay?" Glen asked, distracted enough to put the bag aside.

"Of course." Emry shrugged. "Not the first time some idiot's thrown words at me."

She glanced at the wall clock. "Anyway, I have to go teach some classes. Good luck today, guys, I'll see you at dinner. You've got this." She looked at them pointedly.

Ian took a deep breath. "We won't know the results until midnight."

"Oh, God," Glen mumbled, reaching for the paper bag again. "Oh, God."

* * *

When Emry arrived at the dusty classroom, her soldiers were present and ready, but their teacher was not. "Where's Damon?"

"Headley called him," Ahron said hesitantly. "Just a few minutes ago. Said he's got a job for him to do, so we finished the lesson and he left."

Okay then, Emry thought, turning to the board. "Who can tell me the main types of demons?"

Lucy raised her hand.

"Go ahead, Lucy."

"Golubaya, Belaya, and Chernaya," Lucy said with a smug smile.

"That's right." Emry wrote the names on the board. "And what's special about each one of them?"

Lucy raised her hand.

"Somebody else."

Lucy dropped her hand.

Kalen raised his. "Golubaya look like animals, Belaya look like humans, and Chernaya can look like anything."

"Very good," his leader said. "Which is the most dangerous?"

Anoki raised her hand. "It depends on the demon itself. It could be any of them, depending on the level."

Emry nodded. "Which one do you think poisoned me?"

Silence.

Ella's palm shot up. "Got to be Golubaya, because they seem like animals, and they have claws, so maybe they can release venom as well."

Riggs raised his chin a bit. "It could also be Chernaya. They can look like anything, so maybe they can look like animals too."

"But who said demons that look like humans can't poison you? They're not really humans," Ahron pointed out, sitting up straight. "It could be Belaya as well." He glanced at Emry and his cheeks flushed.

Emry raised a brow at Ahron. "You've got a decent point."

She could see a shy smile blooming on his pale face.

"Any demon could potentially poison you, no matter what they look like. We can never know their power potential with real certainty. We always have to be careful and consider what we don't know. In this case, Ella was right; the demon I fought was a Golubaya, and it looked like a bear."

Kalen choked. "You fought with a *bear*?"

Emry shrugged. "Wouldn't be the first time. When the day comes, you all will."

He looked a little skeptical.

"I can beat a bear." Lucy crossed her arms.

Riggs laughed at her. "Shut up. You can't."

"Wanna bet? I can get *your* nose inside your ass."

"Enough." Emry put out a hand. "Who can tell me a Golubaya's most common forms?"

Anoki raised her hand. "Snake, bear, pigeon, and crocodile."

"Good, but you missed one."

"Elephant," whispered Kalen.

Emry pointed at him and nodded in approval, adding it to the board. "That's right."

"These are just the forms we've run into in our battles," Emry said gravely. "You never know what may come, so you have to be prepared for surprises." She took a deep breath. "Did Damon go through the demons' different levels?"

They nodded.

"Excellent. Explain them to me."

Riggs held up his hand. "Level one is easy, level two is scary, and level three is the scariest."

Emry stared at him. "I see."

They all chuckled, but she raised her hand to make them stop.

"Alright, as Riggs just said, level-one demons are the easiest to slay, but it doesn't make them *easy*. Most of the demons at that level are Golubaya. Level two is far more difficult. When we face a level two, there are usually casualties. Most of the demons at that level are Chernaya. At last, we have level three. All the level-three demons we've ever seen are Belaya. The demons at level three are the only ones who can talk. Are we clear?"

Everyone nodded.

"Good. Any questions?"

"How can we recognize when an animal is actually a demon?" Anoki asked, her hand in the air. "Or when someone is not human?"

"Excellent questions. Have any of you ever seen a demon?"

They all looked dumbly at each other, except for Ella. She moved uncomfortably in her seat.

"Ella?" Emry crossed her arms and gestured to her with her chin.

"I have," she admitted. "Golubayas have blue auras. I was also told that Chernayas have a black one, and Belayas a white one. But I've only seen a Golubaya."

"That's right."

"How come you've seen a demon?" Lucy turned to Ella.

Ella took a deep breath. "It was the last round of the big war," she started.

For some reason, Emry could already feel dread rise inside of her.

"I was three years old. Our neighbors were Tigers, immigrants from Rows, but they'd always seemed nice, so my family trusted them. One night, in the middle of dinner, they burst into our house with a bunch of demons. I was small enough to hide in a closet, but they killed everyone else."

"How do you even remember that?" Kalen asked. "You were so little."

"Some of it I remember, some of it people told me. Old family friends in Seka took me in and raised me. I joined the army because they were running low on money and it's my turn to save them."

"Aww," everyone said in unison. Even rude and sarcastic Ella let out her sensitive side for a moment. Then they all looked at Emry.

Emry closed her eyes. "Ella, on behalf of the Tigers, I apologize for what happened to you." She felt her voice choke. "If you want to sit together and talk after lessons, we can."

Ella shook her head. "I'm okay. I know you're not like those who betrayed my family."

The girl elegantly crossed her legs one over the other, immediately ready to get back to lessons. Admiration and guilt bloomed inside of Emry, but neither was a match for the black void she could feel herself sinking into.

Damon

Millions of thoughts swarmed Damon's mind as he walked to the Slayers building. Emry and the squad were probably going straight from class to dinner, so he knew the hall would be empty.

He sat on one of the chairs Riggs and Kalen had brought inside. As he entwined his fingers and leaned his forearms on his knees, his head hung low.

Damon had done the job that Headley had assigned. A demon had been disturbing a little village not far from Seka, and he was tasked with killing it. When he'd returned to Headley's office to tell him that the work was done, it was empty. Of course, he got curious. He was always a little curious, and it was a rare opportunity.

Hell, he hadn't expected to learn what he did while he was rummaging through Headley's stuff. Usually when he did that, he never found anything interesting. What would he tell Emry?

After dinner, the kids would have free time, and the two of them could talk in private. Should he even tell her what he'd found? How would he tell her? He had to tell her. Emry would tear him apart if she ever found out he'd kept this from her.

As if sensing his guilty thoughts, Emry appeared in the room. Her hair was the first thing he saw, the bright hue bringing life into the dull, colorless room.

"Where are the kids?" Damon looked up at her.

"Dinner," she answered, looking him over. "I'm going soon. I just came to put away some notes from class."

She didn't spare him another look as she went to her room. He wasn't surprised that she didn't bother asking him if he would be joining them. Damon could still taste the bitterness from their fight yesterday.

"Wait," he called out.

Emry faced him and crossed her arms. "What?"

"I need to talk to you."

She sighed and approached him. "Alright, but my friends are waiting."

"Listen," he said, standing up. "I went on a mission today, slayed a Belaya at a village near Reefstone."

"Alright."

"When I returned, Headley's office was open. I rummaged through his stuff."

"Are you kid—"

"Emry..."

She looked exasperated. "*What?*"

Damon walked a little closer. "Headley... I think he might give us some work later this year. Not just you and me, but our team."

She stared at him, green eyes widened with bewilderment. "What?"

"Demons from the east sea are approaching, and people from the eastern line are in danger," he said as he ran his hands through his hair. "There's a chance he'll put us in Ob."

He could feel the tension in her silence, and it scared him.

"Why us?" she mumbled to herself. "Why not a more experienced group?"

"Some of them are already there, gathering information."

"How come we didn't hear anything about it?" Her voice was getting louder now. Her eyes blazed like fire as they raised to meet his.

"Intelligence soldiers are still investigating, but this could deteriorate into war. They're supposed to tell us soon, but there's no official order to do so yet."

"Got it." Emry turned away, but bumped into one of the chairs. With a grunt, she lifted it and threw it at the wall, breaking it into multiple pieces.

Damon cursed and sprinted after her, blocking her way. "Where are you going?"

"To Headley's office. I want to clear up this nonsense," she fumed.

"You can't."

"Damon, move! You know, and I know, that we can't let this happen. They're not ready. We need at least a year before they're put on a battlefield."

He shifted in his spot and looked down at her, praying she would listen. "There's nothing we can do about it. There's nothing *he* can do about it. The commanders won't change their minds just because we disagree!"

"Do you really not care that they could die?" she whispered. He could feel the fury practically pouring from her.

"Of course I—"

Out of patience, Emry tried to go around him, and when he blocked her again, she lunged. Damon's instincts kicked in before the first blow came, but he had forgotten just how fast she was, and it was too late—Emry was already aiming the second one. He cursed as he had to block her legs with one of his, and twist her arms so her back was slammed against his chest and her arms were caught in his.

"Damn it!" she shouted, struggling ferociously.

But Emry wasn't the only one that was hurting. He could feel her blows, and the throbbing from where she'd hit him.

"Stop it," he said through gritted teeth. "Do you think this is easy for me?"

"Let me go!"

Damon twisted her arms a little more, and she stilled. "Calm the fuck down," he hissed. "Then we'll talk."

It took a minute or two, but he could feel her breathing slow down, and the tension in her body subsided. Emry's head fell to the side, and her arms went limp in his grip. Too much. It was a bit too much.

Damon let out a breath and released her. "You know it'll only bring you trouble. It can ruin everything you've built so far, and for nothing. Don't go to Headley."

When he swirled Emry around to look at him, he saw a hollow look in her eyes. Damon struggled to say something comforting, but she just walked away.

Emry

"Hey," Jenna said as she sat next to Emry on the grass. It was already dark outside, and dinner had finished long ago. Emry couldn't bring herself to think of her friends, who were probably wondering where she'd been. But it seemed silly to worry about it now. Her soldiers were going to battle in a few months, and they would probably die there.

"Did Damon send you?"

"Of course," Jenna said, stretching her legs on the grass. "Although I'm not sure why he thinks *I* should talk to you."

"Look." Emry refused to make eye contact. "I don't think you actually want to be friends or whatever Damon asked you to do. I fucking hate my life, and you don't have to get involved because there's nothing you can say that'll help."

"That's not—"

"I have almost nothing good in my life, and when I do get something good, I have to worry about it being taken away from me. Every fucking time."

Jenna joined her in staring straight ahead. "There will be a time when everything will be taken from you, including yourself, but it's not now. This is the army, not a summer camp. So what if you were supposed to have a few more months? Things change. Adapt."

"I don't need this." Emry shook her head. "I just want to throw everything away and leave."

"And where will you go?"

"I don't know. Somewhere I don't have any obligations. Somewhere where nobody knows me. Somewhere where I don't have to survive, where no one is depending on me," she said bitterly. "I don't want to be here anymore."

Occasionally, Emry found herself thinking about it. It was dark, scary, unwelcome, but she wondered anyway. Was there any meaning to life? To *her* life? Everything was pointless. There was no beating around the bush with Jenna. Emry noticed the gleam of understanding in her eyes.

"So, you want to be dead."

Emry just rested her cheek on her knees, looking at her. "Is that such a bad thing?"

"Well, we usually try to make other arrangements for ourselves."

"I don't belong." She closed her eyes, feeling it wash over her. "Not here, not anywhere."

"Maybe you don't."

"And my soldiers are going to die in a battle in a few months."

"Maybe, but sitting here is not going to help you or them. Taking your soldiers to extreme practices and speeding up their classes might, though."

"You're right."

"Of course."

"It doesn't make me feel better, though. Maybe I should really kill myself and get everything over with." She turned her eyes to the darkness again.

She'd never said those words to anyone before, not even to herself, not like that. She didn't know why she chose to open up now, and why to *her*, but she did.

Jenna snorted.

Emry looked at her incredulously. "*What?*"

"You're a responsible human being, and you have people that are depending on you."

"And if I only had me?"

Jenna stared at the sky for a moment and then lowered her eyes to meet Emry's. "Then, maybe. Just in case, I'll tell Damon to keep an eye on you."

"Do whatever you want. I don't care."

"Yeah? You are the leader of the elite group, you ungrateful punk." She sounded angry now. "Some people who didn't do as well as you are looking for themselves right now on the streets."

"I worked for that position for *years*," Emry snarled at her. "Don't preach to me."

Jenna didn't back down. "You were smart, and you knew you had to study. Some people weren't. That's another advantage."

"You've got answers for any fucking thing that comes out of my mouth, right?"

"That's what I do for a living, *Tiger*. It's not fair. Nothing is fair. All you can do is fight. So be a warrior, be a survivor, because that's who you are, and that's what you do."

Emry felt something different with those words. How many times did she have to stand up again after being punched?

"Fine," she said eventually.

"You know what? He should have come here himself," Jenna grumbled.

"He knew I didn't want to talk."

"So what are you doing now? Chirping?"

Emry couldn't help it—she laughed.

Jenna stared at her. "You two are so smart, but I swear to God—you are complete morons."

Chapter 15

Within

Damon

Damon raised his head to a knock at his bedroom door. Emry silently came in and closed the door behind her, leaning against it and taking a deep breath. Her eyes were fixed on the floor. "Sorry about my behavior earlier."

He examined her. "It's fine."

She nodded and turned to leave.

"How was class today?" he asked.

She turned. Something changed in her eyes, in her face. It was there only for a moment, but he always closely observed everything about her, and he couldn't have missed it.

"It was fine."

"Did something happen? You seemed agitated when we met after that."

He stood up. She kept quiet, and it only confirmed his suspicions. He took a step closer.

"Tell me," Damon demanded.

It took a moment before she spoke. "Ella has seen demons before."

He frowned. "It's good that she has experience, isn't it?"

Emry shrugged, but her shoulders were shaking. "When she was younger, her house was attacked by demons after Tigers betrayed her parents..." She took in a shaky breath, and he realized with a jolt that she was crying. "I ran into a lot of soldiers that Tigers have hurt. So many accusations pointed at me, so much shame reflected on me... This girl didn't accuse me, but she's my soldier, and I just wonder if some part of her hates me, too."

Damon gently wrapped one arm around her shoulders, and her tears dropped. Her profile was against his body, her head resting gently against his chest. Touching her was an instinct, but now his heart was beating fast inside his ribcage. He tried to think of something—anything—to say to make this better.

"I'm sorry that it's like this." Damon caressed Emry's arm as he rubbed his cheek against her hair. He added another arm around her, tightening his hold on her. Her pain made him suffer. "It's not your fault. You weren't the one who attacked her. It's not your responsibility, and you know it. She's smart enough to know it too. I'm sure Ella doesn't hold anything against you."

"I just, for once, wanted a clean start," Emry said quietly. She was crying, but she wasn't as agitated now. She was still holding back, and he could feel it. "Without feeling guilty or having any kind of bad history, and I finally thought I did with my own soldiers. I'm used to blocking anything people throw at me, and it always works. But these are *my* soldiers. It's not fair."

"Your soldiers know who you are, and have only admiration for *you*," he clarified. The feeling of her in his arms was more intimate than anything he'd ever experienced. He rubbed her back soothingly. "I know it's been tough lately, but it'll get better."

A knock on the door startled them both. Emry gently pulled away and stepped back while he answered it.

"Hey Luc, how's it going?" he quietly asked the red-headed soldier looking up at him.

"Okay," she replied with a hesitant smile. Damon had only opened the door a smidge, but he was certain that Lucy had seen Emry in the background. "Headley asked me to call you and Tiger to the dining room. Everyone is gathering there for a council meeting."

"Alright. Gather everyone and go. We'll be there in a minute."

Lucy acknowledged his instructions and left for the hall.

Damon placed his back on the door and pushed it closed.

"Thanks," Emry mumbled. "We should go." Something in her eyes was still off, detached. "I can't believe we're going to battle in a few months. Damon, it means we have to change everything we have planned."

He nodded. "We'll have to wait for an announcement, but it's good that we know now instead of later."

"I would have killed him," Emry mused.

"Headley?" A small smile tugged at the right corner of his lips.

"What's so funny?" she snapped.

Damon snickered. "He's an old dog, but he's tough as hell. I'm not sure *I* can beat him."

"Let's just go and get it over with." She went to leave, but he put a hand on her arm and turned her to face him.

"Wait."

"What now? You always tell me to wait. It's getting old," Emry tried to joke, but it sounded forced.

Damon didn't take his hand away. Instead, he looked into her eyes and reached out to hold her forearms. "I don't know where we're going to be sent, or what we're going to face, but I promise you I'll do everything I can to make sure you and the others are okay."

Emry closed her eyes, took his hand, and gave it a little squeeze. He could see the redness spreading across her face, making his heart beat faster. It was ridiculous how a simple gesture could make him feel so overwhelmed.

"I wasn't in the elite group, Damon." She opened her eyes. "I lost friends, plenty of them. I don't want to lose any of the troops with us... Especially not before they even get a chance to train and study."

"I know. We'll do everything we can—as a team."

Emry nodded and Damon could finally see her smile a little when she repeated, "As a team."

Emry

I promise you I'll do everything I can to make sure you and the kids are okay.

His words echoed in Emry's mind again and again as they strode to the dining room. She didn't like that they made her feel better—she wasn't helpless, after all.

The first thing she noticed in the dining room was exceptionally crowded. Usually, people would pick up their food and take it back to their living quarters, leaving the majority of the space unoccupied. The only exception was Friday's formal dinner.

Emry racked her brain for a possible reason, scanning the room for any clues. *Of course, how could I have forgotten?* ICT's finals were today!

"Oh my God," she breathed, prompting Damon to look at her.

"What?"

"My friends, they had their tests today. I need to check on Ian and Glen. Can you see them?"

"You mean your pair of puppies?"

"*Damon!*" She whacked his chest with the back of her hand.

Feigning pain, Damon pointed towards a group of ICT in blue uniforms, where Glen was jumping up and down in excitement. "Looks like they're over there."

"I've got to go talk to them," Emry said. "Find the rest of our squad. I'll join you guys in a few minutes."

She hurried to Glen and grabbed his shoulder. "How'd it go?"

"We're not sure." Ian looked at her with blurry eyes. "But we think... there's a chance we didn't screw it up."

"Definitely!" Glen chimed in. "Tiger, we've been comparing answers since we got out of there, and we both answered almost everything the same!"

"And we knew how to deal with the machinery, so there might be a chance we're going to stick together." A small smile crept across Ian's lips, like he couldn't actually believe it.

"God, I hope so." Emry gave them an encouraging look. "I'm so happy for you guys. I'm going to stay with you until we get the results, okay?"

"Oh, please." Glen danced around like a frantic squirrel. "I don't know if I'll make it to midnight. I just need to know."

"You have to." Ian playfully nudged Glen's side. "You didn't survive that test just to die before they publish the results."

They all laughed.

"And where were *you* at dinner?" Ian swirled around to eye Emry suspiciously.

"I was with Damon. We had something serious to talk about."

The three of them, like a murder of crows, glanced at the man in question. He was standing with their soldiers, a smirk on his face.

"Did you finally make peace?" Glen peeked at her.

"We actually didn't talk about that… but I think we're good."

Ian scrunched his nose. "He had no right to talk to you that way."

"You're absolutely right. Don't think I—"

"Leaders, gather your units," a voice called out. It belonged to Amalric, the chief commander. His white hair was short on his round head, but his narrow eyes were dark and sharp with intelligence. They rarely saw him, yet his presence always demanded respect—and he got it, no contest.

There was something that set Amalric apart from the other commanders. It wasn't just that he was the chief commander—the highest rank—it was also the atmosphere around him. It was rigid and mysterious. Emry admired him for it.

Quietly, the room obeyed, and Emry took her place next to Damon with their soldiers standing behind them. Every single soldier stood at attention, awaiting further instructions.

"Today, the members of ICT completed their final exams. We'll score the results and post them at midnight," the chief commander continued. "To conclude the cycle, we're putting on a ball Thursday night, after your soldiers leave for the weekend."

He almost spat the word *ball*, as if he despised the idea. Why wouldn't he? Emry got it. It was stupid. They were soldiers. Why did they need such frivolous events? To celebrate risking their lives over and over? Working their asses off?

"Only those dressed in black and white will be permitted to enter, and you'll receive an adapted schedule on Wednesday in preparation for the event." Amalric adjusted his hat, which was neatly tucked under his arm. "ICT, once again, congratulations on finishing your finals in one piece. Dismissed."

The crowd saluted the chief commander and watched as he departed.

* * *

Emry and her crew marched back to the Slayers building as soon as they were released.

"He always seems so pissed off," Damon said, shortening his strides to match Emry's. "He just announced a party as if it was a funeral."

The kids laughed.

Emry, who didn't mind being the party-pooper, spoke up. "It's unnecessary. We don't need to throw a ball. I bet he didn't even want to have it, and the council just wouldn't let it go because it's tradition."

Damon stared at her. "You don't like the idea?"

"No." She turned to look at the dark road and noticed that her soldiers were also staring at her. "We're not here to party, and we shouldn't waste time on that."

"Come on," Damon laughed, and she could feel how determined he was to ease the tension she'd created. "It boosts morale. Help me out here, guys. Wouldn't you attend the ball if you could?"

"I would!" Lucy jumped in.

Ella huffed. "I think it's a waste of time, too."

Ahron raised his head from the ground slowly. "I think it's a good idea for motivation and spirit."

Riggs rolled his eyes dramatically, and Ahron blushed with embarrassment. Sometimes, Emry was seriously worried about how easy it was to make him feel like that.

"What about you, Anoki?" Damon asked.

He could see the girl's body tremble for a moment, as if a tremor had passed through her. "I don't like dances very much."

"Why?" Kalen asked from right next to her.

She looked ashamed and hesitant. "In the west side of She'e, they usually organize balls to exhibit girls for buyers. It's a bidding party."

Emry blew out an exasperated breath. "We put so much effort into fighting demons, we never really pay attention to the ones within us."

Chapter 10

Blood Crime

Emry

The next morning, Damon stopped her in the corridor before they went to wake up the kids. "Listen," he ventured, "are you open to do something different with them today?"

She leaned back against the cold, gray wall, and Damon mimicked her movement. "What do you have in mind?"

"I was thinking about taking them to the Black Forest."

"Damon—"

"We won't take them far, just enough so they would be familiar with our surroundings," he said quietly. "I just want them to be ready for whatever may come."

"Alright..." Emry frowned. "But we're not taking them too far."

"Luckily, they have us as instructors. If demons attack, it'll be a great teaching moment." He performed a playful attack, demonstrating how he'd handle one of their foes. "Besides, it's better to do it now than when it's cold out."

Damon

"Rise and shine, you elite rats! We're going on an adventure!" Damon shouted. "You got fifteen minutes. Get ready or get left behind."

The troops shuffled to get ready, excited that they didn't have to do their normal routine, and would instead be out in the lush vegetation.

"You see that crooked tree?" Emry asked, pointing at a bent tree covered in green moss. "You can use it as a focal point. If you walk this way,"—she pointed at one of the yellow trails—"you'll reach Ob. If you choose this way,"—she turned and pointed at another trail—"you'll reach the conjunction between the Black Forest and the White Forest."

"You shouldn't walk to the White Forest, though. You're not ready for that kind of place."

"What's in the White Forest?" Lucy asked.

"Demons, and lots of them," Emry replied. "Mostly Golubaya. Five years ago, it was oozing with Belaya. The forest's name is a direct reference to their aura."

"What happened?" Riggs asked.

"We happened." Emry grimaced. "It was a nasty operation."

"You took part in it?" Damon asked incredulously. His team was there, but he'd never seen her. In fact, quite a few of his friends were killed during that cursed mission.

She nodded, her lips pursing into a sour line. "Myself and five others fought in that battle. Only I survived."

Emyr's eyes met Damon's, and he could feel a connection form between them. It was unlike the other connections he had shared with her. Losing friends in the same battle—people who grew up and fought with you—was something only those who had survived could understand. He desperately wanted to go to her and walk by her side, but they'd agreed on this formation for a reason.

"Does that mean this forest is full of Chernaya?" Ahron asked. "Since it's called the Black Forest."

Damon cleared his throat. "It was once. It's different now, and not because we attacked. Chernaya withdrew twenty years ago, and honestly, we have no idea where they went."

"Great," Ella scoffed. "How reassuring."

Damon laughed. "Nothing is ever reassuring in the army."

He glanced back at Emry. The green in her eyes matched the green around them. He only had a moment to admire them before she suddenly stopped walking, and those captivating eyes widened. He heard loud gasps around him before he returned his attention to the group's front. Riggs clasped his hand over his mouth and ran to a bush to puke.

In front of them were two men hanging from a tree. Their fresh corpses were impaled by long arrows, and their empty eyes were as blank as their expressions. Blood stained their clothes and faces, a clear sign that they had been fighting for their lives. Carved on the trunk above their heads was a Tiger's head painted in red.

Damon's heart was pounding now. It wasn't the first time he'd seen something like that, but it had been a while.

He looked at Emry again. Her mouth was pursed, her eyes hard. She pushed past the others. "Take the troops back."

"What about you?" he asked quietly, struggling to breathe.

"I need to bury them."

She turned to the recruits, her eyes blazing. "Damon will take you to the base now, when you get there—"

"Tiger, watch out!" Lucy screamed.

Emry didn't need her warning; she was ready when they attacked. Two black humanoid monsters surrounded by black auras jumped at her. Though the hollow-eyed figures resembled ghosts, their bodies were thick and hairy.

Merciless and deadly, two tiny knives were all she needed to defeat them. Emry focused on the first demon. With a palm strike, she hit it on the stomach and then slashed it. The demon fell to the ground as the other launched towards her backside. Without hesitation, Emry flung her arms backwards, stabbing it with both knives. Then, with a kick to the chin, she knocked the creature into the air, slashing its throat to finish it off.

Her face, void of emotion, was splattered with blood. Stooping down, Emry lifted the first demon's head for the others to see. "What is this?" she asked, her voice hard and demanding. The kids stood motionless, their voices lost to shock.

"What is this?" she repeated louder, shaking the lifeless body.

Kalen cleared his throat. "That's a... Chernaya."

"Good." Emry nodded and let it drop to the ground. "Now look." She lifted the second body. "You slash it across." She gestured at the bloody cut on the demon's neck. "Just like Damon showed you last week. Do you remember?" They nodded weakly. "Good." Emry released the body, and it landed on the ground with a thump. "Now go."

She stood there, covered in blood, with her own people slaughtered before her. The last thing Damon wanted to do was leave her by herself.

Taking a deep breath, he found his voice. "Come on," he ordered. "Let's get back to the base."

* * *

When they arrived at the gate, Damon spun Ella around to face him. "Run to Headley's office. Tell him what happened, and that Emry and I are still in the Black Forest. Everyone else is dismissed for the remainder of the day." Without waiting for questions, he started to leave.

"I don't get it," Kalen said. "Why would demons kill Tigers and—"

Damon stopped in his tracks, turning to face Kalen. "Demons didn't do it."

* * *

When he finally made it back to her, Damon found Emry on her knees, digging into the hard ground with her bare hands like a wild animal. Strands of hair strayed from her usually neat ponytail, and her sleeves were rolled up, exposing a long scratch on one of her dirt-covered arms.

She looked up as he approached. Without a word, he handed her a shovel, and they silently dug together. When they'd finished burying the bodies, Emry went over to a bush and picked two flowers, each with three red petals centered around a yellow stigma.

After placing them on top of the makeshift graves, she knelt and said a short prayer. This act of gentle piety felt out of place in the gore-spattered forest.

"I didn't know you were religious," Damon said quietly after she arose.

She turned to face him. "I'm not. It's a tradition to recite an old prayer Tigers say when one of us dies. If there were more of my kind, I'd never give it a thought. But with the way things are, if I neglect tradition, there will come a time when nothing remains of our culture. If we let that happen, then murderers like whoever killed these people will get what they wish for."

He'd never thought about it that way. "I'm sorry, Emry."

She rubbed her palms together. "You didn't have to come back here."

"I wasn't going to let you stay here alone."

"I can handle myself."

"I know."

She let out a breath and broke their gaze.

"I'd like to apologize for what I said about you being obsessive." The words left his mouth without him thinking. "You're not. You're just worried, and you have reason to be. I was just... frustrated."

She looked down, brushing some of the mud from her pants. "Frustrated by me?"

"I'm always frustrated by you."

She looked up at him again, her green eyes full of vulnerability and confusion. They stood there for a while, not wanting to break the silence.

"We should head back and let the kids know that we're okay," Emry finally said. "After dinner, we'll explain the situation to them."

Damon agreed.

They both took one last look at the graves before abandoning the scene.

* * *

Damon knew he would find Headley in his office in the middle of dinner. The old man was always first to the dining hall to avoid waiting in a long line.

"Primrose," Headley said, raising his blue eyes to look at his underling. "Glad to see you made it back in one piece. Is everybody okay?"

"Yes, sir."

"Sir, huh? What's on your mind? You never come here unless I ask you to, and even when I ask, I have to drag your ass here by force."

Damon cleared his throat. "I was thinking we should guard the forest."

"We already have sentries at the gates."

"I know, sir, but not in the forest. Sometimes people leave the gates to practice. We should have someone there to watch."

Headley crossed his toned arms. "People who go out of the gates are responsible for themselves, Primrose. That's how it's always been."

"We were attacked by two Chernayas that Emry took down," Damon pressed. "The forest isn't as safe as it used to be. We could lose people, and not only Tigers."

Headley studied him. "Tiger. We have *one* Tiger in the army. You do realize that having sentries there means that you, your co-leader, your soldiers, and the other teams will have to take on more hours, right? That I will have to put at least two or three people there every six hours, day and night?"

"I do, sir."

"Blood crimes happen. Quite often, actually. Now look." He stretched his arms on his desk. "You have two solid points. The thing is, even though you were attacked, it's been a long time since anyone was killed or even injured by demons in the Black Forest."

"So shall we wait for someone to get injured or die?"

Headley glared at him. "As for your other point, you're absolutely right about the danger that Tigers are facing, and if we had more Tigers in the army, it would be a no-brainer. But it's a waste of manpower to keep sentries in the forest just for one person. I'm also more than confident about Emry Tigridia's ability to take care of herself." Damon gritted his teeth, causing Headley to sigh.

"If I get more reports about demons in the forest, I'll reconsider the suggestion. Now, if you're done, go do something useful."

Damon exhaled exasperatedly. Emry was one of the most—if not the most—devoted soldiers he'd ever met. The thought of it being her body impaled in the forest was more terrifying and unjust than anything he could have imagined.

Chapter 17

Festive

Emry

Ever since the incident in the Black Forest, Damon had been acting differently. He was still playful and witty, dazzling people with his smiles, but Emrycould feel something was off by the way he looked at her. She could still see the dead bodies in her mind, but it didn't rattle her. Judging by his reaction, the young soldier figured that her co-lead was never really exposed to blood crimes, and that's why it shook him. But that was a thought for another day. Right now, she was busy struggling to adjust the black dress she had borrowed for the ball.

The sun was setting, painting the sky outside her room with beautiful hues of red and gold. Somehow, despite her own nature, she felt something unusually festive in the air.

Emry's heart beat fast as she thought of Damon getting ready in the adjacent room. What would his tan skin look like against white fabric? Could someone his size even fit into a suit? How would he react to seeing *her*? She hated herself for thinking about it. It was silly. She'd never cared about her looks before, but now, she desperately wished for a floor-length mirror as she played with the black fabric of her dress. Emry could feel it cling to her chest, the fabric flowing down her legs, ending above her knees.

She took a deep breath. Some part of her wanted to get out of the room, but the other wanted to stay there and hide. It didn't matter which part was the loudest, because in the end, she would have to go.

So that's what she did.

In the hall, Damon was talking excitedly to the kids with his back to her. When they fell silent and stared at her, he stopped talking and turned around. His golden eyes widened as they slowly examined her, up and down, again and again.

Against her own free will, she blushed. The white suit he was wearing hugged his muscular torso, his wide shoulders, and his broad back. He was looking dangerous as always, but the formality made him seem deadly, like an angel—a fallen angel of sabotage. Someone who would smile while offering a glass of poisoned wine.

At last, that trademark smirk appeared on his face. "How long were you standing there checking me out?"

She could feel the heat burn all over her body from his remark.

"You were checking *her* out!" Lucy called, causing the kids to erupt with laughter.

"Nonsense." Damon winked. "Are you brats all packed and ready for the weekend?"

They waited until everyone was indeed ready to make their way to the gate. They could see other soldiers hurrying to the dining room. Emry couldn't help but wish for the whole thing to be over. The dress was more revealing than anything she'd worn before, and even though nothing was showing, she felt exposed.

"Don't forget to send us a message when you get home," she said firmly. "We'll be waiting."

"Unless, of course," Damon began with a mischievous smile.

"Yeah, yeah. Unless we want to be punished," Ella finished.

He chuckled. "Seriously. Stay safe and rest up. Next week we're going to step up our game."

When the duo finally arrived at the entrance to the dining hall, it was dark outside and they were surprisingly alone. Loud music and muffled voices danced through an open window, subtly inviting them inside.

"You're beautiful," Damon said. His hands were twitching as if resisting the urge to touch her, and Emry found herself wanting him to. She closed her eyes and felt her blush give her away as she recalled the night before they'd met their soldiers, when he had *almost* touched her. She thought she knew pain, but this was a different kind of ache.

"You have to stop," Emry said, tears of anger filling her eyes. She blinked them away.

His brow furrowed. "Stop?"

"Yes. Stop," she repeated, more angrily. "Stop saying those things, playing with me." She looked away. "This isn't going anywhere, and it's cruel."

She hated him for making her say those words. It was all a game to him, wasn't it? After all, he knew damn well that nothing could ever happen between them. And even if it didn't really occur to him, even if flirting was just his nature—something he did with *everybody*—she was a human being. *She* had feelings.

A dark laugh left his lips. His eyes were bitter and accusing as they fell on her. Suddenly, she realized that he was *pissed*.

"After everything we've been through, that's what you think of me?" he said quietly, menacingly. "You know what? Fuck all of this."

He opened the door and stormed in, leaving her staring after him. What the hell just happened? What right did he have to be the one who was upset?

Damon

"Take it easy with the scotch," Jenna said as he poured himself another glass. "I'm fine." He took a gulp. They both knew alcohol helped him sleep, but never affected him further.

The dining room was nearly unrecognizable. The center had been cleared out to be used as a dance floor, bright and elaborate decorations had been placed over the drab walls, and fancy tablecloths covered the scratched tables.

People were dancing and joking around, even with soldiers from different departments.

Damon tried to mingle and have fun, but his mind was on Emry. He tried his best not to look, but his eyes always wandered in her direction, wanting nothing more than to see her beauty in all its glory.

Ian and Glen, who were also dressed in black, sat with her. Though a few other women from ICT were around, their eyes never left her being—and Damon didn't miss this. The way they were looking at her, the way they constantly offered her food and drinks... He knew what this was, yet she was so damn naïve.

His fingers clutched the glass hard, slightly cracking under the pressure. If they touched her, if they even *thought* about touching her, he knew he would—

"Damon?" Jenna said, placing her hand on his wrist, interrupting his thoughts. "Let's go. The others are finally here."

He blankly stared at her for a moment, prompting Jenna to grab his wrist harder.

"Let's *go*," she sneered, pulling him off to the other side of the room.

Emry

The ball was even worse than Emry had expected. The soft music and merriment did nothing to soothe her feelings. She thought about apologizing—it *was* her fault, after all. However, she didn't feel sorry for being honest. She felt sorry for being vulnerable.

"You alright, Tiger?" Ian asked, offering her a cookie.

"Yeah... I just need to get some fresh air," she said in an attempt to escape.

As she stood, a guy with brown hair and matching eyes stepped towards her. "Hey," he greeted with a warm smile. "You're Tiger, right?"

Emry nodded. "Do you need something?"

Nervously taking a hand from his pocket to adjust his glasses, he continued. "I saw you across the room and just wanted to say that you look absolutely stunning."

"Oh. Thank you, uh…"

He smiled from ear to ear and reached out to shake her hand. "I'm Mike—from ICT."

"Nice to meet you, Mike." Emry shook his hand and turned to her friends, who were watching them without an ounce of shame. "These are my friends—"

"We know him," Ian said, waving his hand in dismissal.

Mike laughed. "Yeah, they do. Congratulations on passing, guys."

"Yeah, you too," Glen mumbled as they kept on staring. Creeps.

She cleared her throat, glancing around for another excuse to leave.

That's when she saw Damon laughing and drinking, surrounded by a mass of his peers. His suit jacket was slung over his shoulder, and the top button of his shirt undone, revealing his smooth chest underneath.

Emry cursed under her breath. He clearly hadn't been phased by what she said to him, nor how he made her feel, and what made her *angry*.

"Do you want to dance?" Mike asked, stealing her attention.

"Hmm? What?" She snapped her eyes to his, a dangerous fire blazing within them.

"I ju—uh… I just wanted to know if you wanted t-to dance. With me." He motioned towards the center of the room.

"I'm terrible at dancing."

"I promise you I'm worse." He held out his hand in invitation.

Emry stared at it, then at him. Mike was tall. Perhaps even taller than—

Damon.

Subtly shifting her eyes to the far side of the room, she looked at her co-leader. He was still partying away, oblivious to the torture she was enduring by watching him and everyone else ignore reality. It was as if he was taunting her—daring her—to try to exist in a world without him.

And so she tried.

Grabbing Mike's hand, she pulled him to the dance floor. Though awkward, it went smoother than she had expected. They talked and laughed; he spun her about… He was an excellent talker, and he seemed nice. It was strange that he wasn't put off by her being a Tiger and that he seemed truly interested in her.

During a spin, Emry caught a glimpse of Damon. His amber eyes were serious and cold as he stared at her. Her heart begged her to pull away from Mike, but her stubborn brain forced her to cling to him closer.

Maybe the friction between her and Damon would create a spark between her and Mike. If she could feel *something* for him—if she could just feel that Mike wanted her as much as she wanted Damon—she could change her feelings like she could change her mind.

When the last song stopped, Emry pulled away from Mike, and he stared into her eyes. She had been so lost in thought that she hadn't noticed his hand on the small of her back.

"I had a great time tonight, Tiger."

"I enjoyed my time with you as well, Mike."

She froze, and her grip tensed on his arms. Was it okay for her to say this? She *did* enjoy their conversation, and the dancing wasn't horrible… Emry wasn't lying.

"Is everything okay?" Mike asked, noticing her strange reaction.

"Mmm… Yeah," she replied, gazing into his eyes. "Everything's fine."

And as he ran his hand through her fiery-red hair, Emry realized that maybe, just maybe, she could be happy.

Chapter 18

Playing Stupid

Emry

The next day, several thumps and grunts beckoned her awake. When she opened her door, she saw Damon struggling to zip one of his bags. "You're going home?"

"Yes," he answered coldly, not bothering to look at her. "Headly came by earlier. Said to send you to his office, pronto. "He threw the bag over his shoulder and marched outside, slamming the door.

Emry closed her eyes and took a deep breath. She would *not* let this get to her, especially not when she was curious about Headley's summons.

* * *

Headley leaned forwards on his desk and curled his fingers into a fist. "I heard about what happened when you took your soldiers to the Black Forest," he explained after Emryclosed the door to his office. "How are you?"

"I'm fine, sir," she answered, unable to conceal the surprise in her voice.

"Good. And how did your soldiers react?"

"They were shocked, but they followed instructions to stay safe." On edge, she shifted in her chair. "Sir, is—"

"Primrose came here. He was quite shaken. Asked me to put sentries in the forest."

Emry only stared. *Damon did what?*

"I'm still trying to understand his panic," he continued. "Do you feel unsafe, Tiger?"

"N-no. I wasn't aware that he came here."

"You know my door is always open. Whatever you need, whenever you need it, we'll figure it out together."

"Thank you. I... appreciate it, but really, I'm okay."

"If that's the case, I'll let this sentry idea go for now."

"Of course." She stood and saluted him, quickly taking leave.

A heaviness settled in her chest, leaving her feeling guilty and defeated.

* * *

When Damon and the others had returned, nothing felt the same. He only spoke to her when absolutely necessary, though he was polite when he did. At first, their soldiers were confused, but as the weeks went by, they got accustomed to the new atmosphere.

Regardless of their situation, Emry kept on seeing Mike. He was humble, and didn't hide his admiration for her. Oftentimes, she'd catch him staring at her while she was writing notes, or she'd feel his hand gently caress her waist as they walked together. It was embarrassing, but she'd actively remind herself that she should feel admired.

Despite her fondness of him, and him for her, Ian and Glen didn't like him. When she tried to pry out the reason, the two of them would say that he was a kissass. Ian's exact words were "This guy is full of crap. I can't put my finger on it, but something is off about him."

"Don't you get that feeling that he's a show-off?" Glen chimed in.

"He's always the first and the last to talk," Ian snorted.

They could have been right, but he'd never been anything but nice to her. She often feared that they would have nothing to talk about, but that was never the case. It seemed like he had an endless list of topics, so she didn't have to talk much. Because of this, she had assumed that Mike had sensed that she didn't like talking about herself.

"Damon's actually not so bad," Glen said. "He's very cool to be around."

"How would you know?" Emry asked with a raised brow.

"We hung out at the bar last night," Ian confessed. "And he got us free shots."

Glen's face reddened, and he quickly tried to reroute the incoming storm from his long-time friend. "He didn't spare us the nicknames. Probably because he doesn't even remember our names."

"Didn't know you guys could be bought so easily," Emry scoffed, rolling her eyes. "The minute he stops talking to me—"

"Has it ever occurred to you that maybe it's hard for him to see you with Mike?" Ian asked.

"No, why on earth would I think that?"

That was a lie. It had crossed her mind. But she didn't let herself dwell on it because it was not something she could afford to pursue.

This new thing with Mike—this *real* thing with a charming guy who wasn't afraid to show his feelings—was something she wanted to pursue. She *needed* to. It didn't mean that seeing Damon was easy. He was kind and warm to everybody but her. She would have been okay with that if she didn't know how caring he could be. Emry didn't want to miss him, but she did.

The trio sat in silence. Ian and Glen knew that speaking any further would be like digging their own graves, and Emry knew that doubling down on Mike or Damon would fuel a fire that even *she* couldn't survive.

She'd never felt so trapped and confused before in her life. Was this what happiness was?

Damon

Damon sat in the bar, slamming back drink after drink. Seeing Emry every goddam day with minimal interaction was torture, but it was one he had to endure. Her words from that night still echoed in his head. How could she boldly say that he was playing with her? Did she actually think so little of him?

The situation plagued him more than anything ever had. Usually, he was a mastermind for handling emotional issues. He'd simply stop thinking about it, and the issue would poof from his brain, never to be thought about again. But with her, it was different.

He could feel his breathing hitch whenever she was within touching distance. He just couldn't let go of the bubbling rage he felt every time he saw her with *that* guy. He needed to get his old self back.

A thump next to him knocked him out of his thoughts.

Jenna slumped down on the seat next to him, clutching her drink. "You know, I was thinking."

He grinned at her. "I can already tell this is going to be a dangerous conversion."

"Maybe. But I can guarantee it will pique your interest." She gave him a pointed look and nudged him with her shoulder.

"Hit me with it," he said, finishing off another shot and ordering another.

"This guy that you loathe so much, the one that hangs with Tiger?"

He tensed and swirled the drink in his hand. "Yes?"

"If you were observant like me, and not sulky all the time, you'd realize that they never kiss. She never reciprocates his touch." Jenna took a sip.

"Why are you telling me this?"

"Are we playing stupid right now? Because that's not my thing."

"Her love life is none of my business."

"Alright then." She finished her drink and left. Sometimes, he thought that she knew him way too well.

"Hey there, handsome."

Damon's attention was once again held captive by a pretty girl with big blue eyes. She situated herself right where Jenna had been only moments ago. Damon recognized the tall brunette as Cara, a Slayer from another team. He had a thing with her that ended three years ago, but not a relationship. They remained friendly ever since, but she'd never really approached him. Until now.

"How are you?" she purred, looking at him expectantly.

"Been busy working my ass off, and yourself?" They laughed together.

"I'm fine. Not a leader like you, but at least they kept me." She winked at him.

"Totally. Some of my friends are stuck trying to figure out what to do with their lives. It's tough out there. Could you see yourself doing anything else?"

"Definitely not!" she snickered and caressed his arm.

They continued to catch up until she finally took the big step.

"Listen." She dragged her chair closer to his, leaning in. "I'll be honest. I thought you and I could have a night to ourselves. For old times' sake."

This was exactly the opportunity he'd wanted. Cara ogled at him, biting her lip, and waiting for an answer. Unbidden, Jenna's words came to his mind.

Damn it.

He couldn't believe himself when he politely rejected her, and went back to the Slayers building alone.

Chapter 19

The Soldiers

Riggs

"Riggs, read the paper before you aloud," Damon commanded impatiently, arms crossed.

Tiger had just finished handing them the papers. Why did Damon ask *him* out of the six students? From the seat next to him, Ahron was giving him a confused look. His glasses sat unevenly on his nose as always.

Tiger returned to her place next to Damon. Their postures were rigid, their jaws set in a hard line. They both looked like statues.

Riggs' hands shook as everyone waited. Prepping to read as instructed, he cleared his throat.

Clang!

Ahron spilled his cup of water on his paper.

"Oh, shoot. I'm sorry," he apologized, avoiding Riggs' glare.

Damon huffed. "Seriously, Ahron?"

"I'm really sorry," he said again.

Tiger gestured for him to read instead. For the remainder of the day, Riggs couldn't focus at all. Dread filled his heart and stayed there until lights out. He waited until everyone fell asleep in the hall, and approached Ahron, giving his sleeping bag a rattle.

"Ahron, wake up!" he half-whispered and half-shouted.

"Wha-what?" Ahron mumbled, reaching for his glasses in their case by his head. "Riggs?" He blinked.

"Today, in class..." Riggs could feel his heart beating erratically. "Did you spill the water on purpose?"

Ahron slowly sat up and rubbed his eyes. He looked so pale in that sleeveless shirt that Riggs thought maybe, if he'd been just a shade paler, he could have been used as a lantern.

"Umm... Yeah." Ahron looked uncertain. "Yes."

"Why?"

He was uneasy, barely looking him in the eye. "I caught you once lying to Ella about one of the papers we had to fill when we just got here. She didn't realize it back then, but I did. You... you can't read."

Riggs turned quiet for a moment. "If you're going to tell somebody, I swear—"

"I won't tell anyone." Ahron interrupted. "Your secret is safe with me. Now, can we go back to sleep?"

Riggs lingered there. He didn't know why, but he didn't want to sleep. There was something risky and comforting about letting someone else know the truth.

"I've never been to school, so I never learned how to read or write. If they discover this, they might kick me out."

Ahron looked hesitant. "When I was in school, "I tutored kids a little younger than me, so I have some experience. Maybe it's not too late to learn."

Riggs knew that it was, in fact, too late for him to learn. He'd tried multiple times, but the letters always got mixed up. Some of them vanished and reappeared. Other times, they changed spots or blurred before his eyes, so he had absolutely no idea why he agreed. Despite this, he accepted Ahron's offer.

Just like that, they developed a routine, practicing at night when everyone was fast asleep. He would wake Ahron up and they would sit next to the table that he'd carried in just for this. The normally fidgety nerd sat tall during these lessons, and his eyes glinted in the soft lantern light as he spoke. It took a few weeks, but eventually Riggs could identify each letter. "Let's try decoding words," Ahron instructed.

"Decode words?" Riggs frowned. "What does that mean?"

With a smile, Ahron said, "It means you'll be able to recognize the basic sounds that make up a written word. We're going to work with writing and sound simultaneously." He'd always seemed so lively when he was explaining things to his friend.

Riggs could only groan in response.

"You're doing a great job," Ahron praised after they practiced more. "Look how well you read that sentence."

Embarrassment and pride coursed through Riggs. He rubbed his nape. "It's all thanks to you."

As expected, Ahron mumbled something and looked down. Riggs could not deny he enjoyed making him blush.

"Hey... Can I ask you something?" Ahron blurted out.

"Uh... Yeah, sure."

"Why didn't you go to school?"

Riggs cleared his throat, not expecting a personal question from his shy teammate. "My father was a Slayer who was killed in action. When he died, I dropped out to provide for my family. My mom didn't like it, but to be honest, I was never smart or disciplined like you, so I didn't mind. Either way, I wasn't going to study, so why not be useful? When my workplace was ruined by demons, I enlisted, and that's how I got here."

Ahron nodded, keeping his eyes focused on the worksheet sitting between them. It was an intimate conversation for two people who rarely spoke to each other. When Ahron was tutoring him, he was more confident than anyone Riggs had ever known, besides Damon. He decided to test it.

"I told you my story," Riggs said, placing his hand on top of Ahron's. "Now tell me yours."

"I—Ah..." Ahron rubbed his hair and took a deep breath. "My father smokes a lot, drinks a lot, and..."

"And?" Riggs prompted.

"He hits me and my older brothers a lot," he whispered into his notebook. "My brothers decided to stay with him. They said that enlisting is worse because I'll die. But... I felt like I couldn't do it anymore. I had nowhere to go, so I came here."

"What about your mom?"

A soft smile appeared on Ahron's face. Enchanting. "She died from pneumonia when I was ten."

Something about the way he spoke about her made Riggs' heart break, but all he could say was "I'm sorry."

Ahron shook his head. "Nothing we can do about it, right?" he asked, but Riggs could see the pain in his eyes. "She always believed in me. Guess I'm the only one who believes in me now."

"I believe in you." He didn't mean to say it, but the words left his mouth without his consent. He was thankful his blush was hidden in the dim light.

With disbelief, Ahron raised his head to look at Riggs. "You do? Could've fooled me."

"You're right." Riggs chuckled. "I'm an asshole."

"Well, you're not an asshole right now, so thank you for that," Ahron mumbled.

Riggs tried to control his laughter. "For not being an asshole? God, you're a piece of work."

Ahron blushed, but boldly looked him in the eyes. "Well, so are you."

Anoki

For Anoki, the best time of the day was the two or three-hour window before bed, when Tiger and Damon would let them do whatever they wanted. No shouting, no running, no classes, no training—just dark, calm, and quiet. Well, as quiet as it could be with five other teenagers in the same room.

Anoki liked to take her time in the evenings with a warm shower, brushing her long, black hair, and unfolding her sleeping bag to read and relax. Her

leaders usually went out the hall and back, crossing with long strides; both strong and decisive—always working, always doing something. They looked like they carried so much responsibility on their shoulders. It made her wonder if she would want to be a leader like them.

Being last to the showers meant no one would be waiting for her to finish. But every time she returned from her nightly routine, Kalen would pop up and head straight to the bathroom. He always did it *after* she came back.

One night, she decided to ask him about it. After he'd left, she got up and followed him. She stopped at the doorstep, staring. There were four stalls, each containing a small shower. They had curtains, but now the curtains were pulled aside. Kalen walked from stall to stall, checking each tap. He was so engrossed in it, that when he did it again, he didn't even notice her. When he was done and turned to check the faucets on top of the counter, his eyes widened in shock and then he let out a scream.

"Shh!" She hurried to him and covered his mouth.

"What the hell are you doing?!"

"What the hell are *you* doing?!"

"Nothing! I just..." He looked at the cells. "It's nothing."

"That was *not* nothing," Anoki insisted. "Is that what you do *every night* after I'm done?"

He froze, probably contemplating whether to tell her the truth or lie. At last, he sighed. "I don't know. It's just something I do."

"What else do you do besides checking the showers?" Anoki asked, her voice raising an octave.

He looked away. "I check the windows and the door to the hall."

That didn't sound weird, but then she remembered him doing a second round at the taps. "Wait, only once, right?"

His face crumpled with shame.

"What's going on?" she asked, leaning against the counter with arms crossed.

He took a deep breath. "You have to promise me you won't tell."

"I can't promise you such a thing."

"Then I'm not telling you."

"Fine." She turned to leave, but he grabbed her arm.

"Wait! Please... just wait."

She leaned against the counter again, studying him as he took a few deep breaths. He was a little taller than her, but at the moment, he looked to her like a lost puppy.

"I escaped from an asylum. Okay?"

"An asylum?" Suddenly, she felt cold. "Why were you there in the first place?"

"Because..." He nodded to the showers. "I don't know why, but since I was twelve, I've had this impulse to check that everything is alright, you know? I don't want our leaders to be angry if there's a flood in the showers, and I don't want demons to break in..."

"Kalen," she said softly. She'd never asked, but he was probably from Ob. "Demons can't just burst in. We have sentries at the gates. Besides, each one of us checks to see if the tap he or she was using is turned off after we finish showering. You don't need to do that."

"I just have to..." he tried to say, his words coming short and fast, each tripping over the other. "I have to."

"Why?"

"Because it's on me to make sure things stay alright."

"What do you mean? It's not—"

"It is." He took a step towards her. "That's how things are for me."

She blinked at him, her thoughts darting to the first week they had shared in the army. "You weren't like this when we first got here."

He blushed. "Every time I move to a new place, I get some relief from the... tension. But when I get used to the new place, it comes back."

"What comes back?"

"The responsibility. Can you just keep it a secret? Please?"

"I don't know, Kalen…" she trailed off, his gaze was making her uneasy. "We have to tell Damon and Tiger." Surely, they would know what to do.

Kalen shook his head frantically. "No, we don't. Please, Anoki, you'll ruin my life."

She ran her hands through her hair. "Do you at least understand that this isn't healthy?"

He closed his eyes and sighed. "Yes."

"What if it throws you out of balance when we're on the battlefield?"

He looked down, and she could see the tips of his ears redden with shame. "We can't tell them. We can't."

She stood there, helpless. Suddenly, she remembered her elderly grandfather back at home. The grandfather she'd loved, the grandfather she'd lost. Last time she felt helpless, he was there, by her side. She remembered her grandpa begging her parents not to sell her for marriage. Feeling suffocated, she couldn't help the ache in her chest or the tears that came to her eyes.

"Are you okay?" Kalen asked, surprised.

"Yeah, yeah, I just…" She took a deep breath. "My grandpa used to give me good advice every time I was in trouble. He had this way with people, you know? He was a spiritual healer back in west She'e."

"A spiritual leader?" Kalen asked, his blond brows raised.

She knew that outside of west She'e, no one really believed in those things. But *she* knew better than that. Spiritual or not, her grandpa knew what he was doing. He always told her to believe in herself, believe that it's not only up to her to save herself, and that she had the power to help others too.

"Listen," she said, "I'll keep quiet under one condition."

He gave her an exasperated look. "What?"

"You're going to let me help you."

Chapter 20

Sweepy

Emry

Emry held the punching bag tightly for Riggs. "Again!" He punched at it again. "Harder!" He lashed out at it, letting out a roar in the process.

The spacious, old room smelled of sweat and dust. She and Damon were training their soldiers in the same building where they'd had their Duels a few months ago.

"You're good," she told Riggs. He was struggling to breathe and his black curls were slick with sweat.

Damon, standing across, looked like the perfect combination of hopelessness and amusement as he watched Ahron attempt to kick another punching bag.

Emry couldn't help but let her betraying eyes run over him, just for a moment. He'd tossed his shirt aside, and worked up quite a sweat. His hair was ruffled and his eyes were wild. She wore a black crop top that now stuck uncomfortably to her sweaty body.

She returned her focus to Riggs. "You're good, but your problem is that you throw a punch to shove, when you should aim to rattle your opponent. Look." She pushed him away a little, and then her arm shot forwards as she hit the bag. It swung with force. "You get what I mean?"

He nodded. "I'll try again."

"Don't push the bag, pummel it."

This time it was better. Though he was stronger than the others, relying on that alone was holding him back. There was no grace in his movements, no calculation. Ahron had calculation, but no force to back it up. And that certainly wasn't helping with his insecurity.

The door burst open, and a Slayer from another team came in.

"Primrose, Headley is calling for you."

"Seriously?" Damon grabbed a towel to wipe his face and hair.

The soldier shrugged. "He said it's urgent, and he said to tell *you*"—he motioned at Emry"—that it might take a few hours."

Damon cursed and looked at her. "Can you finish here?"

"Of course," she assured him, leaning against the punching bag. It wasn't like she had another option.

Behind her, Ahron collapsed on the floor. "Can we take a break? Please?"

Emry glanced back at her team. They looked exhausted as well.

"Yes, but we're going to the armory after that. I want you guys to experiment with more weapons. It doesn't feel like you're all well-suited for a knife." She eyed Ahron in particular.

When the unit reached the armory, she waited for them outside. "Go inside, take what you want, and step out. We'll try to improvise with your choices."

After a few minutes, they stood before her with their selected weapons. Lucy, Kalen, Anoki, and Riggs stuck to their knives, but Ella came out holding a dart gun, and Ahron wielded a long cane sword.

Emry tilted her head to the side. "Interesting."

She pulled out a little black box—the Shadoni box—and laid it on the ground. Upon opening it, dark mist filled the air, and out of the fog came a crocodile demon surrounded by a blue aura. The crocodile, huge and wild, moved its tail rapidly and made its way to the soldiers.

Fists clenched, Emry stood ready to pounce if it tried anything. At last, the creature's dark pupils shrank, and he lunged forwards. Ella stepped back, but Ahron—though shaking like a leaf—screamed as he lunged forwards, using his cane sword for momentum. When he landed on the crocodile's back, he stabbed deep into the thick, green scales. He was still screaming as the demon dissolved into a fog and returned to the open box, stopping only when he hit the ground with a loud thump.

"Ahron, you did it!" Kalen called, running to his side.

"Looks like a stick and uses one to fight," Ella said with disbelief. "It fits."

"I… I did it." Ahron sounded dumbstruck as he rose. He didn't care about Ella's remark. "I actually did it."

"Jumped right on that animal's back." Lucy slapped him on the shoulder.

Riggs stood before him, his dark eyes sparkling as he smirked with mischief. "Not too bad, Sweepy."

Ahron scoffed indignantly, but didn't say a word as Riggs kept grinning.

Emry nodded in appreciation. "That was great, Ahron. Let's go again. This time, don't let one person do everything. In battle, you're going to have to work together."

By the time they finished and showered, it was already past dinner, and Damon still hadn't returned.

When she was making her way back to the Slayers building, she saw a dark figure sitting alone near the stairs. Hesitant, she approached, keeping her footsteps soft and silent.

As she got closer, she realized it was Damon, and before she could say anything, he exhaled her name. "Emry."

"Are you okay?"

A moment passed.

"No."

"Do you want to be alone?"

Another moment.

"No."

Carefully, she sat next to him. He didn't talk, and neither did she, but it seemed to be what he needed. Together, they sat there, staring ahead into the darkness. There was something peaceful in the air, or maybe it was the fact that, for once, she was doing nothing at all.

Emry was still well aware of his presence. She could actually *feel* that something was off with him. It filled her with concern.

"My grandma had a heart attack this morning," he eventually said. "I went to the hospital in Egma to see her."

She waited a minute, taking in his words. "How is she now?"

"She's better. She was already up when I got there, just weak. It wasn't major, but it creeped me out. I spent all day with her, then came back here."

"I'm glad to hear she's doing okay." Emry fumbled with her fingers. "Were your parents also there?"

"No." He closed his eyes.

"Why?"

"They're dead."

"Oh. So a brother, or—"

"Dead."

She didn't pry. It wasn't her business, and he clearly wasn't in any shape to answer questions. They hadn't talked properly in *months*, and it felt like two strangers trying to have a conversation. Emry was uncertain what she could do to make him feel better. He seemed to be completely absorbed in his feelings and didn't even notice her awkwardness. His stare was focused intently on a point ahead in the dark.

"How did today go?" he finally asked.

"It went well. It seems Ahron found the right weapon for himself—a cane sword."

"That's great."

"Yeah."

Silence.

She had to say something. *Anything.*

"Are you and your grandma very close?"

"Yes." A faint smile appeared on his lips. "She's the one who raised me. The only family I've got." He took a deep breath. "If something were to happen to her, I don't know what I would do."

"What about you? Do *you* feel alright?"

He shook his head. "When I saw her in the hospital, I just... I fainted."

Emry shot him a look. "You *fainted?*"

"Then again, at Headley's office, when I came back."

"*Twice*? Are you ill?"

"I don't know, Emry. I don't know." He shook his head, looking lost, and now she started to feel like that too. "Maybe I've been ill for a long time. I don't know what's wrong with me anymore."

This was so out of character from the confident, happy guy she'd known. There was something fundamentally wrong if he wasn't smiling.

"I don't know what to say, Damon," she finally admitted. "Usually you're the perfect one, and I'm the one who's fucked in the head."

He burst out laughing. "Is that so?" Suddenly, he yanked her hand and wrapped it with his own, stroking her palm with his thumb. It was warm around her freezing fingers. "You never see yourself the way other people see you."

She felt exposed, sitting on the grass with her hand clutched in his, but it felt too good to draw back. It felt like he needed it, and she was glad she could do *something* to cheer him up. Even so, she deeply doubted that with her impulsiveness, her anger, and her sadness, anyone was seeing her as more than what she really was.

The silence between them now was serene, not so tense anymore. It felt nice.

"What you said to me back then at the party," he said gently, "it wasn't fair of you."

Emry took a deep breath. She knew confrontation, knew how to stand her ground. She knew how to shout, how to hit. She knew how to walk away. She definitely did not know how to react to accusations presented to her with such tenderness.

"What were you thinking?" He turned to look at her. The gold specks in his eyes twinkled in the moonlight. "I was never playing with you. I was always honest."

"I didn't mean—"

"I thought you trusted me more than that."

There. She could sense a hint of anger in his voice, but also a mountain of hurt.

Emry hesitated, trying to find the right words. "Growing up, I learned to keep my guard up all the time. Do you have any idea how many times people pretended to be my friend, only to try to hurt me later? How many times people were trying to find revenge for dead loved ones by hurting me?" He shot her a dark look, but she continued. "Who I am today is based on my experience. Tigers can't let their guards down. When they do, they get murdered in forests. I never let my guard down, but with you, I find myself letting it down too many times."

Damon's posture changed. He sat tall with confidence. "Really?"

She blushed. "It's not... a good thing."

"You're right," he said, squeezing her hand. "I was impatient. I should have known better than that. I guess I was upset because I cared about what you thought of me. I still do."

"No, you just surprised me. You've always been very patient."

He chuckled bitterly. "Yeah, until I wasn't anymore."

"You've been more patient with me than anyone else has ever been."

He raised a brow, his lips curving into a smile. "Do you really mean it?"

"Yeah, but Damon..." It was hard to find the right words, especially when he was that close to her.

"Emry."

She stilled. Waited.

"I meant every word I said to you." His voice was low and decisive. "Every single one. You never need to second-guess my intentions."

His stare was intense, pulling her into a black hole within those pools of gold, until he finally looked away.

"It was hard to stay away from you," he murmured. "But then again, I needed to try because you're always out of reach, aren't you?"

She closed her eyes. There it was again, both the pain and pleasure that came with him talking to her like that. Was he talking about the elephant in the room? She could no longer dance around it—it was time to take responsibility.

"I have to be, and so do you. You *know* that."

He looked away. "I know."

Chapter 21

Privacy

Emry

"No! Stop!"

Emry shot from her bed and burst into Damon's room, the door slamming shut behind her. Her first concern was his safety. The second was for his reputation—none of their soldiers should hear him screaming in the middle of the night.

"STOP!" he screamed, tossing and turning. His eyes were closed, but his face was twisted in horror. "I said—"

"Damon! Damon!" She tackled the bed and shook him. "Wake up! You're screaming!"

He shrieked as he opened his eyes. As he sat up, his breathing was labored, as if he were trying to expel something from his body.

"Hey," she said gently, kneeling beside him. "Hey, look at me."

As requested, Damon shifted to look at her. He looked like a wide-eyed madman with his disheveled hair plastered to his skin from sweat.

"I need you to calm down. It was just a dream," she said slowly, absentmindedly touching his cheek. "You're alright. Everything's alright, okay?"

It was terrifying to think about what had scared him so much.

Once his breathing had finally slowed, Emry drew back and turned to leave, but his hand caught hers. His eyes were hard, uncompromising. "Stay."

"Damon," she said helplessly, looking around for no particular reason. She couldn't stay with him, though the heartbreaking look in his eyes didn't give her much choice. He looked shaken, scared to let her go, and frightened to be left alone. She took a deep breath. "Alright, alright. I'm here." She sat on the bed next to him. "I'll stay with you until you fall asleep."

He nodded, her hand still locked in his.

* * *

Come morning, all Emry could feel was hot. Burning hot. She opened her eyes as awareness started to flood her mind. Damon's hard chest was pressed to her back, and his arm was tightly wrapped around her torso. She could feel him stir, and the intimate contact caused her body to grow hotter.

Her heart was racing.

What was she doing here?

Damon's terrified ochre eyes flashed in her mind. She wasn't supposed to stay here! She was only supposed to comfort him until he drifted back to sleep, and then return to her room, to her *own* bed. She mentally whipped herself for being so foolish. How come she fell asleep so fast? She felt him stir again and tensed, not sure of what to do. Inwardly, she screamed at herself to get away, but Damon's grip was tight.

"God." His voice was deep and husky from sleep. "I can actually hear the gears inside your mind working."

That was it.

Emry pushed forwards and out of his bed. "Oh, God. I can't believe this is happening!" She paced back and forth in his room, panicking.

He sat up to rest his back against the headboard, watching her intently. "What time is it?"

She glanced at the clock on the wall. "Before dawn. We still have time before we need to wake everyone up."

"I see." He yawned again, not looking bothered. "I'm not entirely sure what happened last night, but... sorry about that." He gave her a lazy smile.

"Damon." She stopped and stared at him. "You were *screaming* in your sleep."

His eyes darkened as he looked at her. He nodded once, not looking surprised at all.

"Does this happen often?" she asked quietly, returning to sit on his bed.

He looked at her like he didn't really want to answer. "Sometimes," he finally said. "I hate that you had to see me like this."

He'd seen her in so many shameful situations that she felt like she owed him at least this *one* moment.

She looked down at the blanket. "Weakness does not cancel out strength."

"Right." Damon caressed her hand, but she pulled away.

"Listen, that can't happen anymore. I—"

"Afraid of what your boyfriend will say if he finds out you spent all night with me?" He was grinning now, the bastard.

Emry ran her fingers through her hair, frustrated. "He's not my boyfriend."

"Then what is he?"

"A friend," she almost barked at him, storming away.

He looked both angry and amused. "Does *he* think that he's just a friend?"

Emry crossed her arms. "He should."

Damon snorted. He jumped out of bed and stood before her. "I saw you with him. You two never touch each other."

He cornered her, making her step back until her back was pressed against the wall. His eyes were wild, challenging.

All she could do was look up to meet them, even though she wanted the Earth to swallow her whole. "Damon—"

"But you did spend the night with me," he whispered, reaching to twirl a lock of her hair with his fingers.

Emry clenched her fists, resisting the impulse to give in to his touch. "Next time, I'll just let you keep screaming."

She pulled away. It was a cruel thing to say, but the only thing that came to her mind that could mend her dignity.

"Don't act as if you didn't like it. When was the last time you slept that well?"

She scrunched her nose, baffled by the question.In her panic, she hadn't realized she had slept through the night. He came closer to her again, his eyes mischievous.

"You were *snoring*," Damon pointed out.

It was the last thing she thought he was going to say. She turned red in an instant. "I was not!"

She took a deep breath. "Did you have any more nightmares?" she asked cautiously.

"No," he said, a gentle crease forming between his brows. "Not after you came. And I always have them, even if I don't usually scream."

She nodded, mulling over this information. "What caused you to scream last night?"

"Probably the same reason I fainted yesterday. Maybe while my guard was down, my mind tried to bring up some memories that I don't want to address."

"What do you mean?"

Shrugging, he continued. "I was five years old when my parents and brother died, but I don't have any memories of them. My grandma knows what happened, but whenever she tried to talk to me about it, I couldn't stand it. I just want to forget and move on, but those nightmares..."

Damon's expression turned vulnerable as he looked at her, and she recalled the terror in his eyes only hours before. Absentmindedly, she used her hand to move his dark hair away from his eyes, but she caught herself, drawing her hand back. He yanked it quickly and pressed it to his cheek, leaning against her touch. Emry's heart started to pound again, and her breaths turned shallow.

"Damon..." He shook his head and let go of her hand. She knew why he did, but it hurt anyway.

A sudden commotion in the hall jolted them out of their moment. They exchanged glances, hurried to the door, and cracked it open to peek outside.

"It's Kalen and Anoki," Damon murmured. His head was above hers.

The two recruits were standing in the hall's entrance, the blond looking extremely frustrated. And guilty.

"Look, I know we agreed—"

"Exactly! We *agreed!*" Anoki whispered. "I'm glad I stopped you. You weren't supposed to—"

"I know, I know." He ran in hand through his hair. "I'm losing my mind. You have to let me check. Just one time, okay?"

She crossed her arms, her chin jutting out. "*No.*"

"Why?"

"I told you—if you have this feeling inside of you, this pressure, this..."

"Anxiety?"

"Yes! Yes, exactly. You check on things, and it makes this feeling go away. But I'm sure it will go away naturally. You just have to *let* it. We need to expose you to this bad feeling, so you'll see you can cope with it on your own. I think."

"But... I can't. This is too much for me."

She sighed. "You know what? Let's go there, together. We won't touch anything, though. How does this sound?"

He sighed and closed his eyes. "Fine."

Anoki nodded to herself. "I get it. Maybe I'm demanding too much too fast."

"You *are* demanding too much too fast," Kalen grumbled, opening his eyes again.

But Anoki was too wrapped up in her own thoughts to listen. "This should be progressive, gradual."

"Or maybe I just can't be fixed." There was sadness in his eyes, an acceptance of fate.

"You don't need to be fixed, Kal. You need to overcome an obstacle, and you will. You're not alone in this! I'm here for you. We'll make it—together."

He looked down and nodded. Emry suspected that he was on the verge of crying.

"Come on," Anoki said, taking his hand in hers. "Let's go."

The duo stepped out of the hall, and Damon gently closed the door.

"Well," Damon said nonchalantly. "Looks like we're not the only ones having issues."

Emry nodded, disturbed. "Do you have any idea what that was about?"

"Actually, no." He frowned. "I can gather some information, but…"

"But what?"

"Maybe we should just let them be."

"Seriously??" She crossed her arms. "What if Kalen has a serious problem?"

"Well… it looks like he's in good hands." He gave her a sly smile.

It was funny how in a matter of moments, she already wanted to kill him.

"He's awake before dawn with one of his teammates."

"So are we," he said, closing the distance between them.

"*We*," she angrily whispered, "are not like them." She gestured at the door. "You can't compare them to us!"

He groaned. "Don't you feel like we'll be invading something private?"

She did, but it didn't matter. "I don't know where *you* grew up"—she sneered, anger coursing through her veins—"but where *I* grew up, there *was* no privacy, only death. And you know why? Because of stupidity and imprudence!"

Now he looked angry. "I lost friends, Emry. Just like you."

"Do you want to lose soldiers, too?"

He ran his hands through his dark hair. "No, but Kalen is a good Slayer. I don't think we're going to have a problem with him."

"I don't give a—"

"Emry,"—his voice turned gentle—"I've kept my secrets for eight years now. You and Jenna are the only ones who know about my nightmares. None of my leaders knew, or if they did, they never said anything. And look at that—I'm still here."

She sighed and turned away, but he stepped closer when she did. "We'll keep an eye on him, and if we feel like there's something going on that could potentially affect his performance on the battlefield, we'll confront him. Think about it. If we find out that he lied about his circumstances before enlisting, we legally must report to Headley and he might kick him out. Is that what you want?"

Damn it! He was right. "I don't like this."

"I know, but..." A sad smile tugged at the corner of his lips. "At least he's not alone in his situation."

Emry looked at him, feeling wary. "Like you've been?"

"Yes," he huffed, trying to escape back to his room.

She followed him. "Look, if you want to—"

"I don't want to talk about it—with anyone. Please understand."

Suddenly nervous, Emry swallowed. "It's just that... I'm worried about you," she admitted.

Damon's eyes softened, and he approached his co-leader once more. Placing his hands on either side of her neck, he let his thumbs graze her skin. He lowered his head so his forehead almost touched hers, and Emry could feel sparks fly violently between them.

"I'm doing *great*," he rasped, closing his eyes. "Right now, like this... I'm okay."

Chapter 22

Over And Over

Damon

On Thursday, after Emry and Damon sent the kids home, they had a meeting with Headley and some of the other unit leaders.

"The situation is that demons, mostly Belaya, are fast approaching at the eastern front," Headley told them from the head of a long mahogany table. "I know we usually provide more time to train novices, but we might not have that privilege anymore. You all need to step up your game."

"Novices going to the frontline in less than a year? This is crazy!" yelled a soldier that Damon had respect for.

Murmurs of agreement emanated from the crowd.

Headley's jaw tightened. "I understand your concerns, but it can't be helped. Intelligence suspects there's something more nefarious lurking."

"Like what?" Emry asked.

"We're not sure yet, but this convergence is *too* sudden. Perhaps something has fundamentally changed in the demons' social dynamics, like their leadership."

"Are they colluding with Tigers again?" blurted a sandy-haired soldier.

Damon despised him for the question, but he couldn't really blame him. All eyes turned towards Emry. He felt her stiffen next to him, but she didn't respond. Instead, she just stared back at them challengingly.

"I find it hard to believe." Headley let out a long exhale. "There's not much left of the Tigers to pursue."

"What about other nations?" suggested someone else.

"There's not enough information to confirm or deny anything. We might send some of you to gather information and fight them off."

Again, murmurs spread through the crowd.

"In the meantime,"—Headley's powerful voice silenced them—"I have a mission that needs to be done by Saturday, and I need volunteers. A sixty-year-old man and two girls, both twelve years old, were killed in Egma. It's been documented that the demons responsible are level two, so I need at least eight people to handle this. Who here wants to take them down and get that big payout?"

Damon didn't have to look to know Emry had raised her hand. Without thinking, he raised his hand as well. Headley nodded at the pair, and six more hands shot up, one after the other. After dismissing the others, he briefed his volunteers.

"I'm going to arrange a bus for tomorrow night to get you to Egma," he informed. "But, if any of you are already going home there this weekend, you can leave in the morning and join the mission on Saturday."

While Emry and Damon were making their way back to the Slayers building, he turned to look at her.

"Come with me to Egma in the morning. We don't have to wait all day for the bus tomorrow."

"What?"

Maybe she thought it was inappropriate, but he had to offer. When was the last time she actually left the base for anything other than a mission?

"Do you have any work to do tomorrow?" he asked casually. "Any watches or duties? I can ask one of my friends to cover for you."

"No, but—"

"Then you don't have to stay here alone. You can stay with my grandma and me."

"I don't know..." She looked apprehensive, pausing at the door. "Are you sure your grandma will be okay with it?"

"Absolutely," Damon assured her as they went up the stairs to the hall. "My grandma has the biggest heart in the world, and she's quite intelligent. You'd love her."

His grandmother was his hero, his inspiration, his biggest supporter. She was different from other ladies in Egma, and he was anxious for the two of them to meet.

Emry looked like she didn't know how to reject his offer without hurting his feelings. "I'd better stay here and study..." she mumbled, but Damon could see the pain in her eyes as she looked away.

"Come on. When was the last time you left the base?"

"I can't even remember. And I've only been to Egma once in my life."

"Really? It's only a few hours away, though."

"I meant to go more often. I just didn't have many opportunities. But, Damon, I really don't want to intrude on you and your grandma."

He could understand why she was worried, but the thought of leaving her alone again didn't give him much of an option. Usually, soldiers got to go home once in a while to meet with family and friends, strip off the fatigues, and have a change of environment. Emry didn't have that. He'd known her for a few months now, and she hadn't returned home even once. Maybe that was the reason she hadn't given him a firm 'no' yet. Perhaps deep inside, she actually longed for a change in scenery.

He grinned reassuringly. "You won't be intruding. My grandma will be happy to meet you. Oh, and don't worry about food. I promise we'll make something delicious."

Emry laughed, but he could see she was nervous. She was hugging herself, looking at her shoes. He wished he could hold her in his arms and wipe away the loneliness.

"I don't know, Damon. Will she be okay with the fact that I'm a Tiger?"

"Of course," he snorted. "I'm telling you, she's the sweetest person. She raised me all by herself, you know." He felt a nice, warm feeling inside of him every time he talked about her. "I think you'd like an escape, wouldn't you?"

Her eyes locked with his. "Only if you're completely sure."

Emry looked unsure, but he could see the spark in her jade eyes for the opportunity to escape.

"I'm heading out," Damon said, stripping off his shirt. "Do you want to go to the club with me? I'll save you a seat at the bar." He winked.

She looked distant; he should have known better. She was a beast of a Slayer—she was strong, fearless. When it came to social events, however, that strength dissipated. He wasn't sure if it was because she lacked confidence in social situations or because she wasn't interested in the company to begin with. The long days that she'd spent studying for the exams took a toll on her, as did her experiences as a Tiger. The more that he got to know her, the more he could understand the damage that her life circumstances had caused her. Picturing her in the bar with him felt kind of absurd, as if she wasn't going to fit there, but he had to offer. He had to try.

"I'm going to ICT," she said, embarrassed.

Rage pumped in his temples, but he tried to conceal it as much as he could. "To your boyfriend?"

"I already told you he's not my boyfriend," she spat. "But yes, I promised to come by after the meeting."

"Then you'd better run along to him." He hated himself for acting that way, but he couldn't help it. It was *his* problem that he couldn't get her out of his system, not hers. He saw her flinch and ignored the sting in his heart.

The look she gave him sent chills down his spine. "You don't have to be like this every time he's brought up. You're so kind to everyone else—How come the people I like are never good enough for you?"

They stood in silence for a moment, Damon unwavering in his rage. When he didn't respond, Emry walked away.

Emry

"So you're actually going away for the weekend?" Ian asked as he and Glen packed for their own trip. "And to *Damon Primrose's* house, of all places?"

Emry rolled her eyes and huffed. "Yeah... I guess I'll meet you at the train station tomorrow morning, and we'll take the train to Egma after you two get off at Nova. Damon said it's stupid to spend my time here when I have to get to Egma, anyway."

"Of course." He nodded, clearly mocking her. "*Damon* said."

"It's nice of him," Glen piped up, sitting on the floor and folding his socks. "And it's a great chance to leave the base for a while."

"Come on! You're so innocent sometimes."

Glen threw a sock at him. "Shut up. She has a boyfriend now."

"I don't!" Emry said angrily. "Damn it."

Her friends exchanged a look.

"What's wrong?" Glen asked.

She sighed and sank into one of the chairs. "Nothing. It's just... Mike is waiting for me right now. Can you guys come with me to his room?"

Ian blinked. "What?"

Glen looked at him pointedly. "She wants us to come with her to Mike's room," he drawled.

"What would I do without you?" Ian fired back.

"I honestly don't know." Glen shook his head.

Ian sighed and turned to Emry. "What's going on? Why do you need us there?"

"I don't want things to get uncomfortable. That's all," she said, pulling at her sleeve. "He's nice and everything, but... I just don't want him to start questioning me about going to Damon's for the weekend. He won't do it in front of you guys."

Ian huffed dramatically. "He wants to know where he stands with you; it's reasonable. Actually, we want to know too."

"Ian, I don't want to have a conversation I'm not ready for. Can't you understand?"

Glen stood and put his hand on her shoulder. "Alright. Let's go."

Emry smiled. "Thanks, Glen."

"You know I'm coming too, right?" Ian asked, his hands on his hips. "I'm just saying that it's understandable that he wants to know what's going on."

"I want to have feelings for him. Really, I do. I'm just waiting for that to happen. I want to have that conversation with him when I actually have something to give. Is that okay?"

Ian's eyes filled with understanding. "Yeah." He put his hand on Emry's shoulder. "Let's go talk to this dumbass."

They crossed the floor to Mike's quarters. His brown eyes lit up when he saw her on the other side of the door, but he frowned when he noticed Ian and Glen.

"Hmm. Hi, guys."

"Hey there!" Glen said, jovially. He gave Mike a clap on the back. "We decided to join you guys."

"I can see that," Mike murmured, closing the door after them. "Tiger, I wanted to tell you that I'm going home tomorrow, but I come back on Saturday because—"

"I'm actually going away this weekend, too," Emry said. "I'll come back Saturday night, so we can hang out then, if you'd like."

"Oh." He adjusted his glasses. "Where are you going? Surely not home to Rows, right?"

Ian and Glen watched them quietly from the rug, leaning against the wall in an attempt to appear casual.

"No," Emry said. "We have a mission in Egma, and Damon's from there. He invited me to stay at his house for the night."

Mike stared in silence. She turned to look at Glen and Ian, but it seemed like they were holding their breath.

"I see," Mike said, easing into a chair. "And you agreed?"

She could have *sworn* she heard them gasp. *Idiots.*

"Why not?" she asked in her best nonchalant voice, but he just kept looking at her accusingly.

"I heard about Primrose. I don't think he has good intentions."

"You don't even know him. I've been leading alongside him for months now."

"I don't like this."

At that moment, Ian decided to be useful, loudly clearing his throat. "At first, we didn't like the guy either, Mike, but he's actually okay."

Mike tossed him a nasty side-eye. "We're not exactly in the same position here."

"What is that supposed to mean?" Glen scoffed.

Mike's eyes snapped to Emry. "Nothing. I'd like to have a talk with Tiger without you guys."

Ian and Glen looked at each other and stood to leave. Emry sighed as they clapped her on the shoulder on their way out.

"Sorry," Ian whispered as he passed her.

"We tried, girl," Glen whispered before closing the door after him.

Mike approached her tentatively. His brown hair shone in the lamp's light. "Listen. I feel like there's something between us, something more than just friendship. I know we've never said it out loud, but don't you feel the same way?"

Damn it. "I... Look, you know I've been through some hard shit." She looked away. "Relationships, even just friendships, are hard for me."

He scratched his nape, looking more miserable than before. "I know, I know. It's just—we've been friends for a while now. We're not jumping the gun. You know I think you're beautiful." He came even closer. "And smart." He caressed her hair.

Uncomfortable with the proximity, Emry took a deep breath and gently pushed him away. "Mike, I don't know if I'm ready to take it to another level yet."

He grimaced and took a step back. "And yet it's fine to go to another guy's house?"

She snapped. "Look, I don't owe you anything. Do you have any idea what it's like for me to actually leave the base for the night? To go to someone else's house? I have nowhere to go. *Nowhere!* You have no idea how I feel about a gesture my teammate is making for me because you've never been in that position in your life!"

"We never talk about any of that," he said, stunned.

She backed away and realized that he was right. This guy was so fond of her, but how much did he understand her? How much did he actually know about her to like her so much? Yeah, they had their conversations, but they usually revolved around him, and it hadn't ever bothered her before. But he never actually got to *know* her, and she never actually wanted to open up to him. He wouldn't understand.

She sighed in defeat. "You know what? I'm sorry. I should go."

He shook his head. "No, *I'm* sorry. I didn't mean it that way." He tried to approach her again. "I really like you, and sometimes I just forget that you need more time than I do."

"How about we discuss this more when I return from the mission? I don't know if time is even the issue."

He grimaced. "Okay." But it didn't seem like it was.

After they parted, she couldn't help but rethink everything she had been so certain of. She had thought that at some point, she would develop feelings for Mike. She was so sure that she would get over her feelings for Damon and move on, that having another guy in her life would do the trick. She still wanted to try. She had to try, but was any of that fair to Mike, considering that it was still not happening?

Chapter 23

Egma

Damon

"You ready?" Damon asked the next morning as Emry stepped out of her room. Her long hair was up in a ponytail, and she was carrying a little satchel on her back.

"Yes."

"Got everything you need?"

She paused, frowning. "I think so."

He chuckled. "I'm just messing with you. You really don't need to take anything. We'll have everything for you at my house."

It was clear that she was nervous. Damon wondered how the conversation with Mike had gone the night before. Even thinking about that guy irritated him.

When they left the gate, he turned to go right, but she stopped him. "Where are you going? The train station is this way." Emry pointed to the left. "I told Glen and Ian I'd meet them there."

"Who said we're taking the train?" He felt pure joy from her bewilderment.

"How do you want to get to Egma? Flying?"

"I've got a car," he said, continuing right. "We don't need to be packed like sardines in a train cube."

As they walked, he could feel her awe, even in the silence that prevailed between them. He knew that owning a car was a rare luxury reserved for the rich.

They walked past the sands to where his car was parked at the margin. The Black Forest wasn't far, and its trees lined the road, looking both inviting and scary. Emry's eyes were glued to the car, and he gave her a moment to take it in.

"I can't believe you actually have a car."

Damon grinned as he opened the passenger door for her. "Come on. Get inside." He tried not to smile at how carefully she climbed in next to him. Her eyes darted everywhere—the buttons, the handles, the seats.

"I just need you to buckle your seatbelt," he said, demonstrating for her. The trains and army buses never had these.

She pulled at her own. "What's it for?"

"It's to prevent injuries or even death. If I have to stop abruptly, or if I accidentally hit something, it secures you to your seat. When we drive, you need to buckle it."

The truth was, he never buckled his own. Now that she was with him, he knew he had to if he wanted her to do it as well.

When Damon started the car, Emry jumped a little at the roar of the engine. He laughed, turning the wheel. Like an excited little kid, she sat upright on the edge of her seat.

"This is crazy," she said. "You can see the entire road up close from here. In the train, you can only see the view from the little side windows."

He nodded. He didn't even notice it anymore, but she was right. "It *is* quite amazing."

"How did you learn how to drive?" she asked, still looking around.

"My grandma taught me."

He liked to drive. He rarely found himself alone on the base, but when he was driving, he was always driving alone. It usually took him about five hours to get home, and even though he was terrified of having flashbacks while driving, he usually enjoyed the silence. Driving, in some way, felt like meditation. The fact that he had so many memories of his grandma teaching him to drive was a factor, for sure. It was as if the good memories he associated with driving pushed away the hidden ones from the back of his mind, not allowing him to mess up when he had to concentrate. Now, having Emry next to him, driving felt different.

"So, when you said before that I could take the money from the finals..." she began, looking away from the road for the first time.

"I meant it. I have more money than I'll ever need."

"Were you born rich?"

"Yes."

"Then what the hell are you doing in the army?"

He knew this question would come eventually. Most soldiers were there to escape poverty.

"Don't you sometimes feel that you were born to be a Slayer?" he asked, turning the car right.

"I do, with every cell of my body. I'm a soldier—I'm a Slayer. And I despise demons more than anything because of what they have done to humanity, because they've never accepted any peace offer we've ever given them, because they enjoy celebrating death. When I go on a mission, I feel more like myself than anything. But I couldn't have known that at twelve, Damon. Back then, I enlisted for money."

He sighed. "I was a difficult kid. Numb. Detached. I couldn't focus on anything at all. Then out of nowhere, I would turn violent. There's a lot that I can't remember, but the period before I enlisted was not pretty. My grandma was advised to put me in the army. For some reason, enlisting had a good effect on me, so I stayed."

Maybe it was foolish of him to think that neglecting talking about his past would eventually erase it, but it was hard to act differently after years of yearning for just that.

"Is it still hard for you to talk about it?" Emry asked quietly.

His jaw clenched. His eyes were focused on the road. "Yes."

It *was* hard. She could never know how hard it was for him to open up to her like that, but after she'd been exposed to that part of him, he felt like it was only fair to try.

She drew to her window, peeking outside. Her long ponytail was resting at the side of her neck. "Okay."

He took a deep breath. "I don't really *know* what happened, nor *why* I have these nightmares. And talking about the past..."

Why was Damon still rambling? She turned to look at him. He was tempted to stare at her instead of looking at the road.

"You know what? Forget it." He could feel his vision blur, feel the shaking of his hands. What was he thinking? He was driving, for God's sake. They had to stop talking. From the corner of his eye, he saw that she observed the difference in his posture, the urgency of his tone, the way his jaw clenched.

It was the first time he'd actually talked about his childhood, and even though there was a part of him that wanted to burn himself for letting Emry see it, there was also a part that felt safe confiding in her. Inside the warm car, he could feel a new kind of privacy, of serenity. He wasn't scared to expose his shame, he realized. Not to her, anyway. Damon trusted Emry, but he was scared of the terror it would bring upon him.

He could still feel her studying him. Making sure he was aware of her movements, she reached out and placed a hand on his shoulder, giving it a squeeze. Her hand lingered a moment before sliding down to his arm. She gave his arm a squeeze as well and carefully drew back.

There was something in her touch that made the darkness go away. He breathed in relief, and she returned to gazing out her window. The tension broke, and just like that, they were driving in peaceful silence, just him and her.

Emry

Emry groaned in protest as she felt her body being shaken gently.

"Emry, wake up. We're here."

"What?" She turned her head and blinked at Damon's grinning face. "Did I fall asleep?"

"Sure did. Looks like my mere presence is helping you." He winked.

She smacked his arm, but said nothing.

It was a tad chilly when they got out of the car. The air felt different; everything felt different. Looking around, she saw tall trees, vibrant leaves, and thick bushes. No doubt, this was Egma. Egma was famous for her colorful nature—lakes, stunning landscapes, and diverse flora and fauna. Unlike the Black Forest, this place actually felt *alive*.

"Come on," Damon said, gesturing to the mansion before them.

She was frozen in place, mouth agape, earning her a funny look. The house was gigantic and intimidatingly opulent.

"This is where you live?" Emry asked in a small voice.

He laughed. "Last time I checked, yes."

The humor had returned, she noted. The sun's rays outlined his face, and his black hair fell away from his golden eyes. She was staring dumbly at him, but luckily, Damon didn't seem to notice as he started towards the mansion.

"When I don't live in the room a few feet from yours, I live here."

She nodded and followed.

When they entered, she could see that the inside of the mansion was luxurious as well—paintings lined the walls of a massive living room with a mahogany table. The room opened into the kitchen, making the space seem even bigger. She looked around, feeling slightly embarrassed.

He gently took her satchel from her. "Let's go find you a room to sleep in."

"Where's your grandma?" Emry asked, following him to the second floor landing.

"She's probably playing cards at the club instead of resting like the doctors have advised." His face soured when he said that. "You can stay here." He opened a door that led to a small room with a bed, a table, and a closet. "I know it's not much, but—"

She shook her head. "Don't kid yourself. It's perfect."

He smiled, then pointed at another door closer to the staircase. "That's my room, if you need anything."

"Are you sure your grandma will be okay with me staying?" she asked for the millionth time.

He rolled his eyes and tugged her hand to follow him. He caught himself and released it quickly. "Do you want to cook dinner with me? Or are you still tired?"

"I—"

"Damon?" They both jumped as they heard a low, feminine voice coming from the doorway.

Damon tossed Emry an excited look and hurried down the stairs.

The lady was around sixty-seventy years old, with chopped black hair, tea-brown eyes, and pale skin. Her floor-length, long-sleeved dress was elegant, as was her silver necklace. Her eyes, surrounded by wrinkles, were shining happily. Nevertheless, she acted with restraint, smiling gently and nodding her head.

"You look good, dear. How are you?"

"I'm great, grandma," he said, engulfing her in his arms. "Better than the last time I saw you. How are you feeling?"

"Fantastic," she said. That's when she noticed Emry quietly trying her best to remain unseen. "And who is this young lady?"

His grandmother looked at her intently, and she couldn't help but feel scrutinized.

Damon's smile didn't falter. "This is Emry. I told you about her. We have a mission here tomorrow, so I offered her a place for the night."

"I remember." Her eyes lit up with a spark that had Emry feeling like she was in trouble. Nevertheless, the dignified lady offered her hand. "I'm Damon's grandma. You can call me Mima."

Emry shook her hand. "It's a pleasure to meet you. Damon's told me a lot about you."

"Really?" Mima glanced at him, raising a brow. "I didn't think you'd be gossiping about me, boy."

Damon chuckled warmly and took Mima's coat. "You'd be surprised."

Chapter 24

Internal Force

Emry

Evening fell, and darkness enveloped the mansion. Emry found herself sitting at the head of a decorative dinner table with Damon and Mima on either side.

Despite the warm welcome, Emry felt out of place. Sadness lingered in her throat as she idly listened to Damon and his grandmother chat away. She longed to feel wanted, to feel needed, to feel an inescapable happiness wrap itself around her, and pull her into its embrace. But for now, she was satisfied with just witnessing it. Knowing that someone had it, even if it wasn't her, was everything.

"So how have you been since you were discharged from the hospital?" Damon asked Mima, as he shoved noodles from the steamy broth into his mouth.

"I've been well, thank you," she answered. "Have I not taught you any manners?" She gestured at him eating. Emry laughed, and Mima shook her head. "Does he eat like that at the base too?"

"Every time," Emry said, laughing at his scowl.

He shrugged unapologetically. "I'm always starving, especially now. We haven't eaten anything all day. Just so you know, she always does that." He gestured at Emry. "Playing with her food instead of eating it."

Emry felt herself redden, and he smiled in victory. She gave him her best glare.

"Is the food not to your liking?" Mima asked.

"No, no, everything is delicious," Emry hurriedly said. For some reason, she *really* wanted the older lady to like her, and she was nervous. "I had no idea Damon could cook like this," she said, using the opportunity to throw a jab at the cocky guy next to her.

Mima laughed. "When he comes home, he always cooks."

Of course. "Apparently he's good at *everything*," she mumbled to her soup.

They both stared at her, and she blushed.

"Really?" Mima broke the awkwardness by looking at Damon incredulously. "I doubt that."

"You should." Damon put the napkin to his mouth. "It's a bald-faced lie." He smirked at Emry.

Mima just shook her head. "Don't let him get to you, girl." She looked at Damon. "You're always full of mischief. You never change."

"Mischief? Me? I have no idea what you're talking about."

"Now, Damon, you never had any respect for authority as a kid. I thought you might have developed some in the army."

Emry snorted into her soup. Yeah, respect for authority, like breaking into Headley's office when he's gone and snooping through his papers. They both stared at her again. All of a sudden, she felt embarrassed—her reaction came automatically, and now she didn't know what was appropriate to say. This time, no one was going to save her—they were waiting.

"If there's one thing Damon can't do, it's respect authority," she said honestly, like the idiot that she was.

Mima looked at her, and then at her grandson. "Maybe you could teach him something."

"I should have known you two would bond over mocking me." Damon turned back to his meal, not looking offended at all. "I can't wait to hear what you say about the cake I baked."

When they were done, the cake was brought out, and Emry could feel her mouth water at the sight of it. She only saw cakes when they were served dessert on Friday nights, but those desserts were never like *this*. Damon had crafted a fluffy chocolate cake and smothered it in a rich chocolate sauce.

Emry helped clear the table, but instead of returning to the dining room, he stayed in the kitchen to wash dishes. She couldn't let him do that.

"I'll wash them. Go have some time with your grandma," she insisted.

"I have plenty of alone time with my grandma, thank you. Now, go keep her company."

"Damon, seriously, you can't expect me to relax when you—"

"Emry," he said, facing her. His hands were soaked with soap. "Just go and have a piece of cake with my grandma. Can you do that?"

Mumbling to herself, she went back to the table.

"Is he giving you a hard time?" Mima asked, placing a slice in front of Emry. Emry stared at her plate for a moment; that piece of cake was the most beautiful thing she'd ever seen.

"Not really," Emry admitted. "He's just being annoying. I tried to help him wash the dishes and he wouldn't let me."

Mima chuckled. "*So* rude of him."

Emry bit her lip timidly. "I don't know how to be a guest. I haven't been one for a long time. I'm just trying not to screw this up."

Mima looked unsatisfied somehow, and that was all it took to make Emry nervous again. Maybe she misspoke. Was that too honest?

"I'm sorry," she sputtered. "Maybe I'm not being polite enough. I grew up in the army, where the only manners that mattered were extraversions of strength, so that's all I know." She tried to sit straighter. "I really wish I knew how to talk to you, but I don't. I don't have pretty words. I don't have pretty anything. What I am is all I have to offer."

It was heartbreaking to admit, but it had to be done. For the first time since meeting this woman, Emry could feel relief—even with a pounding heart.

After a long silence, spoke. "Being a Tiger in this world must be difficult."

Emry breathed. "You have no idea."

Mima smiled softly to herself and raised her spoon. "I was a little girl myself once, with nothing going for me. No money, no family."

Emry looked at her, surprised. "Really?"

"Oh, yes. My father was from Nova, my mother from Egma. We lived here in Egma until demons killed them. But they were so poor that there was nothing left for me, and I found myself on the streets."

Emry had a hard time picturing that proud, dignified lady on the streets. "What happened?"

"Well, dear, when life is coming at you, you have to come back at it. I lived on the streets, but I did it with pride. I was also always very good with cards." Her dark eyes glinted, a smile coming to her lips. "I was young, but I was a fast learner. I memorized cards, memorized movements, and facial expressions. I learned a few tricks, and I knew my way around a gambling hall. You know why I never got caught?" She took a sip from her drink.

"Why?"

"Because I was very good." She laughed. "But also because I was a woman." She put the glass down. "And women were thought to be gentle, stupid, and naïve. That disadvantage worked better than I ever thought it would. With every man who looked down at me with disrespect, I made a fortune."

"That sounds incredible," Emry murmured, trying to imagine such a life. "*You* sound incredible."

This woman had the same magical countenance that Damon always had. How had she not seen it before? She even had the same mischief in her eyes.

Mima regarded her with a hard expression. "Aren't *you* incredible?"

Emry swallowed. Now that politeness was cast aside, and they were being honest, she tried to offer the most truthful answer she could. "You are incredible," she said again, gently. "It seems to me that you hold so much power inside of you. And I—I have been fighting all of my life. I see the work done, but I'm not like you." She looked directly into her eyes, her voice soft. "I don't have that internal force. I'm a broken mess."

Silence prevailed between them, and then Damon strode over and slumped in his seat. "You two have a nice talk? Exchanging ways to insult me?"

Suddenly, Emry felt exhausted. "I think I'll retire for the evening, if that's okay. I feel a little tired." She rose from her seat.

"Are you alright?" Damon frowned. He was at the edge of his seat in an instant.

"Yes," she said sincerely. She turned to Mima. "Thank you."

Mima nodded at her, and Emry thought she could identify understanding in her eyes.

"Sleep well, dear."

Damon

Damon watched Emry ascend the stairs. He heard his grandmother clear her throat and turned his face to her.

She was studying him with that wary expression that she always had when she tried to break something into pieces. "She's very beautiful, isn't she?"

"Indisputably." He grinned in return.

She cocked her head. "How well do I know you, Damon?"

"Very well. You've known me ever since I was born."

She paused, then gestured at the stairs. "The way you look at her—you've never looked at anybody like that before. Not me, not your friends, not anybody."

He knew she couldn't possibly know that, as she had never met any of his friends besides Jenna, but still, he tried not to squirm in his seat. He could lie, he could try to deny it, but he knew it was pointless.

He sighed and cupped his glass. "I *can't* look at her, or we'll both be kicked out of the army."

"Then what is she doing here?"

Damon raised his eyes to look at Mima. He didn't want to have that conversation, but it didn't seem like he had a choice. "I told you we have a mission tomorrow. She's always staying alone at the base and never goes home. I just wanted her to have a family meal for a change."

Her eyes were still fixed on his face. "You should have stayed away, not invited her here. Her circumstances don't matter."

He exhaled exasperatedly. "I tried to stay away. I couldn't. *I can't.*"

She sighed, as if accepting fate. "You need to be careful."

Careful of what? Careful of falling even harder for Emry? Careful of the army finding out? He didn't find it in himself to ask. Instead, another question bubbled inside of him, urgent and loud.

"How does *she* look at me?"

His grandmother was a master of reading people. She would definitely know.

"What?" An amused smile was playing on her lips.

Damon exhaled. He knew that she'd heard him the first time. "You talked about how I look at her. How does *she* look at *me?*"

She held his gaze for a moment. "As if she is very confused."

He blinked. "What?"

"That's how she looks at you."

"Great," he grumbled, disappointed.

"Don't get me wrong—I do like her." His grandmother leaned back in her seat.

He could feel the tension leave his chest. "You do?"

"Yes." She nodded once. "I do. But she's a piece of work, Damon. It's not going to be easy."

But he already knew that, didn't he?

Chapter 25

The Deal Breaker

Emry

Emry couldn't sleep. She kept imagining Mima's life. It was absurd that only when she'd told Emry her story could she actually see it in her. Maybe it was due to how clever the woman actually was; the perfect illusionist. Maybe she only showed you what she wanted you to see.

Dinner had been so lovely, but being alone in the small room, in such a large bed, felt lonely. She was used to being alone, but somehow the joy she'd experienced earlier made her crave more of it. It was something she couldn't have. She was overcome with frustration and exhaustion, but sleep never came.

Emry wished she could be more like Mima: frightening, yet full of restraint and dignity. She felt like a tiger: wild, untamed, and angry, lashing out every now and then. She was always scared, and therefore always ready to lunge. She was so tired of it. So tired of everything.

Gently, she slipped out of bed and tiptoed into the hall, not entirely sure of her own intentions. Hesitating there, thinking about going downstairs for some water, she heard him.

This time, he wasn't screaming. It was so faint she actually had to stop and make sure that she'd actually heard something. Instead of screaming, his voice reached her in small whispers—tormented, agonized.

"Please, stop," he begged.

She couldn't take it. She opened his door quietly, walked to his bed, and knelt next to his frantic body.

"Damon. Damon, wake up!" She gave him a little shake. He let out a groan and sat up, eyes wide.

He was panting, just for a moment, before he closed his eyes and let out a long breath. "Did I scream again?"

"No, but... I heard you."

A tired grin appeared on his face. "Were you eavesdropping on me?" How could he even joke right now?

"No!"

"My very own stalker. If you want, I'll let you watch me sleep."

"What a privilege. You're so full of yourself!"

"I knew you'd like that." He turned his head and his eyes scanned her face. His smile faltered. "What about you? Having trouble sleeping?"

"As always." She looked away. She didn't want to tell him about the loneliness she'd been feeling, about the frustration with herself and her life.

"Sit with me a little." He patted the space next to him. "Just until you feel sleepy. I can't sleep now either."

Emry hesitated, but his eyes were staring at her so intently that she lost focus and slowly crawled into his bed. She sat before him, with the blanket entangled around them. It felt as if they were just little kids having a sleepover.

"Did you have a good time today?" he asked quietly, almost whispering. His knee was practically touching hers.

"Yeah," she answered in the same tone. "A lot." She fiddled with the blanket a bit before she caught his eye again. "Thanks for inviting me over."

Something twisted in him. "You can come here whenever you want."

She almost felt like crying, and she hated it. "Don't be hasty. Maybe your grandma wouldn't like me hanging around."

"Shut up," he snorted. "She likes you."

"She does?" It felt pathetic just how happy that made her.

"Mima told me so herself. Why are you so surprised?" He inched closer.

She thought about the conversion she'd had with Mima. "I'm afraid I didn't give a good first impression."

"When do you ever?" He cocked his head, laughing. "I wouldn't worry about that. She's very observant, Mima sees through anything."

Emry nodded. "She told me about herself. She's incredible, Damon. You're lucky she's your grandma."

He drew himself more of the blanket. "Did you two talk about me?"

"Yes," she said sarcastically. "We said your soup was disgusting and your cake was awful."

"No! Not the *cake*!"

She laughed. "You're so used to everything revolving around you."

"Is that so?"

"Yes," she said matter-of-factly. "You're the center of attention everywhere you go."

"Including yours?"

"Sometimes." She blushed. "But I don't have much attention to begin with."

"Right," he said, not looking very pleased.

She eyed him. "I don't think you need any more attention. You already have enough of it."

"It's better to have good quality over a large quantity, don't you think?"

"Are you calling me quality?" she snorted. "Your expectations are very low, then."

"You're kidding, right?"

"I'm not much of a joker."

"Speaking of not coming off well..." He shook his head. "You're not much of anything, and I'm too much of everything. Did I get it right?"

"Pretty much." Unable to help herself, Emry smiled at how accurate it sounded.

"If that's true, then why do you have the ability to stop my nightmares when I can't control them?" he asked quietly.

She drew in a breath. "I don't know, Damon. I wish I could find a way to help you stop them."

"You already help," he murmured, scowling.

"I hate seeing you like that."

Somehow, it was easier to open up in the dark. She felt closer to him than she'd ever felt. Damon grabbed her hand and looked away, but Emry could see the pain in his eyes. She looked down at their clasped hands instead. It seemed like he was touching her every time he needed comfort. She should have let go, but she didn't. In the end, even if everyone wanted him, she was the one he let in. She was the one sitting with him in the middle of the night.

"My grandma knows," he said suddenly. "She knows what happened to my parents, my brother, and me, but I don't want to know. Every time I'd try to hear it, I'd faint or panic. And even if I didn't grasp anything at all, I'd still have even worse nightmares than before."

She bit her lip and squeezed his hand. "I'm sorry. Maybe one day you'll be able to hear it. I'm happy that at least you have your grandma."

He raised his head, and his hair fell across his smiling face. "She really did a number on you, didn't she?"

She chuckled. "Absolutely."

"Are you close to anyone from your family?"

"No." She paused, and the smile died on her lips. "I haven't seen them in a year. They welcome me when I come home, but they don't really know me." She couldn't help the bitterness in her voice. "And I don't really know them, either. I... I take care of them, but I don't have them."

It was shameful. Other soldiers were completely alone in life, with no family and nowhere to go. She *had a* family. They were alive and breathing, but they weren't *hers*. Her parents and sister were always uneasy when she came to visit, so she stopped coming home. Even if they didn't say it to her face, Emry could feel their distance, how they politely waited for her to leave. She didn't even belong in her own home, and was just as unwanted there as everywhere else.

Suddenly, she felt Damon raise their clasped hands and entwine their fingers. "You have me," he rasped. His amber eyes were smoldering, intense. "Always. When you're angry, when you're happy, when you can't sleep, even when you feel like you want to set the whole world on fire—I can take it all."

She blinked away the tears that threatened to escape her eyes. He couldn't possibly know how much his words meant to her.

"Thanks, Damon…" she finally said, not knowing what else to say.

He yawned and fell back on the mattress, pulling her down beside him. "Stay," he breathed. "I know we're not supposed to do that again, but just… stay."

She rested with him as he closed his eyes. For a moment, just like the creep that he joked she was, she watched him sleep.

Damon

It was the middle of the night, and Emry didn't know that she was clinging to Damon. She rested her body next to his, and her hair tickled his jaw. He could painfully feel every inch of her that touched him, and it spurred his mind. If she were awake, he could have easily flipped them so her back would be pressed to the hard mattress and he would be pressed to her front, lips finding hers. He could easily make her writhe and moan, restless underneath him, begging him, whispering his name.

The picture in his head became too vivid. He gently untangled from her and got up. She frowned before her green eyes fluttered open, confused.

"Just need a moment," he said gently. "Try to sleep. I'll be back." Did she know what she was doing to him? Did she have any idea?

When Damon reached the balcony at the end of the corridor, he sighed and ran his hands through his dark hair. The wind soothed his burning body. Before him, he could see darkness embracing the trees, the hills, the valleys, the swamps. Egma was indeed beautiful, and he had missed his home.

* * *

The first thing Damon noticed when he woke up was that he hadn't had any more nightmares that night. The second thing was that Emry was sleeping next to him, her head turned to the wall. Her scent, a mix of sugar and pepper, enveloped the bed, and it was messing with his mind. He sighed and rubbed the sleep out of his eyes.

Damon met Mima in the kitchen, and she greeted him with a slight raise of her brow, sipping her coffee.

"Morning." He smiled at her. "How do you feel? Did the doctors say you could drink coffee?" he scolded.

"I feel wonderful. I'm not going to have another heart attack. I'm sure of it, so don't lecture me. Do you need to leave soon?"

"Yes. We won't take the car back to the base, because we don't want any demons following us back here. We'll just take the bus."

"Where's Emry? Is she awake?"

"She's still sleeping in my bed."

Mima cocked her head, and he gave a slight shake of his.

"Not what you think."

She studied him. "Be careful, Damon."

He exhaled, mixing it with laughter. "Careful of what, grandma?"

"Careful of your heart," she said gently. "She's a special one. She and I have something in common that not many people have. But I'm not sure how she'll choose to lead her life. If she gets caught in her own flames, I'll be heartbroken to see you burned as well."

He took a deep breath, letting the words sink in. There was something terrifying in them, because he could feel their truth. As always, his grandmother had hit the nail on the head. He stepped closer, set aside her mug, and took her hands in his. "Thank you for worrying about me, grandma."

He looked into her eyes—eyes that were usually full of intelligence and wit, sarcasm and wisdom—and they were shining with genuine feelings of tenderness and concern for him.

"You're a precious boy, Damon. You always have been."

He smiled, cherishing this moment with her. "Promise me you'll try to slow down. You're not the only one worrying, you know."

She laughed heartily. "I have a week full of pool exercises with the other rich snobs from the country, and card games."

He laughed. She'd never change.

Emry

Emry found Damon and Mima standing together in the kitchen. She hoped she wasn't interrupting.

"Morning," she managed, passing her eyes between the two of them. What did guests usually do when they woke up?

"Did you sleep well, dear?" Mima asked, handing her a cup of coffee. Damon huffed and grabbed his own mug from the sink.

"Yes, thank you. Your house is beautiful, and I had a great time here," Emry answered.

"We should get going soon," Damon said. "Are you ready?"

"Yes." She felt the soldier in her rise again. *Thank god.* "Do you know where we're going?"

"Yeah. I'll lead the way."

After Mima and Damon said goodbye at the doorstep, the older lady turned to her.

"It was a pleasure to meet you," Emry said. "I hope we'll have a chance to meet again."

Mima nodded, then sighed. "Come here, girl."

Emry was taken by surprise when Mima pulled her into a tight hug. When she let go, her eyes were fierce.

"You are not broken—you're a deal breaker. You're the thing that makes everything else shift to one side or another. You're the most valuable condition, and you're everything that counts. Remember that."

Chapter 20

Accusations

Damon

The pair walked between crowded trees, pushing their way through branches and rocks, until they reached a lake. Its water was clear and blue, glinting in the sun. Damon could hear Emry gasp. Having grown up in the beautiful area, he was used to it., but it was probably her first time. He stood back as she took a few steps forwards.

"It's beautiful," she said in awe.

"Never seen a lake before?" he said, stepping beside her.

"Only once or twice," she said. "Rows is a desert. We don't have lakes there."

Crunching footsteps behind them shattered the moment. They both immediately drew their weapons, only to find their squad approaching from the rear. Short greetings were exchanged before the soldiers prepared for the demons' arrival.

"Good timing," Emry said. "I can sense the demons coming." There was a fire in her eyes that wasn't there before.

"Careful," Damon said. His grandmother's words were ringing in his ears. "Headley said they're level two. It's probably not going to be pretty."

"It's *never* pretty."

"Which species are we going to face?" asked one of their friends as he drew his bow.

Damon swapped glances with one of their squad, a girl he knew was also from Egma. "I think Chernya. Don't you, Claire? It's been a while since I've been here."

"Yes." Claire nodded and stepped closer to him. She was holding her knife out defensively, obviously nervous.

"Be ready," said another Slayer.

It only took them a few moments to arrive. Shadowy monsters jumped from the treetops, lunging at them. Their eyes mirrored black, their bodies tainted black. Their small heads were disproportionate to their bulky bodies. Tiny, useless wings attached to their backs flapped angrily.

The archer was the first to shoot. His arrow caught one of the demons in the air, sending the creature spiraling to the ground in a bloody fit of screams, dying upon impact. Another arrow was drawn, and chaos began.

Like in any other battle, Damon gained elevated focus. Drawing his knives, he slashed without looking, relying mostly on instinct. He tried to do most of the work while also being aware of his teammates, but it was difficult. One of the demons managed to stick its talons into his shoulder blade, and he growled in pain.

With a *whoosh*, a knife suddenly flew over his head and hit the demon in the face. The taloned demon loosened its grip and fell to the ground. When Damon looked over, he saw Emry's deadly look. Her hand was still in the throwing position. She nodded at him once and then spun to face another demon trying to sneak up behind her.

He'd taken down a lot of them, but it seemed like they were gathering around Emry. Her eyes were wide, her pupils dark and shrunken. She didn't look scared. She looked ready. She lunged, but there was no way she would make it by herself. Damon ran towards her, slashing with his blades, but other people needed help as well. It was a clumsy maneuver, but in the end, he reached her. To his surprise, even though her body was covered in bruises, she was practically glowing. Knife in each hand, Emry was breathing hard, but she was taking them one by one.

A disturbing thought reached his mind. Were the demons gathering around her, or was she the one running inside the chaos?

The crisp sound of bones being crushed shifted his attention, and he twisted to the right. There, a grinning demon was tightly holding the archer, exposing its black teeth. Razor-sharp claws extended from its right hand, and Damon's mind blanked.

In an instant, he was next to the demon, slashing its nape, earning a high-pitched screech before it fell, lifeless. The surprise of his own speed left Damon satisfied, but curious about his own limits.

On the ground, the archer writhed, but he nodded, signifying that he would be okay on his own. Damon returned the gesture and tried to find Emry among the mayhem, but couldn't. *She was right there. Now she's... gone.* Panic surged through him. His eyes grew wild as he spun around, searching for his co-leader.

He shouted for her. "Emry—!"

A talon hit him directly below his shoulder blade, digging its way into his flesh, and with a groan, Damon was forced to the ground.

Was this how he was going to die? Surely, he'd expected something more heroic than that.

He sneered, thinking of how he'd lectured Emry to be careful on missions. The demon towered over him, arm lifted, claws ready to strike. It opened its mouth to speak, but froze seconds later. A wet *squelch* was heard as its body fell to the ground, exposing a frenzied Emry.

"What the hell..." She panted and brushed her bloodied hair from her forehead with the back of her hand. "What the hell were you doing?!"

"I couldn't find you!" he spat, getting to his feet.

Her eyes, once wild and protective, were now riddled with a cold anger. Damon immediately realized his mistake, but it was too late to backtrack, and he didn't give a damn.

"You tried to find me?!" She closed the distance between them.

"Yeah, I did," he said with a scoff. He turned and pointed to the archer, who was tending to his wounds. "That could have been you. Hell, *that* could have been you." Damon motioned towards a demon splayed on the ground. "So, yeah. I sure fucking did, Emry. I'll always try to find you."

Beside them, the light from a flare gun soared into the sky, illuminating the fire in Emry's eyes. A bright-red dust scattered down around them, and reality sunk in.

"The bus will be here any second," she said, not sparing him a second glance. "Make sure you get seen by a medic."

Sheathing her weapon, she brushed past him and made her way over to an injured Slayer.

* * *

Damon had saved Emry a seat when the bus came, but she chose to sit with someone else. She seemed to be in a good mood, laughing with them, but he didn't feel like joining the conversation. He didn't believe her behavior, either. Since when was she chatty and friendly? That wasn't her. Instead, he talked to Claire and the others nearby.

"You know what?" a Slayer loudly said. "We need to celebrate that we're all alive!"

Everyone cheered.

"It's going to be night when we arrive. Let's go to the club!" suggested another. "We'll make ol' Colin give us free shots."

"What do you say, Primrose? You in?" someone else asked.

All eyes turned to Damon.

"Hell yeah!" It felt forced, but Damon joined his friend and everyone cheered. "We just beat a bunch of level twos and we're all alive."

"Will you come, Tiger?" a male Slayer asked.

"You know what? I think I will," she said, turning to face him.

* * *

When they unloaded the bus at the base, Emry quickly walked to the Slayers building, avoiding Damon.

He hurried to catch up to her, his shoulder throbbing. "You know... I was saving you a seat back there."

She ignored him, making her climb up the stairs.

"Come on! What is your issue?"

"Oh, I don't know, Damon," she said irritably. "Perhaps it's the fact that you almost *died* searching for me."

"I was looking out for you. Is that so terrible?"

With a sharp movement, Emry snapped to face him. "Yes!"

"Seriously?"

She growled. "Do you have any idea how it makes me look when you're protecting me in front of others? I'm your fucking *co-leader*, not your subordinate! I'm capable of handling myself, *and* I saved your stupid ass!"

A flash of anger bubbled inside of him. "You're unbelievable. Your pride is smothering your ability to understand the situation. You'd rather be dead than let someone help you!"

"Even if that were true, it doesn't concern you!"

"Duly noted. Won't happen again." Damon left, slamming the door behind him.

Emry

Damon's words repeated themselves in Emry's head. His accusations hit her hard. She had to let it go for now. She *would* go to the club and try to socialize for a change, try to have a good time. Emry damn well deserved it, too. Her thoughts were hunting her. Was she too innocent? She told him he didn't get anything, but did *she*? Was she a total idiot? Maybe. Probably.

Hesitating in front of her disheveled closet, she picked out some black leggings and a fitted, black shirt. Now, people could actually see the shape of her body, and it felt... different. She closed her eyes, deciding that she wouldn't change.

Emry took a deep breath and made her way out of their quarters, only to see Mike at the entrance.

"Hi," he said, looking stunned to see her. His eyes roamed down her body, surprised at what she was wearing. "I just heard that you came back. I thought you'd come to see me, but… Are you going to the club?"

She took a deep breath and gestured for him to walk with her. The sky above grew darker as the sun set.

"Didn't you go home for the weekend?" she asked.

"I did, but just for a day. I told you I was coming back on Saturday."

Did he? She couldn't remember. "Oh, well. How are things?"

"Fine…" he said, and she could sense he was being apprehensive. "Are you okay?"

"I'm fabulous."

"Are you sure? I just —"

"Yes, yes. I'm sorry, the mission was tough and I don't really feel like talking right now."

"But you *do* feel like going to the club," he accused.

She stopped walking. "Mike, I can't do this right now."

"You can't ever." He stopped walking and crossed his arms. "How was it at Primrose's?"

"It was fine," she said impatiently. "We went there, we ate, we slept, woke up, slayed some demons, and now we're here."

"Then why are you so pissed?" he demanded.

"Because you keep talking even though I just said I didn't want to." She could feel rage building inside of her again. She had to move, she had to step away from him. "Just leave me alone!" she hissed and left him there, watching her go.

Chapter 27

Get It Right

Emry

Even though winter was slowly showing its face, the inside of the club felt warm and stuffy. It wasn't as packed as it usually was in the middle of the week, but everyone who'd been on the mission was now on the dance floor, and more people had joined the celebration. Though it was nearly pitch-black, neon lights flashed along the floor, outlining the path to the bar.

Standing alone against the wall, Emry watched the moving figures swaying with the music as if they didn't have a care in the world. Feeling brave, she grabbed a drink and downed it in one go. She could feel the warm sensation in her chest and nose, bringing tears to her eyes.

Coming up for air, she spotted Damon at the far side of the room, talking to Claire, another Enigman. They were laughing, drinks in hand. Emry didn't miss the way Claire's eyes sparkled as she dangled on his every word. She gripped her glass tightly, suddenly disappointed that it was empty.

When she turned back to the bar to order another, she noticed a guy from her squad, staring at her a few feet away. "Yo, Tiger! You actually came!"

Emry scooped up her drink and made her way over to him. "Owen! Hey!" she called, hoping she had gotten his name right. "I was phenomenal today. I deserve a freaking break."

She chugged her drink, because damn it, she didn't have it in her to make small talk while sober. Besides, she just wanted to forget. She didn't want to see Damon or Mike, She just wanted to sit with random people and drink. Her head was spinning, her thoughts were out of order, and her heart was aching, but she didn't care.

They were cheering at her, laughing.

"You shouldn't have done that," Owen said, gesturing for her to sit next to him.

"Yes, she should have!" squeaked the girl beside her, Ruth. She was ordering them both two more drinks. "Come on," she urged, her eyes dancing as she gripped the glass Colin handed her from behind the bar. "Let's get wasted!" she called as she sipped her drink and shook her head. Her golden curls were shaking with her movements.

"You two are going to be alcoholics at this point," Owen teased.

"Whatever," answered Ruth. "Tomorrow's Sunday. We can be alcoholics tonight. Tiger, we don't have any soldiers coming tomorrow, right?"

Emry was busy sniffing at the yellow liquid at her glass. "What is it?"

"Pineapple!" Owen said.

"Try it!" Ruth shouted.

They cheered as Emry roared and let the drink slide down her throat. The prickling sensation felt good—too good. Soon she found herself giggling like a schoolgirl, ordering more drinks, and feeling that warmth inside of her again, and again, and again.

Damon

Damon swirled his glass in a circle. Truth was, he didn't feel like drinking tonight. He'd finally managed to get Claire off of him, and now that he was finally alone, he thought about ditching the club and going to see if Jenna was at the Intelligence building. He could use his best friend.

He hadn't seen Emry and figured she'd stayed at the Slayers building. As he approached the bar to pay and leave, he saw a big gathering of people yelling and cheering. He stepped closer to see what the fuss was all about and had to double-check to make sure he wasn't hallucinating.

In the middle—swinging her hips—was his co-leader. He'd never seen her like that; her cheeks were red, and she was... laughing. *Everyone* was looking. Emry slumped into a seat, and the guy next to her bent to wrap his arm around her shoulders, laughing hysterically.

"Okay," she called. "Who's having a drink with me now?"

She stretched to take a bottle from the bar, pouring down shots. Her admirers, sweaty from dancing, cheered her on.

"Damn it," he mumbled. People made way as he walked inside the circle. "You"—Damon wrapped his arm around her waist and whispered in her ear so no one would hear—"are coming with me. Now." When he pulled her off the chair and close to his body, she hit him with an *oomph*.

She giggled as her body made contact with his. "Why?" she whispered back innocently. "Is it wrong that I'm having fun like you always do?" She watched him with joy and curiosity.

He pulled her out away from the crowd, not bothering to look back at their disappointed stares. "You worked too fucking hard to have your reputation thrown away like that," he fumed, coming to a halt. "Can you walk?"

"Why? You want to carry me now?" Her eyes were red and wide open as she looked into his. "Maybe I'll let you."

He felt stupid because his heart was actually pounding over this. "Come on," he said, tugging her forwards. "Let's get out of here."

She was giggling all the way to the Slayers building and up the stairs.

"You..." She pointed a finger at his chest, throwing her head back in a laugh. "You are such an asshole."

Incredible. She managed to insult him even while drunk.

"You're going to regret behaving like that tomorrow. I just saved your sorry ass."

"Oh?" She blinked at him. "Thank you, Sir Damon." Emry took a deep bow, nearly falling over in the process. As she stabilized herself, she ran her hands through her long hair. "That's what you wanted to hear, isn't it?"

He stood there, tired, angry, and frustrated. No, that wasn't what he wanted to hear. "Just go to sleep, Emry."

"Why? So I won't go back there?" She cocked her head, her eyes enthusiastic. "So you won't need to worry about me? Are you angry because you always do?"

He took a step back, startled. She wouldn't have said any of this to him if she were sober.

"Emry, you had a lot to drink. We should get you in bed to rest."

"No," she said angrily. "You don't get to tell me what to do. You said awful things to me today, you *jerk!*"

He closed his eyes and took a deep breath. He wanted to lash out at her, but it wasn't fair. "Listen. I don't think it's a good idea to have this conversation right now. Let's talk tomo—"

"No!" She stomped her foot. "Let's talk *right now.*"

Her green eyes were stronger, decisive—and he hated the influence that looking into them had on him. She was pissed off and drunk, but everything about her glowed.

"You told me that I'm *playing* with you! That I'm leaving everyone *miserable!*" Emry jabbed her finger at his chest again. "But what about *me?* What about how miserable *I* am? You don't get it! You don't get *anything!*"

"Then tell me!" he shouted. "Tell me, so my thick, stupid head will finally get it right."

Silence prevailed as she observed his outburst through a haze. She burst into laughter, and Damon felt both frustrated and ashamed that he actually yelled. He took a step forwards, ready to carry her to bed, but froze when their eyes locked.

"I want you," she said."

His mouth went dry. She burst into another wave of giggles.

"And I'm—" She choked. "I'm *so* stupid. I am *such* an idiot, because…" She took a step closer. "I want you. I want you all over me." The intensity of her stare could burn him and he wouldn't look away. "I want you so much it *hurts.*"

Emry's words were ripping Damon's heart in two. He could feel it breaking, being burned alive by the rage brewing inside of him. How many fantasies did he have of her? How many daydreams had he jerked himself out of? He would have given anything for her to be sober right now, but she wasn't.

With a heavy, tired heart, he forced himself to step away from her. "Come on," he said softly. "Let's get you in bed."

* * *

"Will you slow down? This isn't a marathon," Jenna said as she followed Damon to the Slayers building.

Damon took a deep breath and slowed his pace. "Sorry."

"Uh huh... Anyway, it's very unlike Emry to get drunk," Jenna mused. "What exactly do you need from me?"

"Just change her clothes. She spilled alcohol on them," he grumbled.

"I see. Are you gonna tell me what *actually* happened? You're all riled up."

He sighed as he turned to look at her. Her brown eyes were serious. "We had a fight when we came back from the mission."

"Why did you fight? Did you not have a great time at your place?"

"We did." Damon ran his hands through his dark hair. The wind was chilly, helping him clear his mind. "But when we came back, she got angry at something really idiotic. You know Emry; she's got a temper."

"Yeah, I met her," Jenna muttered. "What was she mad about?"

"Some girl was talking to me, asking for medical help. She didn't like it." To his surprise, his friend kept quiet. He turned to look at her. "What?"

She raised her eyes to meet his. "How did you deal with that?"

"I was angry." A sardonic laugh escaped his mouth. They were climbing up the stairs now. "She's always around this ICT guy—" He stopped in the middle of his sentence.

They paused one floor below Emry, caught off-guard by the guy in question looking around and anxiously messing up his brown hair. When Mike turned and saw them, his eyes narrowed.

"Where's Tiger?"

He apparently didn't know he needed to climb to the last floor. *She's never brought him here before.* Jenna wordlessly went into their hall, leaving the two alone.

He was the last person Damon wanted to talk to, but he didn't want any trouble. "Emry's upstairs, but she's resting."

"Really?" Mike laughed and shook his head. "Did you take her back from the club?"

"I did."

"Why did you do that?"

Damon could feel his blood rushing in his vein. "She got drunk and started to do stupid shit, and *you* weren't there to help."

"She asked me to leave her alone," Mike hissed. "Said she didn't want to talk to me."

"You know what?" Damon took a step closer. "She told me she didn't want to talk to me either. I was still there."

"She's a strong, independent soldier who can make her own decisions," Mike growled, gesturing wildly. "All I did was respect her wishes. *You* didn't."

"Okay," Damon said menacingly. "You want to fight? I guarantee that's not a good idea."

Mike took a step back, suddenly aware of what was happening. "I want you to stay away from her."

Damon appreciated him standing his ground. "Yeah?" He raised his brow and took a step closer. "You know I can't do that. She's my co-leader."

"That's an excuse," Mike started, but Damon had already turned his back. He didn't have any intention of continuing this conversation. Right as his foot hit the first step, Mike said, "You can never be together."

"Come again?" Damon whipped around.

"You heard me." Mike raised his chin, but Damon could hear the shake in his breath. "I've been seeing her for months now. Do you think I'm that much of an idiot? Whatever there is between the two of you, it can't happen. Both of you will get expelled." He clenched his fists so his hands wouldn't shake. "So stay away from her!"

"Or what?" Damon left the steps and came closer.

Mike was breathing hard as he looked into Damon's eyes. "Or I'll report you."

Damon chuckled, then thrust his hand forwards and let his palm wrap around Mike's throat. In an instant, he was pinned against the wall, twisting and shrieking, but to no avail.

"I'm usually a patient guy," Damon growled. His hold tightened. "I'm also the best Slayer this organization has and one of the leaders of an elite group. Who do you think people will believe? You?" he mocked. "You know what? Let's start with you telling people about what happened to you here."

Mike stopped struggling, confusion plaguing his face. "W-what?"

Damon smashed Mike's head against the wall, and he fell to the ground, unconscious. He shook his head at the motionless form and turned around, only to see Jenna watching him with amusement from the stairs.

Chapter 28

Dread and Pleasure

Emry

Emry woke up with a massive headache and zero memory of the night before. Panic started to creep into her mind until she saw the chair next to her bed. She dragged it closer and saw a box of painkillers and a note on the cushion. She frowned at the handwriting. It wasn't Damon's neat and elegant script; it was nearly illegible.

> *You got drunk in the club and made a complete fool of yourself. Damon took care of you. I changed your clothes.*
>
> *Jenna*

Emry groaned and took the painkillers. What was she thinking? She barely ever drank. She felt angry with herself. All she could remember was having a fight with Damon and then yelling at Mike on her way to the club. Poor Mike. He didn't deserve that.

She looked at the clock and realized that she needed to hurry. It was already noon, and she had sentry duty at the north gate. When she stepped into the hall, she found Damon sitting in a chair, tying his shoes.

"Hey." She leaned against the doorframe, studying him.

"How are you feeling?" he asked, not looking up. Was he still angry about their fight from last night? Did she do something wrong while she was drunk?

"Awful," she admitted. "My head is pounding so bad I actually want to rip it off."

Without looking at her, he let out a hoarse chuckle and then stood to leave. It stung.

"Damon." He froze, his back to her. "I'm sorry you had to drag me here last night, but are you really that upset about it?"

Finally, he faced her. His eyes were almost animalistic, feline.

"Look. I'm sorry… I shouldn't have gotten drunk." She shook her head with regret and massaged her temple. "I didn't intend for it to happen."

"How much do you remember?" His voice was stiff.

"Nothing. I only remember walking to the club." She took a step closer. In the end, he'd helped her out, even though he'd probably been angry with her. "I'm sorry about yesterday. I didn't want to fight." She tried to sound as sincere as she felt.

He took a moment to observe her cautiously, as if she didn't make any sense at all. "It's fine," he eventually said, turning away. "Forget it."

"Seriously? What now? Did I do something else that pissed you off?"

He didn't answer, and her panic returned in full force.

"Damn it," she cursed, following him down the stairs. "You have to tell me."

"It's nothing," he said, but she could feel the anger in his voice. "Let's just move on."

"No. What did I do?" She blocked his path, going backwards down the stairs.

"Emry, be careful," he said, irritated. "You'll fall down."

"Then tell me what I did! It's my right to know."

"Other than drinking way too much? You said things you probably shouldn't have. That's all."

She felt her cheeks redden. "What?" she whispered, stopping in her tracks. "Whatever I said that pissed you off so bad last night, remember that I was *drunk*."

"*Yeah,* I'm very much aware of that." He stopped now, too.

"What did I say to you?"

He gave her a long look, his lips pressed to a thin line, and then he simply walked away. Emry felt like she could actually kill him, and that feeling didn't diminish over the next six hours of her watch.

* * *

When Jenna passed by the gate, she raised an eyebrow. "Tiger, how are you feeling?"

"Like shit." Emry blew the hair away from her face. "Do you have time to sit with me a bit?"

She was getting antsy inside the tiny shack designated for the watchers. Some gates had impressive towers, but not the north gate. She usually would've enjoyed the isolation, but Jenna was apparently around at some point the night before. Damon certainly wasn't going to tell her what happened, so it was worth a shot.

"Hmm." Jenna looked at her up and down. "Unfortunately, I do. Have you eaten anything?"

"I haven't."

"Then I'll go fix you something to eat first."

When Jenna came back, she handed Emry a plate and sat on the floor so no one would see that she was there. Guards weren't allowed to have company while they were maintaining the area.

"Tell me," Emry said, moving the raw vegetables on her plate to the side. "What did I do last night?"

Jenna watched her curiously. "You don't remember?"

"No."

"Did you ask Damon?"

"Yes." Emry's grip around the plastic fork tightened. "He wouldn't tell me anything, but I have a right to know."

"He was really pissed off. I've been trying to figure out what you did."

"So you don't know what happened?"

"I don't know what you did before Damon got angry and brought me in to deal with you. He usually isn't like that. He has patience—sometimes *too* much patience. Something triggered him last night. Must have been you, no?"

Emry huffed loudly.

"You know," Jenna said, chuckling, "I don't have much patience either."

"You?"

Emry glanced down at her. Jenna always seemed like the very model of wit and apprehension. Everyone said she was one of the most talented Intelligence soldiers they had. Jenna raised a brow, and Emry's interest was piqued.

"What's *your* story, Jenna? How did *you* end up here?"

Jenna returned her stare to the wooden wall of the shack. "After my parents were killed in the Great War, my older sister and I had to survive on our own. I was twelve. She was eighteen, and very stupid." She readjusted her position. "She heard rumors on the streets about a place called the Honeymoon Kingdom. My sister was never one to actually seek a stable job. She wanted to make money, and she wanted to make it fast. She didn't want me to help because I was doing well in school. Apparently, this place offered her a job in which she could make a lot of money, just like she wanted."

Emry looked at her intently. "It was a brothel, wasn't it?"

"Of course, but she took the job anyway. She came back every night, drugged and exhausted. She could barely talk. The first week, she got paid in cash. After that, they paid her in drugs."

Emry nodded, staring ahead through the window. "So she went there, and you were taken here by the government?"

"Hmm." Jenna flicked a tiny piece of dirt from her shirt. "Yes, but not exactly."

"What do you mean?"

"One night, she didn't come home. I went to the brothel, and I saw her body through the window. In that fancy mansion—where every carpet was red and gold, with pictures on the walls and mahogany tables—was my sister, passed out in the corner. Some of the men were drinking and doing... other stuff, but one tried to wake her up. He slapped her, but she didn't budge. Then he turned to the rest and shrugged. They just started laughing. I realized she was dead."

"What did you do?"

"I learned their business hours. I knew who was working and when. It took me weeks, and I had to drop out of school. I stole a tank of gasoline and learned how to pick a lock. Every month, the owners of the club closed for one night to count their money before opening again. When that night came, I made sure to lock them in. I also made sure to drench the building with gasoline, and threw what remained inside the window with some burning candles." She leaned back. "Then I ran to a hill and stood there, watching the whole place burn. The flames rose to the sky while I listened to their screams."

Emry's breath hitched. She studied Jenna and felt a chill wash over her. "You did well."

"Yeah?" Jenna chuckled. "I think so too."

"But how did you get *here*, in the army?"

"I wasn't careful enough. Someone had seen me starting the fire, and I was sent to prison. That was where I stayed until someone visited me—Hamilton."

"Our chief commander?"

Jenna nodded. "Wanting to know my thought process, he sat with me in my cell and asked me to tell him exactly what I did, step by step. He was probably impressed, because he got me out, under one condition."

"He wanted you to become Intelligence," Emry summarized.

"Yep. Anyway, as I said before, I don't have a lot of patience, but acting on an impulse isn't going to get me anywhere. I do my best to keep it together so I can do my job. That's life."

Emry sighed, staring without really seeing anything. "That's life, but sometimes I don't like life much. Thank you for telling me what happened."

"It's not a secret. I would have done it again if I could. But you get it." Jenna cast her a look. "You get the warmth."

For the first time that day, Emry smiled.

* * *

Making her way back from her watch, she took a detour to ICT to speak to Mike. She figured she should apologize for her behavior the previous night. When she knocked on his door, it took him a few moments to respond.

"Yeah?"

"It's me," Emry said behind the still closed door. "Do you want to talk?"

She heard nothing for a moment, then he opened the door, and she held her breath.

"Damn," she mumbled, her eyes widening at the sight of him. "What happened to you?"

He had a bruised neck and a swollen eye. He sat in front of her, looking uncomfortable in his own room.

"Why don't you ask Primrose?" he asked. His voice sounded different, as if it was hard for him to speak.

"Damon did that to you?" she asked incredulously.

"Yes, *Damon* did that to me," Mike mimicked. "Do you believe me?"

"Yes, I just..." She fumbled for words. "Why?"

"Does it matter why? Look at me!"

She did—and he looked horrible. Still, Emry wanted to know.

"What happened between you two last night?" Her heart was beating fast. She knew they didn't like each other. She also had a vague idea why, but she didn't dare say it.

Mike looked away. "Ask him."

"To hell with that," she snapped. "I'm asking *you*."

He just shook his head. "Are you..." He suddenly looked so vulnerable, and Emry regretted her tone. "Are you interested in him?"

She tried to conceal her horror at being asked that. "Where is this coming from?"

He looked down, defeated. "I think he has feelings for you."

His words sprung hope inside her heart, like little buds right before the blossom. She prayed that Mike couldn't see her feelings on her face. Above everything, no one could think that there was something between her and Damon. It would put everything at risk.

She tried to look indifferent. "You're confused, Mike. He's my co-leader, and it's not just that. He's got tons of girls flirting with him every day." She couldn't help the bitterness in her voice when she said the last part. "He wouldn't be interested in me."

It was true, but it was also the reason she was so miserable. She looked at Mike—this sweet guy who'd been so thoughtful towards her. God, why couldn't she make herself love him?

In the end, he kept her locked out. "Just ask him."

She went back to the Slayers building and waited for Damon inside the hall to do just that. She tried to use the time to study, but it was difficult to focus when all she wanted was to remember what had happened while she was drunk.

It was late by the time he arrived. For some reason, his clothes were covered in weeds and soil—perhaps he'd been on duty outside. He stopped when he saw her sitting by the desk, and Emry turned in her seat expectantly. She went over and took his hands in hers, lifting them up for inspection. She wasn't surprised to see his knuckles bloodied, and when she looked into his eyes, he seemed completely unfazed. They shared one intense look before he pulled away and brushed past her.

"Did you hit Mike?"

"Yes."

She blocked him from slipping away to his room. "Why?"

He stepped in front of her, impatient. "You don't really want to know."

"You need to tell me what I said to you, Damon."

"It would change *everything*."

"Hasn't that already happened?" she almost yelled, desperate. For some reason, she just needed to know. She couldn't go on like this. Her heart beat faster with fear, but she kept her eyes steady on him.

He took a step forwards, his eyes fixed on hers. They were so close now. Was there any space left between them? Desire shot through her body, so strong it was almost unbearable.

"You said you wanted me," he whispered. "So much that it hurts."

Emry felt as if the world had stopped spinning for a moment, like reality had frozen. She broke away from him. "Oh my God." The weight of it all hit her. "Damon," she pleaded, her cheeks so hot they burned. "I'm sorry, I was drunk. I wasn't—"

"You're *sorry*?" he repeated. "Are you going to tell me that it was just some stupid bluff meant to mess with my head even more?"

She didn't have anything to say, so she just stared at him, desperately trying to think of an explanation. At last, she came with the same excuse. "I was *drunk*, Damon."

"So you're saying..." He took her hand and pulled her into his body, his arm curled around her. His hands were sliding up and down her back, and she closed her eyes, breathing hard. "That you're not painfully aware of me when I'm close?" His voice was soft in her ear. "That when we touch, you're not aching to be pressed against me?" Frustration crept into his voice. "That I'm totally on my own in this?"

She took a deep breath and opened her eyes. "Damon..." Her hand automatically raised to caress his cheek.

His head dropped to her neck, their bodies pressed tightly together now, and she could feel every muscle and bulge of Damon's physique. Dread and pleasure shot through her, igniting everything inside. Emry's hand sought out his muscled back to keep him close to her. She gasped, trying to arch her body even tighter to his.

He stepped away from her, callously tearing his body from hers. "You were very clear about how you wanted things to go between us."

She ran her hands through her hair, trying to think. "We're co-leaders. What was I supposed to do? Why do you think I—" She stopped. *Stupid.*

"What?"

She wished the ground would open up and swallow her whole, but she knew it wasn't going to happen. All she could do was look into his eyes and tell him the truth.

"When I started this friendship with Mike, I intended to develop feelings for him so I would forget about you," she admitted, not daring to look at him. She hated herself for saying it, but there was a certain relief to finally being honest. "Because you and I... nothing can happen between us."

Her heart never beat so fast, her hands were never that shaky, and her body was never that warm. This was the worst kind of danger.

A miserable smile crossed his face. "And how's that been working out for you?"

She crossed her arms, embarrassed. "Not great, but what was I supposed to do? Just sit there and wait for you to pick some girl from your waiting list? Because I'm not okay with that. I'm not okay with you being with someone else. I tried not to care, because I didn't want to get hurt."

"I know," he said quietly. "I live it every day. Every day that I have to see you with *him*."

She didn't miss the venomous tone that crept into his voice.

He stepped closer to her. "All those months, I had to stay away and watch you walk with Mike, watch you laugh with him. I had to be there to witness it, so close, but so far away from you."

Her fingers folded into fists as she looked down. *She* had done it to him—made him watch her trying to move on, knowing that it could never be him, that he could never have a chance with her. Emry couldn't help but think about how painful it must have been for him, because she knew how painful it was every time she'd been reminded that he could never be hers.

She heard him sigh, and then felt his arms engulf her, gently tightening, pulling her in. "Stop tormenting yourself," he whispered. "That's not what I want."

She released a shaky breath and let herself relax in his arms. "I'm sorry," she mumbled into his chest.

"It's okay." He caressed her long hair from top to bottom. "But you need to break it off with him."

She pulled back to look at him. "There's nothing to break off. He knows that we're just friends." She'd made sure of that. She'd never told him otherwise, never said that she was ready for more.

He shook his head. "The guy lives in some kind of delusion that you belong with him. You need to tell him that you don't," he said quietly. She could hear the barely restrained anger in his voice.

"I'm going to lose him, then," she concluded, heart beating fast. "He won't be my friend anymore. What happened between the two of you yesterday?"

It was never easy for her to make friends, and the sadness of losing one was harder than she'd anticipated. The loss washed over her like a wave of melancholy and loneliness. Sure, she'd wanted to develop feelings for Mike, but having him as a friend meant even more.

He crossed his arms. "He said some things that I really don't think he'd like you to know. Anyway, he deserves to know that he really doesn't have a chance with you."

Some part of her wanted to argue. Some part of her still wanted to fight that palatable thing that was so strong between them. Maybe it wasn't too late. Maybe she could still develop feelings for Mike. Maybe she could still escape this trap.

One look into Damon's eyes told her the answer. Grumbling, she walked out the door and slammed it behind her.

Chapter 29

Cherished

Emry

Emry found Mike fixing electrical wires in the infirmary, grimy from the dust. "There you are," she said.

He looked up from the cables that he'd been inspecting on the floor. "What's up?"

She gestured at the chairs. "We need to talk."

"I knew it was coming." With a mirthless laugh, Mike stood up and took a seat on a chair next to her.

She studied him for a moment. "I like you. I really do... but I think we should be on the same page." She folded her hands. "You're a friend, and that's all I'm comfortable with."

"You talked to Primrose, didn't you?"

"It doesn't have anything to do with him. This is about us."

"Us," he mused, resting his elbows on his thighs. "I wish there *was* an us."

"There is! I want to stay friends." Could he hear the pleading in her voice?

Mike looked angry. "You knew I had feelings for you all this time. Why wait until now to tell me the truth?"

"I wanted to try, to give it a chance. It doesn't come easy to me, Mike." Emry looked at the cables on the floor. "I thought I could rewire my feelings. But I appreciated yours—I still do. I just can't return them in the way that you'd like."

He snorted, then looked away. She felt a pang of guilt inside.

"Come on. Any girl will be lucky to have you. *I* would be lucky to have you. But you wouldn't really want me—you don't really know all the crap I 've to deal with. You deserve much better than this."

"Don't do that." His voice was shaking. "Don't tell me 'It's not you, it's me.'"

"But that's the truth." It was, even if he didn't want to hear it.

Mike stood up and returned to the wires. "I think you should go. It's late, and I still have work to do."

Emry bit her lip and nodded. His words cut deeply, but she understood.

"I guess I'll see you around." He gestured at the door.

With that, she opened the door and ventured out into the cold night. It hurt to be treated like that by him. She'd never wanted to hurt anybody, but at the same time, she also felt relief. Now, she didn't have to try anymore. A part of her was glad that she didn't have to pretend to be someone that she wasn't. She'd never felt like she could actually show him her true self—the ugly, angry, impatient sides of her.

For a long time, she'd wanted to be a different girl—a patient one, a serene one; a girl who smiles and flirts, who enjoys life, and is surrounded by friends.

At the end of the day, she couldn't give him something that wasn't real, and she couldn't be something that she wasn't.

Damon

Damon turned his head at the sound of the door opening.

"I talked to him," Emry said as she burst inside.

She was upset, and he could feel it. It didn't detract from the fact that she looked so beautiful, her long hair swaying back in the gust from the door, her green eyes vivid and gleaming. She stepped closer until she was mere inches from him. He stood, and Emry hesitantly reached up and touched his face with the tips of her fingers, barely a brush. She traced his jawline, his nose, and his eyes. His eyelids fluttered closed as he relished her touch.

Damon sighed in quiet contentedness and wrapped his arms around Emry, bringing her even closer. She gasped, and her hands tentatively slid to his chest. He could feel every heartbeat, every spark on his skin, every breath that he was taking. He had never been more focused, and there was nothing he had ever wanted more than this moment right now.

Her hand found its way to entwine in his hair, and he rested his forehead against hers. All of his nerves were on fire, calling him to close the distance between them, but he waited.

Emry

There was a gentleness in the way he was looking at her. She'd never seen him look at any other girl like that—and she'd seen them all. Deep down, she'd known. She'd known that whatever was between them was special. She'd known that the words that he'd said to her were true. She'd known that she was not just another distraction or charity case.

When he pulled her in, when she finally got to trace his face with her fingers, she'd felt it—the flammable vibration between them—waiting to be ignited. Her heart was pounding as he pulled her even closer, and she could feel herself tremble with excitement. His eyes were intently focused on hers, dark and frustrated. She realized that he was waiting for her—his way of asking instead of just taking. He wanted it to be her decision. Emry closed her eyes and tentatively pressed her lips against Damon's; the smallest touch.

Everything exploded.

He groaned as if he couldn't hold himself any longer. His hand on the small of her back pushed her so she was flush against him. She moaned at the contact, and his tongue slid into her mouth, touching, soothing. Standing on her tiptoes, she kissed him hard, lips eager for his, as he turned them so her back was pressed against the wall. His arms were tight around her, caging her with his hard body. Every part of her heated to an unimaginable level.

Damon shifted his hands around her thighs to lift her. Her legs twined around him, and his hands gripped her even tighter. He pulled away, just for a moment, and though his breathing was labored, she didn't miss the animalistic possession in his eyes. Her legs tightened around him as his lips went to her jaw, his tongue following their path, pressing and delving into her skin and down her neck.

"Damon," she gasped his name, unable to help her soft moans as his lips, softer than hers had ever been, made their way down her neck and to her chest.

She could feel just how much he wanted her from the press at her lower stomach. She arched her back against the wall, her voice breaking off as he caressed her breasts, his fingers just lightly brushing the sides. Her hands, still buried in his hair, forced him back to her lips. Every part of her body felt on fire, and her heart was thundering in her chest. Nothing had ever felt so good.

"Bedroom," Emry murmured softly against his lips, clutching him tighter. "*Now.*"

Wordlessly, Damon kept her body molded to his as he carried her to his room. With one hand he held her—*he was so strong*—and with the other he shut the door. She smiled on his lips as he pressed her against the closed door. She'd never had this experience with anyone before, never been made to feel this way. Every new sensation felt natural, felt right. She untangled one hand from his hair and it made its way under his shirt, lightly brushing his skin, up and up, until his shirt finally came off.

"Emry," he whispered, and she pressed herself against him again, rubbing her body against his. He groaned, tormented, as his head fell to her shoulder. He was breathing hoarsely as her fingers lightly caressed his naked back. His lips found hers again as she arched herself into him.

The last thing she thought he was going to do was pull away.

But he did. He was breathing hard, pressing his forehead against hers, and then, softly, groaning in protest, he let her slide down until her legs reached the floor. He still held her, making sure she was steady. She blinked in bewilderment. His eyes were closed, his face hard.

"Did I…" She was still out of breath, suddenly feeling insecure. "Did I do something wrong?"

"No, no." Damon cupped her cheeks, touching her so gently that she felt herself blush all over again. "No," he rasped.

"Then what—"

"What's going to happen afterwards?"

Emry stepped away from him. "After what?"

"After tonight," he began, never breaking their gaze. "What's going to happen?"

Realization trickled in. "Nothing. Nothing will happen after tonight."

He turned around, running his hands through his dark hair. Even now, she couldn't stop herself from watching his muscles tense and relax.

Damon faced her again. "I choose you, Emry. But I need you to choose me back."

"What do you mean?"

He came closer, taking her hands in his. "I don't want a one-night stand. I want a relationship. I want everything. I want *you*."

She took a deep breath, closing her eyes. "Damon—"

"I don't care about the risk," he murmured. "No one has to know."

She stood there with his hands in hers, but all she could feel was that dark void threatening to swallow her again. "I can't do that." Her voice was hollow, even to her own ears. "I provide for my family. If I get kicked out, they might find themselves on the streets."

He nodded and let go of her hands. She desperately wanted to punch something, to throw something. She crossed her arms and looked aside.

"What if I provided for your family?" he suddenly asked, and her eyes snapped to him. "I have money, more than I'll ever need."

"No." Her voice was strict and uncompromising. "I can't, Damon. This is *my* job. I have to be the one who does this for them. I've worked my ass off all these years to make it on my own. I don't take charity."

Could he understand? She had to make it on her own. She had to.

"Tigers are accused of everything," she continued. "We betrayed the human kind, so it's our fault that we get murdered. You think the police care when blood crimes are committed? They support it," she whispered. The bitterness of her words burned in her chest. "You probably know that people from different places are now in Rows, buying lands at suspicious prices, trying to make something out of nothing, and getting rich. Do you know how often Tigers are being accused of seeking their help? For getting it? It's so humiliating, every single time." She fought back the tears of anger in her eyes. "It's a shame when we dare to seek help. I won't let myself be that. I won't have anybody pointing at me, laughing at me. I've worked too hard to get to where I am today to turn into *that*. I'll do it on my own."

Damon pressed his palms around her forearms. "I understand."

She let out a breath. "Now what?" She had to stop herself from standing on her tiptoes to kiss him again. They both looked at his empty bed. "I can't believe you did that." Emry couldn't help but scowl.

"Yeah, me neither," he grumbled, and Emry couldn't help thinking that maybe he was just as disappointed as her. "Hey," he said, his features softening, a small smile playing on his lips. "I love you, Emry."

His words knocked the air out of her. She knew he didn't expect her to say it back. His smile was full of sincerity and reverence, and she felt so cherished that she almost started crying. Instead, she pushed herself into his arms, her head buried in the space between his shoulder and neck.

He tightened his arms around her. "It's going to be okay."

She really wanted to believe that.

Chapter 30

Tired

Damon

"This is madness," Damon whispered to Jenna.

They were sitting in one of the dusty, gray corridors of the Intelligence building, as they always did. The sun was coming up.

Jenna suppressed a yawn. "I hate working late," she said, not listening to him at all. "But everything has been so hectic lately."

"Of course," he told her, alarmed. "If there's a real change in the demons' leadership, as you think…"

"That's *my* opinion," she said grumpily. "Ten other Intelligence members disagree. They think the demons are moving their temples across the island. I think they're right, but I find it hard to believe that's all."

Damon shook his head. "I'll take your word over ten others."

They remained in contemplative silence until he spoke again. "It means Headley is going to talk to us tomorrow. Damn it."

"Probably. You need to remember that you don't know anything about what I just told you."

"We've been doing this shit for eight years, Jen. I think I'll remember."

"I don't know. You're all over the place lately." She looked at him pointedly. "Where's Tiger?"

He stayed quiet for a minute before he answered. "In her bedroom, probably trying to catch some sleep before the kids arrive tomorrow."

"I should do that too," she grumbled. "Those airheads are going to wake me up in four hours."

"Poor you," he mocked. "Some nights I don't get any sleep at all, like tonight."

"But I'm not you. I need to sleep if they want me to use my brain for them."

"I love her, Jen."

He just said what they both already knew. She didn't look surprised in the least.

"Will you really risk everything you've ever worked for to be with her?"

He gave her a small nod. "If she'll accept it. We can be discreet. It's not like we'll tell people."

She shook her head, but she was smiling. "It's a bad idea, Damon. But it's also beautiful."

* * *

"I'm sending your teams to Ob next week," Headley said the next day. His blue eyes were exhausted as usual. "You'll be fighting on the east line. The purpose is to push back the demons that are threatening Reefstone, and gather information for Intelligence. As you've already been told, Intelligence suspects something fundamental is being changed within the demons' hierarchy, and we need to understand it better in order to prepare for what's to come."

"What kind of information do we need to gather?" Damon asked, alert and ready despite watching the sunrise.

Next to him, Emry was dead silent. They were sitting with Al and Liz, two leaders of another team that would be sent with them to the east.

Headley sighed. "There are letters that level-three demons wrote to each other from Ostrov Demonov to the shore and back. We want them."

"Letters written in Shadoni?" Al asked. There were few Slayers who could read the demons' language.

Headley nodded. "Might be encrypted, but we can count on our Intelligence to figure it out."

Emry took a deep breath. "Where will we find the letters?"

"Next to the shore. There's a big abandoned building they use as a headquarters. They think we don't know, but we already have the landmarks. The letters are supposed to be there, guarded by demons level two, maybe three."

Emry huffed, and Al started laughing. "You're kidding, right?"

"It's a suicide mission," Liz scoffed. "Our soldiers aren't even a year in."

Headley looked at them exasperatedly. "I understand that it's tough, but it is what it is. Back in my day, we had a similar case. I was fourteen years old, going to my first battle after only three months. Your soldiers have had more training than I did."

Damon took a deep breath. "Please give us the details. We need to prepare." There was nothing left to do but be practical.

"Who will be leading the mission?" Al asked.

"Me," Headley said, to their surprise. "I'm coming with you."

By the time the leaders were dismissed, they had more information and more causes for concern.

"We have a week." Emry's voice was hard as she and Damon strode down the corridor in sync. "We're going to make the most of it; our soldiers should be ready for what's waiting for them at the east line."

He couldn't help but agree. The troops weren't ready for a battle, but he and Emry would give them their best chances. They had to.

"Emry," he rasped. "We're going to make it."

When they gathered their soldiers and told them, they were just as shocked to hear that they were going to fight. Ahron was trembling, but overall, they took the news bravely.

Each day, their co-leaders got up early to train them, counting the passing minutes, calculating times. A week wasn't a long time. Classes were cast aside in favor of training sessions.

Damon feared his relationship with Emry had regressed to feeling no different from those long months they spent fighting. They were nothing more than two stubborn leaders, polite to each other, harsh and protective towards their soldiers.

They didn't talk about the words they'd exchanged. They didn't talk about the way they'd touched each other. They didn't talk about any of that. During those days, it was easier to forget. There wasn't enough time to think or ponder. There were too many drills and too many instructions. There were also Shadoni boxes full of demons to practice fighting. Emry wouldn't even look at him if she didn't have to. They were both focused, determined to do their best to prepare their team for the mission ahead of them.

But at night, when he didn't have anyone to bark commands at, it was harder. He wanted to talk to her, wanted to know what she was thinking. His nightmares were disturbing him again, and he had a hard time fighting them. The longing to touch her was painful.

But he was still fighting.

Emry

Emry tossed and turned in bed. She had been sleeping so little at night and working so hard during the day that every night felt like it was going to be the night. *Tonight,* she would think. *I'll finally fall asleep.*

But sleep never came.

She was drained. Every bone in her body ached. Her mind screamed at her to fall asleep, but she just couldn't. Admitting defeat, she gave up and went to see Damon.

When Emry softly knocked on his door, she wasn't even mad at herself. Yet, it didn't help the butterflies swirling inside her stomach. Would he reject her again? Would he understand? She knew that when he'd confessed to her, she'd made the right decision. She didn't regret it, no matter how hard the pinch inside of her heart felt.

She heard his deep voice, hoarse from sleep. "Yes?"

Emry silently slipped inside, feeling unsure as she stood next to his bed. He'd been sleeping on his side, but now he was fighting to keep his eyes open for her.

"I'm so tired," she said.

Damon raised his blanket. Relief spread through her as she crawled inside, resting her back against his front. He put the blanket over the two of them. His body heat radiated to her, keeping her warm and cozy, and she instantly found herself dozing off. From inside their little cocoon, he wrapped his arm around her and tightened her to himself with a soft grunt.

That night, she slept thoroughly. When she woke up in the morning, a little earlier than she had to, she blinked at the pale rays of sunlight coming through the window. She turned and propped on her elbow, looking down at Damon's sleeping figure. He was never this quiet and serene. Emry couldn't help herself. He gently let her fingers hover above the bridge of his nose, his forehead, his cheekbones. She couldn't help herself. She loved to touch his beautiful face. It was almost as if it was sculpted.

She almost jumped when he stirred. "You're awake?" she whispered, her fingers stopping at his cheek.

"Yes," he answered, eyes still closed. "But I'll pretend to be asleep so you won't stop."

Emry was glad he couldn't see the blush that spread over her cheeks. She pulled her fingers away, and he blinked the sleep away. She was staring down at him, her long hair pulled to one side.

"I could wake up like this every day," he mused.

Damon's eyes were staring into hers and he looked so honest that her emotions got the best of her and she acted on impulse. She bent down to kiss him, lips gently brushing his. He groaned, his hands moving to her waist, pulling her into him. Her hand snaked around his neck as she pushed herself down to his body, wishing to feel more of him.

He carefully flipped them so her back was pressed against the mattress, and he was on top. Her hand was slowly roaming down from his shoulders until it reached his lower back. She gently pushed, pressing it snugly against her. He let out a frustrated sound and moved his lips to her neck as she gasped. His kisses burned down her neck, his tongue following their path to taste her. Her eyes snapped closed and all she could do was whisper his name.

He stopped, hovering over her, his breaths mixing with her own. "Emry," he mumbled, pulling away. He flopped onto his back, his hand on his forehead.

She looked at him in confusion, but then she understood. "Right. I'm sorry."

Was she? She wanted him back, right where he was. She could feel the burning need inside, the unfulfilled tension. Emry just *wanted* him, goddamn it. It was hard not to grab his thin shirt and pull him back to her.

"You should be," he rasped, eyes still closed.

He was breathing hard, but an annoying thought crept into her mind. Was it easy for him to reject her? Was he even a little frustrated?

She sighed as she felt her body cool down. "Thank you for letting me stay here last night."

"Of course." He let out a breath and opened his eyes. His stare was strained now. "We need to be at our best for our soldiers."

She wanted to scream at him to snap out of it, to not fall back to the same patterns as before. She wanted to tell him that it wasn't fair for him to be angry that she couldn't be with him, that it was already tough—but she couldn't. She'd made her decision, and he was entitled to his feelings on the matter.

She swallowed, feeling the disappointment swell inside of her. "Yes. You're right."

Chapter 31

The Slayers

Ahron

Ahron glanced up briefly from his place on the hard ground. It was already getting dark, but their leaders weren't finished with them yet.

Ever since they'd learned about the impending mission, Tiger and Damon had done whatever it took to bring the best out of them. Now, the leaders gave them just ten minutes of break time, but he couldn't bring himself to stand.

His and Riggs's late hours of studying and reading had come to an end. They just couldn't keep themselves awake. Neither soldier stayed up to talk or read anymore. The minute their leaders dismissed them, they would collapse on their sleeping bags from exhaustion. Even Anoki and Kalen, who they found occasionally huddling and whispering in the dark, were immediately asleep.

As if he needed more reasons to not get up, a nauseating scene was unfolding right in front of him. Riggs, covered in sand and dirt, was flirting with Ella. He could see how flushed she was beneath the gray dust smeared on her face. She laughed loudly, her curves swinging in the older boy's direction, and he grinned, looking absolutely pleased with himself.

Ahron had to look away.

After dinner that evening, Riggs yanked at his sleeve as they were stepping out of the dining room and into the chilly, dark night. He pulled him to the secluded back of the dining room, but Ahron was not in the mood.

He crossed his arms. "Can I help you?"

"Oh." Riggs grinned at him, and Ahron hated how his heart gave a flutter in response. "Aren't we feisty today?"

He immediately felt uncomfortable. "What do you want?" He was too tired to be played with.

"Why aren't you looking at me?" Riggs cocked his head.

Ahron *knew* that he knew this movement was enticing.

"Maybe you're not much to look at."

Riggs snorted. "I think I'm very much to look at. See," he declared as he rolled his sleeve and flexed his biceps.

Ahron blushed at the sight. "Did you drag me here to show me your muscles?"

Riggs rolled his eyes. "No, I dragged you here to understand why you've been so grumpy ever since practice today."

"I'm not grumpy, and even if I were, it's none of your business," he mumbled in reply, avoiding his gaze again.

"So it has nothing to do with me and Ella?" Riggs's eyes glinted dangerously as he took a step forwards.

"N-no," Ahron mumbled, taking a step back. He cleared his throat. "I like Ella."

For some reason, Riggs's pretty face was frowning. "Yeah, I like her too."

"Good." Ahron turned his back so he could leave the perplexing conversion and Riggs's toxic presence behind. He managed a few steps before he could hear his voice.

"But she's not my type."

He froze and turned to see that Riggs's expression had grown serious, frustrated. He didn't dare come closer. Instead, he forced himself to ask, "So what *is* your type?"

"Oh, I don't know." Riggs sauntered towards him. "Apparently, there's something really hot about thin, pale guys with noodle arms who get excited when they teach me how to read."

Ahron took a few deep breaths, his heart going crazy against his ribs. This was the night before their mission. If there was a time for honesty, it was now.

"If you're messing with me, I swear I'll take my stick and whack your head off."

Not the most romantic declaration, but Riggs was grinning as he took a step closer to him. "You know, you're not the only one with a powerful stick."

Ahron's breathing became short and ragged, but the cursed, beautiful creature in front of him just laughed and walked past him, whistling.

Kalen

Slowly, with time, it got easier and easier to resist the urge to check the bathrooms outside the hall. For many years, Kalen had felt like a prisoner. When he didn't check, his thoughts would swirl in his mind, never letting go. Now he figured that somehow, even without checking, the tension would eventually go away. Maybe he didn't have to check in order for the anxiety to go away. Maybe he could just suffer through it until it went away. It wasn't easy, but a little bit of his control—control he didn't have for a long time—was slowly returning to him.

Kalen had a long way to go, but this was a start.

Damon and Tiger gave them twenty minutes of free time before lights out that night, and he wanted to talk to Anoki. He knew she may have wanted that precious time to herself, but he had to talk to someone who knew what he'd been going through, and she was the only one.

As the months had passed, he'd found himself seeking her—maybe a bit too much. But it wasn't just her help he sought. In her own way, she was captivating. Being born and raised in Ob, he'd never met anyone like her before. At night, when he couldn't trust himself to not check, Kalen would wake her up. She'd pull him outside, no complaints, and they would sit on the grass. There, where it was just them in the night, she would tell him stories from her childhood.

If their leaders found out, they would both be punished, but he found those moments his favorite of the day.

He used to think that living in West She'e was a nightmare. He never thought that there might actually be good things about living in the controversial land. Usually, people from West She'e were troubled because of the bizarre traditions of their homeland. However, Anoki told him West She'e wasn't just about praying to trees and child brides.

She'd told him about exquisite, dark-red fruits whose sweet taste lasted for hours. She'd told him about the yellow flowers that dusted the fields. Anoki told him about her grandfather, a loving man, a man who had begged her parents not to marry her off.

"Hey." Kalen tapped her shoulder in the hall, and she turned around. He could see the tiredness in her eyes. He wanted to smooth the wrinkle on her forehead with his thumb, but he held back. "Do you want to sit with me a little? It's okay if you're tired and would rather not."

"Are you okay?" she asked.

"Yeah, just want to talk."

They walked outside to the little nook that was hidden behind the big building. No one ever came there, and it felt like it belonged to just the two of them. If someone else ever found this little place, he would be devastated.

Anoki leaned against the stone wall, sighing. "The last few days have been terrible."

He laughed, leaning next to her. "Maybe Tiger and Damon are planning to kill us before the mission takes place, so they won't have to go."

"Are you afraid?"

"A little bit," he said quietly. "But this is what we came for, right?" Kalen laughed, but it was strained. "I just didn't think we would get there so soon."

Tomorrow. Just thinking about it made his heart skip a beat.

She turned so she could look at him, and he suddenly understood how close they were sitting, and that he'd been staring at her the whole time.

She must have noticed it too, because she moved back a little. "I feel the same, but I try to be strong."

"You always try to be strong."

She laughed. "Sometimes, trying isn't good enough. Sometimes, I wish I was more like Tiger."

"She is tough, but sometimes..." He shrugged apologetically. "I feel like there's a price to that, you know? She isn't like anyone else. It's like her whole atmosphere is dark. I wouldn't want that. For you," he added quietly.

Anoki sighed. "There's always a price to everything. I appreciate how you can be so bright and cheery, even after everything you've been through."

"A lot of it is thanks to you," he admitted in a whisper. "You make me better."

He could see the shadow of a flush on her dark cheeks, and it made him feel proud.

"You never told me what it was like in the asylum that you escaped from," she suddenly whispered, and he groaned. Why did she have to bring it up now? "Come on." She gave him a little shove. "You never tell me anything."

Kalen laughed at her playfulness, and decided that maybe he could actually talk about it, for her. "It wasn't a good experience."

"We're not here because of good experiences."

"I guess we're not. My parents discovered that I was checking on things when I was fourteen, and they sent me to this asylum in Ob. There, things got worse. There wasn't much food, and most of the time they made us eat... things." He really hoped he didn't have to elaborate. Just having those visions in his mind made his stomach swirl. "They made special food for us that I... I just can't..."

"It's okay." She brushed her hand against his arm. "You don't have to."

Kalen sighed in relief. "The doctors were harsh, and they used a whip if you didn't oblige. One day, I took a brutal beating. I just couldn't help but check on the hall lights. I was bleeding afterwards and had to be transferred to a proper hospital."

"Didn't the doctors in the hospital figure something was wrong in the asylum if they'd beaten you? No one beats anybody in She'e. All of our treatments are based on herbs and, well, talking—giving advice."

He shook his head. "It's not like that in Ob. There are strict rules, and if you don't obey, you pay. Even in a mental facility."

Anoki put her hand on his shoulder again, and he was grateful for her touch. Her hands were so soft despite their hectic training outside.

"When did you escape?" she asked.

He stiffened beneath her touch. "When they started to use a special new method: electricity."

He could hear her gasp. "What does that mean?"

He turned to look at her. "They were electrically shocking us."

She didn't break his gaze, though he could see her chest rise and fall.

Encouraged by the look in her dark eyes, he continued, "It wasn't bad for everyone. The patients were always confused after treatment and couldn't remember things, but I think it can be a helpful method if they study it. Some of the patients actually got better, even though they had to bear the marks."

"Marks?"

He sighed and pulled his blond hair away from his forehead, and she gasped. On his temple was a red circle, faded, but still there.

She adjusted her position, eyes not leaving his mark. "Does it hurt?"

He shook his head.

Slowly, she raised her fingers, and he closed his eyes as Anoki touched the spot. "I'm sorry, Kalen."

He shook his head. "I survived to find you," he whispered. "It's more than I could ever dream of." She blushed and looked away, but her hand fell to his. "That's why I ran, anyway. I couldn't stand it, and I'm pretty sure some of the other patients were thinking about escaping as well. It's better to die here—as a Slayer, with a knife in my hand—than die from bad treatment alone in an asylum."

Her lips were trembling. "I thought so too. I thought it was better to die on a battlefield than have my body up for sale."

He squeezed her hand. "I think you did the right thing."

"Yeah?" Tears welled in her eyes. "Sometimes I miss my mom. A lot. You probably think it's stupid since she agreed to sell me, but…" Anoki fumbled with her shirt. "I think she just doesn't know any other way to live."

Kalencould see how hard she was trying not to give up and cry.

"Can I hold you?" he asked quietly.

She nodded, and he scooped her into his arms. Her head rested on his shoulder. "I rent a place in East She'e, and you know, I'm protected there because of the feud with the west, but… sometimes I miss my home so much."

For the first time, *he* was the one comforting *her*. Not so useless anymore. He rubbed her back and rested his head on hers.

"I know. I know."

Chapter 32

Come First

Damon

The drive across Ob was tough. They'd easily crossed Seka's plateau, but Ob was made up of mountains and valleys. They probably wouldn't have slept well on the bus anyway, but driving up and down the mountains didn't help. By the next afternoon, their soldiers were tired and irritable.

Ahron gulped from the back. "I'm going to be sick."

"Just hang on," Anoki encouraged. "I think we're close."

"Just swallow it," Lucy said, before Riggs kicked her in the shin. "Ouch! *What?*"

Damon shook his head and smiled. He glanced at Headley, who was in the seat adjacent to the driver in brown fatigues. His blue eyes were fixed on the road, hard and focused.

He snuck a peek at Emry, who was sitting across from him. Her green eyes were staring at the road that was vanishing and reappearing as the vehicle rounded the mountain's curves. He wanted to know what she was thinking, how she was feeling. He always did. He yearned for a moment alone with her, but he knew there was a reason he had stopped her a few nights ago.

It felt like they were taking a step forwards, and then two steps back. She was right there, but she was distant. Her eyes were cold and hard, and her hand was resting on the handle of her knife. Emry was tense, and Damon could feel it. He could also feel her excitement. She was silent, but as always, she was eager and ready for a fight.

He took a breath and leaned on his backrest. Not long ago, he had promised her that he would do whatever he could to make sure she and the kids were safe. He intended to keep that promise. Still, he wasn't without concern. They'd trained their soldiers the best they could, but it was their first mission as a team. The kids were going to face level-two demons, maybe even three.

Damon arched his spine to look back at Jenna and two more Intelligence soldiers. At the last minute, Headley had insisted on bringing them along.

"None of us speak Shadoni, and we'd need translators. If there's information in the letters that would compel us to stay there, it's better we find out before choosing to come back to the base," he'd said.

It was a smart decision. Some of the Intelligence soldiers were studying Shadoni, making them quite precious to the army. Shadoni was a hard language to learn, and few could actually figure it out. Of course Jenna was one of them, but it didn't prevent her from grumbling all the way to the bus. Damon had laughed at that. Even the smartest, most talented representatives could act like sulking children.

They were less than an hour away from the east line. He could already see the clear, blue waters of the sea sparkling from a distance, but the air was cold. He was certain it would begin to snow soon.

Behind him, Damon heard Kalen mumble, "Even though I grew up in Ob, I've never been to this area before."

"Of course not." Lucy brushed her shoes. Her short, red hair had grown a little and now reached below her chin. "Since it's close to the shore and Ostrov Demonov, it's dangerous and full of demons."

"People live here, though," Ahron said. "That's why there are so many missions in Ob—to protect them."

"It's risky. I would never live here," Ella declared.

Anoki turned to look at her. "Really? The residents know it's risky to live here, but they take it upon themselves to populate the area, otherwise demons would conquer the land."

Ella didn't even blink. "So let those fools do it."

Riggs laughed and placed his arm above her head on the seat. "She's right. If people volunteer to live in danger, it's their problem."

"I don't think so," Ahron suddenly said, his dark eyes examining Riggs. "I think it's brave. You're being very ungrateful."

"There's a thin line between courage and stupidity." Ella rolled her eyes.

"Well, someone has to do it," said Ahron, lifting his chin. "And I see it as a sacrifice that needs to be respected."

Ella cocked her head, her brown eyes observing him. "Since when do you speak so much?"

"I don't know," Riggs' smile was mischievous. "I find it adorable when he stands his ground."

Damon suppressed a laugh as Ahron turned as red as a tomato. He'd figured there was something between the arrogant, bad boy and the pale, shy "Sweepy." He didn't know exactly what was going on, but there were a few nights where he had caught them sitting together in the hall. He knew Emry had caught them too, of course. He was surprised that she hadn't mentioned it to him.

Again, the urge to talk to her was overwhelming. Ever since their morning together, they hadn't properly spoken to each other. He didn't know what to make of it. He could still feel her pressed to him, just like in his dreams—the good ones.

He groaned and went back to listening to the ramble of his soldiers.

Emry

It was dark when they finally arrived. They parked next to an old inn a few miles away from the shore. When they stepped out, Emry suddenly felt her heart thud in her chest.

This wasn't a regular mission. She was used to going on missions alone or with teammates, but never as a leader. She looked back at her team. They were chatting, but deep down, she knew they were scared, trying not to make a big deal out of what already was a big deal. She wasn't scared for herself or even

Damon, but the kids were a different story, and her approach to this mission would have to be different. Emry averted her eyes and met Damon's. He'd been watching the others too, and she had no doubt that the same thoughts were passing through his mind.

They settled down in the small building and then hurried for a meeting with Headley and the others who had joined them. Their soldiers, along the rest of the Slayers, were given some time to rest.

"What do the letters look like?" asked Liz, a female leader.

"We're not sure what they look like," Headley said. "That's one of the challenges. They could be hidden inside anything."

"What do we think we will find in the letters?" Emry asked.

"Information," one of the Intelligence soldiers said. He had dark skin and a somber expression. "We want to know the meaning of some contradicting information we've gathered and deciphered."

"Something is going on with the leadership," Jenna added. "And it seems like we've been deliberately fed the wrong information. We're being set up, and we need to know why."

"Coming here isn't something the demons expect us to do," Headley said. "Most of our squads are scattered around Egma, Ob, Nova, even Rows. They know we don't have enough people, and even though they're now aware that we know about the headquarters on the shore, they don't think we'd spread ourselves thinner."

Emry nodded. "So our teams are being compromised."

All eyes turned to look at her.

"Tiger—" Headley started.

"I apologize. That was out of line."

What was she thinking? Why did she say that? Of course they were being compromised. That was their job. That was what soldiers were getting paid for. After all, they were just street rats with no futures and no families to mourn them. They were what was left when humankind decided to move on.

Why did it hurt so much now? Emry had never cared before. She'd been rather thankful for the opportunity, as she should have been. She was a proud soldier, a fighter with fire in her eyes, but she'd never had soldiers before. She felt stupid for wanting something else for them—better chances, brighter futures.

Headley nodded once and let it go. She could feel Damon and Jenna's eyes on her, and she hated it.

After they finished, Headley sent them to sleep. The inn was fully booked by the army, but they were ordered to sleep in pairs in case of an unexpected attack. Emry and Damon silently moved across the corridors, checking on their soldiers' rooms, making sure everyone was in bed.

"Everyone's asleep," Emry whispered as she stepped inside the room she would be sharing with him.

"Must be exhausted from the drive," he responded.

She hummed in agreement and walked to the bed on the far side of the room, not looking at him. Emry took off her uniform top, leaving the black, long-sleeved shirt underneath.

"About what happened at the meeting," Damon said, then paused as she faced him. He looked like he was contemplating his words.

"Forget about it. It was stupid of me to say and it won't happen again."

"I don't want it for them either, you know."

Her breath hitched. "We've spent months training them, eating with them, laughing with them, commanding them, caring for them, making sure they made it home. All of that for what? For them to be used as pawns? The worst thing is that it's always like this. I shouldn't even care at all."

"They deserve more than that, I know," he said gently. "But they're talented, Emry, and they're smart. You know that. We've trained them way better than I was trained in my elite group, and probably better than you were, too. I actually believe we have a good chance tomorrow."

"You do?" She peeked at him hopefully, nearly uncrossing her arms.

"I do," he answered, strong and decisive.

A wave of relief washed through her. It was almost ridiculous how his confidence reassured her. "Tomorrow, Damon…" She saw him tense, but didn't care. "If one of our soldiers is in trouble, it must be our first priority. We are responsible for them—we're their leaders. The kids come first."

Emry saw his lips press into a thin line. He nodded once. "The kids come first."

Their words denoted finality, like something had just changed in the air between them, like thunder in the dark sky outside. It was a vow.

Chapter 33

Anything Funny

Damon

Maybe he should have left it at that. Maybe he should have let the promise between them be the last thing they said to each other before going to sleep. But he couldn't bear the thought of leaving it like this, especially not before a mission; especially not before he had to focus; especially not before they would risk their lives.

When Emry turned to her bed again to go through her things, he crossed his arms, not making a move. "You're mad at me."

She didn't answer him. Typical Emry. She crossed her arms and looked at him in silence.

"Let me get this straight." Damon took a step towards her. "I tell you that I love you, that I would risk everything for you. Yet you're *angry* with me?"

"I'm not angry with you," she said defiantly, but her voice was suspiciously quiet.

"Then what is it?"

"Are you even attracted to me at all?" she asked dryly, as if she was bored with the conversation. He caught the way she was clutching herself, the way she tried to look like she had no interest in his response.

She was utterly perplexing. He took a step even closer, frowning. "*What?*"

She shifted, uncomfortable, and he could see her blush spread across her cheeks. "I practically threw myself at you, *twice*, and you rejected me."

Oh.

He chuckled as he took her hand and gently drew her into his arms. Damon missed this. He missed holding her. "You are such an idiot," he mumbled into her hair.

"That fact is well-established, as you and Jenna keep on reminding me all the time." Her words were muffled against his chest.

He rubbed his cheek against her hair, sighing. "I *am* attracted to you—too much. I want you too much. All the time." He felt her shudder in his arms as he caressed her hair. "But if you want a piece of me, you're going to have to take it all."

He would not compromise on that. There was something between them that felt different than anything he had ever experienced. For the first time in his life, he wanted to do things right. He wouldn't have her for a night, knowing that nothing romantic could ever happen between them. He was alright with risking it all, but she had to be as well.

"Damon..." She pulled away so her face wasn't buried in his shirt anymore. "I'm not poetic like you, but it's not..." He saw that she was genuinely struggling with her words. "It's not like that for me. I care about you so much that it's frightening me, and I'm... I'm scared." Her cheeks were burning. "And I also have to gather some common sense, keep my job and my military career, because I'm nothing without it. I have *nothing*."

"You're not nothing. You've never been nothing. But I understand. For the record," he said, pressing his forehead against hers, "resisting you was the hardest thing I've ever done."

He heard the hitch in her breath, *felt* it. Just her body pressed to his right now was messing with his mind. Did she really think he was immune to her influence?

She sighed as she wrapped her arms around him. "I don't know what the right thing to do is. I've never felt like this before, never thought I would, because how I feel about you... it feels like you're holding a knife to my throat."

"Huh." He grimaced and pulled away a bit. "You were right; you're definitely not a poet. That sounds horrible. You're horrible."

"Shut up." She laughed and smacked him.

Damon felt a light surge of happiness. It cost her something to say it, but she still did. He knew how hard it was for her to talk about her feelings.

An unexpected knock at the door made them both jump. They pulled away, and he cleared his throat. "Come in."

Jenna entered, closing the door behind her. "I interrupted something, didn't I?" She glanced at the two of them, her brown eyebrows raised. "I don't give a damn. I'm supposed to sleep in the same room with the other two Intelligence soldiers. You know what that means? That the three of us would end up dead in case of attack. What are we supposed to do? *Bore* demons to death? This is stupid. The army is stupid. I'm not doing it. I'm sleeping here tonight."

"Seems we're not big fans of the army tonight," Emry declared. "So you came to the right place. You can sleep next to me, if you want, but I move around a lot, so I might disturb you."

Jenna shook her head. "I'll set up right here. I need a mattress, a blanket, and a pillow. Be back soon."

The co-leaders found themselves momentarily alone again. "Will you be okay?" Emry asked.

He didn't notice that he had stiffened again. "I hope so," he said quietly. "I usually don't scream. I hope I don't break my streak tonight."

She bit her lip as she stepped towards him. That insignificant movement drove him crazy. "What if I sleep next to you? Jenna would have a bed for herself."

He hesitated. "It's better for us to get good sleep, especially tonight, but..."

She frowned. "I promise not to try anything funny."

He laughed; the pout on her face was adorable. "*I* might try something funny." He drew her close again and nuzzled her neck. Emry smelled so good; the same smell that always managed to calm down his nerves—or turn him on. He felt her arms tighten around him, and his body went rigid. He sighed into her neck, then pressed his forehead against hers again. "Hardest thing," he murmured.

At that moment, Jenna burst into the room, and they quickly separated. "If you two are done," she barked. "I could use some help." She was carrying a mattress that dwarfed her tiny figure.

"About that…" Emry twirled a lock of her hair, clearly enjoying the fact that Jenna had carried the heavy mattress for nothing. "You won't need that."

Emry

The next afternoon, they didn't have to do anything but prepare for the fight to come.

Even though sleeping in Damon's arms had helped her rest, it also left her unexpectedly broken-hearted. Emry remembered her feelings from yesterday, the fact that in the end, they were all tools to be used and tossed aside. If one of the soldiers died, no one would care. The army would find another miserable soul to replace them.

It wasn't the first time she'd had those thoughts, but this time, she just couldn't shake them off. Damon was sitting with their soldiers in one of the rooms, trying to rest and pass the time. She excused herself, saying she had to go to the bathroom, even though all she really wanted was to be alone.

The scent of ocean wind was piercing, but Emry didn't mind. She sat a few steps away from the inn, facing the beautiful, crystal-blue water. The entire area was surrounded by gray and blue shadows of mountains that wrapped the sea like a canopy. The sun illuminated the world between the peaks, making the sight even more breathtaking, almost magical.

Here, she could relax and have a few moments to herself. It was as if something inside of her broke, and now it wasn't just about the kids—it was about everything. How many times did she have to say no to things that she wanted? How many times did she stop herself from making the wrong decision? She had tried so hard, worked so hard, and for what? She finally wanted someone who wanted her back, but she couldn't do anything about it.

What was the point of her life if she could never afford anything to make herself happy?

What was the point of having those thoughts? When she was older and wiser, would she feel sorry for the girl she was now? Would she regret all those years of agony, of pain, of constant worry? Maybe. But she didn't think she knew how to be something else.

The constant mourning weighed heavily upon her. Mourning Tigers, mourning friends, mourning the broken relationship with her family, the options that had been taken from her. Who knew what she could have been if things were different? If she wasn't a Tiger? If she wasn't poor and desperate? It probably didn't matter, because this was her life. This was who she was—nothing shiny, and very easily forgettable.

Her thoughts were interrupted by someone coming up behind her.

"There you are." Jenna slumped next to her. "It's so *cold* here. Why the hell can't you be miserable inside?"

Emry blinked at her, a little shocked. "What the hell? Go away."

"I will," she shot back. "Damon wanted me to find you because there are some things to arrange for your team before you guys go. He's already in the room, whetting knives. But I guess I'll just tell him you'd rather sit alone outside."

She stood to leave, but Emry stopped her. "Wait."

Jenna sat down again and looked at her. "Talk."

"Do you ever feel like life is pointless? Especially for people like us?"

Jenna sighed, staring at the mountains ahead. "It's always deep with you, isn't it? I used to feel that way. You shouldn't do this before a mission, you know."

Emry ignored her. "You don't feel that way anymore? When we die, even if a few people mourn us, we'll be gone. Some people are memorable, changing the world. We are just the garbage of humanity." Somehow, it felt both painful and good to say those words.

"You want to know what I think? Trying to be something big in this world is stupid. The dead don't care if they've changed the world or not. Even if they do, even if tons of people remember them after they die, they'll eventually be forgotten. The world keeps rolling, the world keeps moving on. Nothing lasts forever, not even a memory."

Emry took a deep breath. "Exactly. Life is pointless and stupid."

"It *is* pointless." Jenna nodded, smiling slightly. "And it's stupid."

"Then why keep doing it?" Emry burst with frustration.

"People are prone to ignore those points that you just brought up. They usually see their situations and chances as better than they actually are. We have to be biased in order to be healthy. But even if we weren't, at the end of the day, life can be fun, it can be nice, and it can be lovely, even for people like us. It's an experience. It's made for us. Who said life had to have a great meaning to count? So only powerful people can be happy? Honestly, most of the happiest people I've ever met were the stupidest ones. You shouldn't seek happiness in the greatest things that happen to other people, but in the smallest things that happen to you. They belong to *you*, to *your* experience. Right here, right now, this is *your* moment."

The words echoed in Emry's head as she tried to memorize them. "Thanks, Jenna. I hope that it will be enough."

"I hope so too." Jenna glanced at her. Her brown eyes were more focused than Emry had ever seen them. "I like you, Tiger. If the day comes, even if I'd be more concerned about Damon, I'd hate to watch your sun go down."

"I'm not going to let it," Emry said, feeling a surge of surety inside of her, of power. "I'm a predator. We don't die easily."

Jenna gave her a nod, then rose to her feet and offered her a hand. "Let's go."

Emry took it. Somehow, she'd managed to form a connection with Damon's witty best friend, and she held it close to her heart.

Chapter 34

Power and Peace

Emry

When evening finally came, Emry and Damon gathered their soldiers in one of the inn's meeting rooms. The kids stood in a circle, waiting for the leaders to speak. Emry and Damon exchanged looks.

"Emry and I wanted you to know, regardless of what happens tonight, we're very proud of you," Damon said.

They all looked so tense, the way they should have looked.

Emry nodded. "You've been giving us your best. We have seen it during classes and training. We just wanted to say that we're very grateful to have you under our wing. Remember that above everything else, you're soldiers. You're going on a mission, and it's your job to make sure that it goes as planned. Tonight, we fight for humankind, for *us*. This is for our family, for our friends, for our teammates."

Damon nodded. "We're not exactly sure how the demons are going to hide their letters, so we can't rule anything out. We're going to destroy this place if we have to."

"It's just like how we trained with the Shadoni boxes. Each of you has your own style. Tonight's not the time to learn new techniques."

"If a team member needs help and you can help them without risking yourselves, do it," Damon said firmly. "If you can't, don't. It's that simple."

They all nodded in unison.

Damon passed his stare between them. "Weakness does not cancel strength."

Each Slayer repeated the words after him.

* * *

Night fell, and darkness surrounded the inn as everyone waited to depart to the shore. Headley stood in the hall, barking orders. The other four leaders finalized plants with their units, and the Intelligence soldiers stood there watching everything from the side.

Emry and Damon passed between their soldiers, making sure everyone had their weapons. Emry was surprised and proud to see that her soldiers had that sparkle in their eyes, coupled with fear. She realized how lucky she had been to be chosen to lead the elite group. Those kids were special. They didn't only see the danger; they saw the opportunity to prove themselves, and most importantly, the opportunity to strike the enemy.

Emry knew that they were ready. She also knew she and Damon would give everything in them to ensure each kid made it. She was not going to lose anybody tonight.

"Are the Intelligence soldiers coming with us?" a Slayer asked.

"We're not here to kill shit—that's *your* job. *We* get to sit in a drafty building, taking bets on which one of you idiots will come back injured. Yippee…" Jenna snorted and threw her hands up in fake celebration. "Really, Headley? This lot is the best you've got?"

Emry could see Damon laughing from the corner of the room, his head peeking above his half-packed satchel.

"Couldn't we have brought someone else instead of her?" Al muttered to Headley.

"We could have, but she's the best we've got," the commander declared.

"If I were you, I would keep my mouth shut," Emry added, raising her eyebrows at Al. "You have no idea what she is capable of."

The soldier grumbled something to himself and walked to the bus.

Emry went to stand beside the already-running vehicle, making sure to pat each one of her soldiers on the back as they climbed inside. She was grateful she'd had that conversation with Jenna earlier, because her usual pre-mission mood was finally returning. Emry felt the same prickle of excitement, the vibration on her skin, the preparedness, the beating of her heart. She was a Slayer, even when she had trouble accepting her fate.

Ever since she'd made her first kill at age thirteen, a year after she was drafted, she'd known that not only was she good at it, but that she also enjoyed it. She remembered the dark blood on her tiny hands so many years ago. She raised her arms to look at them, but instead of being mortified, all she could feel was wonder.

Power.

She'd realized that the only way she could actually express that, could be who she really was—was on the battlefield.

She enjoyed the neat slashes she made on her enemies, how fast she could move and dodge a knife thrown at her. Battles made her feel alive. It helped her lash out, radiating that constant rage inside of her.

After a battle, the hot, bubbling anger inside of her would subside, giving room for exhilaration and joy. She always thought that being on the battlefield would be the greatest feeling she'd ever have, because what more could a broken girl demand from a broken world?

But being with Damon was different. Sometimes, she felt the same frustration, anger, and violence, but sometimes just being next to him helped. She enjoyed talking to him, even enjoyed his jokes, banter, sly lines, and innuendos. He was caring, solid, and strong next to her.

The memory of the two of them under the blanket, talking late into the night flashed through her mind. Secret words, secret vows. There was something between them. It was different from slaying. With Damon, there was gentleness in that joy, something quiet and hidden.

Peace.

She blinked as she realized that Damon was still inside the inn. Most of the Slayers had already gotten on the bus, and she was supposed to follow, but she hurried back.

Headley hung back with a few Slayers, but it was clear they were about to leave. Their heads raised in surprise as she walked inside.

"Tiger, we need to—" said one of the soldiers, but she didn't listen. Instead, she grabbed Damon's hand and pulled him into one of the rooms. She didn't care how it looked.

He frowned in confusion as he looked at her. "Is something wrong? Did anything—"

"No, no." She shook her head. Astonishingly, she wasn't nervous at all about what she was about to do. She wanted to savor the moment—the adrenaline in her veins, the biting coldness, the feel of his hand in hers, and the way that he was looking at her.

Emry took a breath and wrapped her arms around him, hugging him. She closed her eyes. She could feel his arms silently wrap around her, no questions asked. Emry had to tell him. Missions were missions, and if something happened to her tonight, she would want him to know. She still couldn't help but wish for just a few more moments alone with him.

She took another breath as she pulled away to look into his eyes. "Damon... I love you."

His golden eyes widened, his mouth slightly agape, but they didn't have the chance to talk as they heard footsteps approaching to burst through the door.

One of the Slayers was gesturing at them. "We need to leave."

Emry nodded and walked after him. Damon's hand fell into hers, squeezing it. She didn't care that she didn't get to hear his response. She got her moment. Now he knew, and she could fully dedicate herself to the mission ahead of them.

Chapter 35

A Monster

Emry

Emry had never fought alongside Headley before. Now, leading the mission, he looked more deadly than she had ever seen him. His gray hair was covered in the darkness, but his eyes glinted with danger and severity. His looming broadsword was resting on his shoulders as his eyes scanned the area.

They were standing just outside a dark building on the shore. The howling wind scattered their hair, freezing every inch of skin left exposed. The water sparkled even in the dark, but Emry was sure the waves were icy. She held her knives tightly, with Damon next to her and their soldiers behind them, waiting for command.

"We must move in silence," Headley said. "But do not expect silence to greet you. On my count." He turned his back to them and whispered, "Three... two... one!" He then twisted the doorknob. It didn't open, so he kicked it down, disappearing into the still darkness.

Headley switched the light on, and they could see the demons waiting, standing still.

There were *so many* of them. She noticed Chernaya, with their humanoid outlines. Their bodies were coal-black, eyes submerged inside their face, lips shut the same way. Belaya stood in the middle, looking like humans. Only their faint white halos gave them away. With a sinking feeling, she realized some of them had no halo at all. Those demons were level three—the only ones who could talk.

"*You*," hissed one of the creatures. His white hair made him look old. He took a step forwards, his big, bloodshot eyes focused on Headley. "You are not supposed to be here."

"How dare you," hissed another. This one was younger, his hair and eyes black. "*How dare you!*"

"Give us what we want," Headley demanded, "and no one gets hurt."

The white-haired demon cackled. "We can't do that."

Headley shrugged. "In that case…" He gave Damon a single nod.

In the blink of an eye, Damon was beside him, his knife dripping with blood. The demon's head was titled, mouth agape, blood spurting from the slit in his throat. He looked shocked. The creature probably hadn't realized what was happening before it was over. Damon tossed his body to the ground, his hands stained with blood, and all hell broke loose.

Emry was forced to defend herself, swinging out both blades, but she felt Damon return to her side. She couldn't spare a moment to look at him—slashing, dodging—her sight became a mess of moving bodies, blood, and colors.

Headley was incredible, and Emry suspected that Damon might have a reason for his slight admiration of the man. He launched forwards, putting himself before his soldiers, just as she and Damon had.

There were too many of them, and out of the corner of her eye, she could see that Riggs was struggling with one. The demon managed to make him drop his knife, but Lucy stabbed it in the back. It collapsed slowly, and Riggs reclaimed his weapon.

She caught Kalen being smashed to the ground, another demon standing above him with a club, but then a little arrow pierced the demon's skin. It was stunned for a moment, and Kalen used the opportunity to clumsily get on his feet and stab the demon in the side of its neck—just as he had been taught. He nodded at Ella, who had already resumed fighting.

She couldn't help how full her heart felt. Full of pride and contentment because her soldiers had been studying. They'd gained something from the constant training, and now they were working as a team, just like they had been taught.

The demons managed to scratch and hit Emry, but she was still standing, and she realized two things. One, they were genuinely surprised by the ambush, giving their team an advantage. Two, Damon was actually taking most of the heat. He was next to her, but he was attacking instead of defending. He was trying to make the demons go after him, and it worked. Was he trying to protect her? That wasn't their deal.

She could see the other humans busting through walls and pounding on shelves, trying to figure out where the demons had hidden the letters. Al used one of the few remaining demons as a battering ram to get inside a hidden room.

Soon, Damon and she were drawn away, and Emry could finally access the inner rooms. She knocked on the feeble walls, searched through books, all the while fighting. The soldiers were everywhere, destroying the place more and more every moment. She even bumped into Anoki and a surprisingly steady Ahron.

"Damn it!" She couldn't find anything, and it seemed like no one else had had much success either. She went deeper into the hall, trying to find anything that remotely resembled a letter. They couldn't have come here for nothing— they just couldn't. But it seemed like she was at the end of the empty room. Now what?

"Damn it!" she hissed, punching the wall in frustration. Chunks of drywall fell to reveal a narrow staircase. A sly grin stretched her lips as her eyes hungrily scanned the stairs.

She glanced at the rest of the room, full of bodies and weapons clashing together, and decided to go up alone. She couldn't afford to make the other demons aware of the fact that she'd found the staircase. Emry ran up and reached a narrow room full of earthenware, books, and pictures. What was with this place? Why were there so many books?

She took a step forwards, ready to raid the place, but then she shivered. She moved on instinct, not aware why, but the slash on her shoulder a moment later was a painful clue. She winced, clutching it as she turned around to face another demon, a level three. He was smiling at her, his knife dripping with her blood.

"Looking for something?" the demon asked. He had blue eyes and black hair. Emry knew that if he were human, some girls would have considered him attractive.

The painful throbbing didn't scare her. Sometimes, she was astonished by how much pain drove her. The hot bleeding in her shoulder made her *stronger*.

Her mouth stretched to a smile again, and she could see the demon frown. "Yes. And you are going to give it to me."

As always, she was too fast. The demon didn't see it coming, but he moved just in time, causing her knife to slash his cheek instead of his throat. Emry dodged his attempt to constrict her and slashed his thigh. He winced in pain, and she took the opportunity to go for his abdomen, but he managed to catch her wrist and bring her down. She rolled as he tried to stab her face, and the floor was smeared with blood.

The demon hissed in pain from his as she got up on her legs, panting. Her marred shoulder was getting harder to ignore, but Emry knew it was going to be okay. The desire to end the demon's life was strong, but she had to keep him alive.

She reached into her pocket for her combat rope and dangled them in front of him. He clenched his teeth, breathing heavily, and she lunged at him again. Her knife slashed his arm, making him drop his, and he screamed as she quickly tied his arms together.

"Not so arrogant now, are we?" she chided. Her body was hurting. She felt the blood rushing in her veins, but she had to gain strength from the pain. She had to gain power from weakness. "No one is going to hear your screams." She turned him around to look into his eyes. "No one is going to be here for you when I cut you open. You're all alone."

These were the exact words she'd heard in her dark daydreams, thinking of what was going to happen to her if things went wrong—the way she was going to die.

Right now, the demon wasn't being held in a daydream. This was real, this was life, and she could see the terror in his eyes; the terror she needed and was going to use.

"Why would I speak?" he hissed at her. "You will kill me, anyway."

"Not necessarily," she said, slowly wiping the blood from her knife. "What's another living demon? There are already so many of you, desperate to kill us all."

She wasn't sure yet if she was lying or not. After all, it wasn't his life that she needed.

"If I'm going to die, I'm going to die with dignity."

"Dignity," she snorted. "The dignity that you have when you kill people, and then blame it upon humanity? The dignity you had when you started The Great War? You're playing the victim because slaughtering all of humankind didn't pan out." She shrugged, taking his hand in hers. "Alright, then. Lovely fingers you've got." She sliced off the tip of his index finger and the demon screamed as blood gushed from the wound.

"Somebody..." He blinked back tears, but they still streamed down his face. "Somebody will hear me."

"You're kidding, right?" Emry asked dryly. "They're busy fighting downstairs. Everybody's screaming. It's just you and me here. Now, where are the letters?" The demon started sobbing, and Emry grabbed him by the shirt. "I'm not repeating my words, but I don't mind repeating my actions. *Speak.*"

"I won't," the demon cried. "I won't."

"I'm going to find them, with you or without you." She threw his head against the wall, though not too roughly. She still wanted him conscious. She gripped her knife tighter and let it graze his ear, leaving a trail of blood. "Do you think you will speak properly after losing your hearing? Because I actually don't know. Want to test it?"

The demon was looking into her eyes again. "I'm a demon," he spat. "But you are a monster."

Her eyes snapped to him. "I know."

"And you don't care?" the demon asked.

"You'd love that, wouldn't you? To play with human weakness," she snarled. "But no, I don't. Only monsters can take down monsters. You always have to lose something. Sometimes, it's yourself." She let her knife graze his other ear, and he gasped with pain.

"Stop!"

"Tell me what I want to know."

"No!"

"This is your last chance." Her voice was steady, and she could feel his body tense. Emry pressed the knife to the side of his neck and looked into his eyes.

His voice broke. "There's a red book hidden in a socket inside the floor, next to the last bookcase. There." He tried to gesture with his head.

"Stay here, or I'll make sure to cut down your legs before I kill you."

She hurried to the last bookcase, used her knife to open up the gap in the floor, and pulled out the red book. She flipped through the pages, revealing sheets of paper, tucked and folded. She clutched the book and went back, but the demon was gone.

"Damn it," she swore under her breath, running down the stairs. When Emry arrived at the bottom, she saw that he was in a corner talking to another level three, and they both turned to look at her.

They ran at her simultaneously, and her heart pounded, emphasizing the danger. She was scared, but she had been scared too many times before to make it something special.

Suddenly, a knife flew into the abdomen of the demon she'd tortured, making him fall to his knees. She frantically glanced back and saw that Headley was the one who threw it.

Emry quickly slashed the other demon across the chest, and he returned by stabbing behind her knee. The pain was terrible, but she couldn't fall to the ground or he'd have her. She managed to cut through his eye, making him scream and clutch his face, trying to salvage his eye. She wanted to finish him so badly, but she had to get to Headley before he got away.

"Headley!" she shouted. He turned towards her. "I got it. Let's go!"

His eyes widened for a second, and then he gestured around, making sure the other soldiers heard and repeated the message. Seeing the other Slayers make their way to the exit brought her relief. It was finally going to be over.

But then she heard a whistle.

She spun around to see the same demon that she'd fought against. He was standing next to the stairs, clutching a switch. He smirked at her, and then he pulled the lever.

The room filled with a jarring noise as fire erupted from the middle. They were going to burn everybody, not just the humans. Screams rang out as the situation worsened. Emry was going to try to make her way to the exit, but four demons were heading her way, intent on dragging her down with them.

Then she saw Riggs staring at her, unsure of what to do.

"Riggs!" she yelled, tossing him the book. He caught it, his eyes wide with shock, but there was no time for it. "Go!" she shouted. And the demons closed in on her. Even if she could take the four of them down, she knew she wouldn't make it in time before the fire ravaged everything.

Horrified, Riggs clutched the book and ran. Emry exhaled as she saw him flee. She was glad that the letters were in the right hands, and silently made peace with the fact that she would not survive long enough to learn what information they held.

Emry turned to face the creatures surrounding her. They were simple demons, level one, but she was injured. She breathed hard as they were about to attack. Then, a few tiny arrows hit three of them, and they grimaced. Emry glanced back and saw Ella sobbing with her dart gun held out. She was running towards the exit, right before the fire cracked in the exact place she'd been standing. Emry mastered all the energy that she could find within herself and cut down the demons. When the last one fell, she turned to see the tall flames closing in. It was too late.

Chapter 36

Flames

Emry

Emry collapsed to the ground. The fire surrounded her, crackling ominously. She coughed, trying hard to breathe.

The pain in her shoulder, in her leg, *everywhere*, was taking over. She was bleeding, but she could still walk, if there were anywhere left to escape to. She'd never make it through the high, burning flames in this condition.

She sat there as she saw the morning come up through a window. They'd won, the letters were in their hands. The sun was rising, lighting the world with frail rays of light. The sky began to look brighter.

Emry would die here—on a mission, as a soldier, as a leader—after taking the enemy down with her. She would die here, and the sun would rise again. Everyone would try again, but she wouldn't have that chance anymore.

The heat was already too much. The flames grew to suck up every bit of oxygen she needed. Pillars of smoke rose up to the ceiling, making everything hard to see, tainting what little air was left. She looked down and saw the floor smeared with her blood.

Her family would forgive her for dying. All her life, she'd done everything she could to provide for them. They would have to learn to survive without her.

Emry was grateful for meeting her soldiers, for being their leader. She was grateful they were safe. She had given them everything she could, and all that was left for her now was to hope it was enough.

And meeting Damon... Every glance they'd shared, every touch, every nighttime conversation, even every fight... He was there for her—as her co-leader, as her partner. He saw her as more than just a Tiger. He saw her as herself. She loved him, and she was content that he knew. It was enough. It had to be.

She looked at the flames surrounding her. How many times had she fantasized about it being all over?

Yet, at this very moment, she knew.

She didn't want to die.

Damon

Everyone was running with Damon across the shore, trying to escape the chaos. Damon could hear crying and screaming all around him as they ran through the cold, the cruel wind slapping their faces. He watched Riggs tearfully hand Headley a red book. He had no idea how his soldier had managed to get his hands on it, but he didn't care.

"My team!" he screamed. "To me, now!"

His soldiers hurried to him, and he mentally counted them, taking in their conditions. They were okay—trembling—but okay. His mind went on, not wasting any time. "Where's your leader?" he growled.

"She..." Riggs sobbed, his muscles shaking. "She threw me the... the book. It contains the letters. I don't know how she found them, but the flames were too strong..." His voice broke. "She told me to go. I'm... I'm so sorry," he choked.

Headley's voice was heard from a distance. "Everyone, away from the building! I repeat, away from the building!"

"Tiger was fighting against some demons, and I shot them, but then she got trapped in the flames," Ella whispered. She was in a state of shock. "She's not going to make it."

Anoki burst into tears, but Damon had no intention of comforting anyone. His soldiers were safe on the shore, surrounded by the other unit, and he had to go.

He ran back to the building, his shoes filling with sand. He could feel the smoldering heat as he neared the collapsing building. Everyone was shouting at him, but he couldn't even process what they were saying. He didn't care.

Headley's powerful voice woke him from his trance. "Primrose!" The flames, even from a distance, cast light on his face. "Step away! That's an order!"

Damon growled at him. "Emry's in there!"

Headley's eyes filled with an emotion that Damon couldn't comprehend. "You can't go back. You'll just die with her," he said, taking a deep breath. "She's gone. Step away from the building, and go back to your soldiers. Now!"

He didn't cast Headley another glance. Damon ran inside the building, taking his shirt off in the process.

"If she gets caught in her own flames, I would be heartbroken to see you burned down as well."

"Damon!" he heard his commander yell behind him. It was the first time Headley had ever called him by his first name, but he couldn't focus on that. He couldn't focus on anything but Emry.

The heat inside was beyond anything he'd ever experienced. His vision was blurry, everything was red and orange. He galloped forwards blindly, the flames scorching his skin, marking him, but Damon clenched his teeth as he moved forwards. He went deeper inside the hall until he found her.

Emry was curled up on the floor, the surrounding flames miraculously leaving her alone. The smoke did no such thing, and he lunged forwards, praying that she was still breathing.

"Emry!" He coughed as he shook her. She coughed weakly, eyes closed, and he was horrified to see the floor painted with blood. Something nagged him at the back of his mind, something that usually made him freeze, maybe one of the flashbacks he sometimes had. But he couldn't afford it, not now. He cursed as he lifted her in his arms and put his shirt over her face. "Damn it! *Breathe!*" he cursed again, as he tried to run to the exit.

Why did it have to be her? Why did she have to be the one who was left behind?

Damon knew that even if he died tonight, he wouldn't regret his decision to come back for her. *"Breathe!"* he commanded, clutching her body tighter to his chest as the inferno ate at his skin. The pain was unbearable, and it was getting harder and harder to breathe. He had to get them out of there before he fainted.

He took the last steps towards the exit when he noticed Headley shouting and gesturing with his arms. Apparently, some soldiers had found a few buckets, and were filling them with sea water to pour on the flames. The ice cold water pushed back the grasping red tendrils with a sizzling sound, soothing the fire and giving Damon a chance to escape.

When he finally stumbled to the freezing-cold shore, he almost fell down onto the ground, Emry still in his arms.

"Take her." He coughed, shoving her into Headley's arms. He was going to lose consciousness, but all he could think about was that she had to make it.

Headley took her and his eyes widened with anger, and maybe something else. "Primrose, your arms... Your *legs*—"

"She's lost blood and needs a hospital."

That was the last thing Damon managed to say before everything went black.

Chapter 37

Favorite

Damon

A little kid was sitting against the corner of the wall, sobbing. His body was shaking, blood all over his clothes and face. The wall, the floor, everything was drenched in gore.

Screams of a woman were heard in the background, but Damon couldn't see her. Then his vision retreated.

Now he could see a shadowed figure standing, only its back visible. It held a knife smothered in blood as it marched towards the kid. Damon wanted to help, but he couldn't do anything as he watched the figure stab the child, again and again. His screams were all Damon could hear until his vision turned white.

Damon woke up, his breathing labored. It was a nightmare, just like the ones he'd had before. He didn't scream this time, not aloud anyway. His nightmares followed the same pattern, always that kid, always that shadowy figure, but sometimes they were even worse than that one.

His body was painfully burning. His shirt was gone, and his chest was bandaged.

Someone had put him in a bed with white sheets and a white pillow in a nearly empty room. It took him a few moments to piece together everything that had happened. A few minutes later, Headley opened the door and stepped into the room.

"Primrose, how do you feel?" He took a chair, put it next to Damon's bed, and sat down—all business. "Your soldiers are outside. They insisted on waiting for at least one of their leaders to wake up before I sent them back. I had no reason to deny that request."

Damon groaned in pain, but tried to conceal it. "Are they okay? Where's Emry?" He sat up.

Headley's hard eyes met his. "They are all okay. We lost people during this mission, none of them yours. We're in a hospital in Ob, not that far from the shore. Your co-leader is in another room, but hasn't woken up yet."

"Will she be okay?"

"That's what the doctors said."

"Do they know she's a Tiger?"

"Of course not."

Damon closed his eyes and took a few deep breaths, then he attempted to get up. He had to see his soldiers. He had to see *her*.

"Stay," Headley's low, authoritative voice commanded.

Damon sighed and looked at him in silence. He knew what was coming.

"To be clear," Headley's voice was rough, "she is my favorite of the two of you."

"That's good to know, sir."

"Shut up."

"Yes, sir."

Headley spoke with his jaw clenched. "On the battlefield, we lose soldiers. Sometimes, the best that we have." He took a deep breath. "This little stunt that you pulled could have cost me not only one of my best, but both of them. You've disobeyed a command, Primrose. It's a very serious offense. You could go to jail for that."

Damon didn't have the energy to be angry. "If you expect me to regret saving my co-leader's life, then you got it wrong. I will take any punishment they decide to give me in military court."

Headley let out an exasperated sigh. "I won't take it to court. See this as a warning."

Shock erupted inside of him. Damon knew that this was serious and that he wasn't supposed to, but he couldn't help the smile that spread on his face. "So thoughtful of you, *sir*. Thank—"

"Don't thank me," Headley answered sharply. "You *punk*."

Damon rolled his eyes. *Like cat and mouse.* "Are you sorry that I saved Emry's life?"

"No. That's why you're being given a pass here. But rest assured that other commanders wouldn't look at situations like this the same way in the future."

"I know." Damon nodded. Everything hurt, but he didn't care. In his own harsh way, his commander was looking out for him. "Where are my soldiers?"

"They're eating outside. I'm going to send them back to the base. They're exhausted, and we don't need them here anymore."

Damon frowned. "What about Al and Liz's team?"

"I'm going to send their soldiers back, too. Al and Liz are going to stay here, at least until the Intelligence unit finishes translating the letters."

"They're still here? Is Jenna here?" Damon asked, rising up a bit. His mood was better in a matter of seconds.

Headley shook his head. "No, they're not. They're still in Ob, but they're hidden. I hope that I won't have to send you guys into hiding as well. If we have any reason to think that the demons figured out that we're in this hospital, I would have to. We can't risk civilians. We're not *demons*."

"How is the translation going so far?"

"Not good. The letters are encrypted, and it takes time to translate and break the encryption. We have the best three from their department, and yet…"

"Jenna is on it," Damon said. "So don't worry. She's the best, just like *me*." He offered a grin, and Headley scowled.

"Don't let me regret the one compliment I ever gave you."

Damon regretfully laughed. "Never, sir."

Headley cast him a look. "You know, the doctors said you should have died when we brought you here. But instead, you're healing up rather quickly."

"Really?" Damon rubbed his nape. "Well, lucky me."

Headley huffed. "I'm going to call your soldiers in so you can talk to them."

"What about—"

Headley faced him again. "The doctors are optimistic. They said that *Tiger* should wake up any moment now."

Damon felt the tension leaving his chest and shoulders. That was the one thing he really needed to hear. "Thank you."

"Tell me something, Primrose." Headley's voice was so harsh that Damon felt himself tense again. "Why did you go back? If it wasn't for a miracle, both of you would be dead right now. Why risk your life just for the tiny chance to save hers?"

Damon felt trapped. "She's my co-leader, sir."

Headley accepted the lame excuse, but Damon had the distinct feeling that he didn't believe him at all. Nevertheless, he stepped out, and soon, Damon's soldiers came in to greet him. He couldn't believe the relief that he felt when he saw them. He made them sit before him and asked how they were doing.

"Great," answered Lucy. Her dark eyes glinted. She had a wide scar across her cheek, but she didn't seem to mind. She had done well on the mission, but he hadn't missed the older soldiers coming to her aid.

"What Lucy means is that we're recovering," Anoki said. "And we're glad that it's behind us."

Damon observed how close she and Kalen were sitting. "I am so proud," Damon said quietly, sincerely, passing his stare between them. "All of you did well, and now you deserve to rest. Headley is taking you back."

"How are *you* feeling, Damon?" Ahron asked tentatively.

Damon widely grinned at him. "Don't think I missed how many demons *you* slayed, *Sweepy.* Remember our little conversation from a while ago? Sometimes the shy ones are the wildest." He winked, and Ahron blushed. "As for your question, I'm in a bit of pain, but it's more annoying than anything. Tell me, did you go visit Emry?"

They looked at each other. "We did," said Kalen. "She hasn't woken up. We hope she'll get better."

He took a deep breath, and his soldiers looked at him with concern, as if they had any idea how much he cared. Maybe they didn't. "You all get some rest until new orders come," he eventually said. "Ella, you shot the demons that attacked Emry before you had to run. While Emry and I are gone, you're in charge. Don't let me down."

Ella blushed with pleasure, and her friends smacked her on the back and patted her shoulders.

They left, and Damon let his head fall to the pillow again, just for a second. He wanted to rest, but his body was urging him to move, to go find Emry.

"Just so you know, you're a real bitch, but congrats and all," he heard Riggs say from the hall. He could almost *see* the smugness on his face.

"Takes one to know one," he heard Ella taunt.

"Finally, we agree on something," Kalen grumbled, and a wide grin spread across Damon's face.

His soldiers were going to be okay.

Emry

Emry didn't want to wake up. The light behind her closed eyelids was too bright. Her bones were aching and her shoulder pain was excruciating. But as always, life demanded an answer.

She opened her eyes and blinked a few times to get used to the searing light. She tried to remember what happened. Her head was pounding, and she felt like a mess.

She had been surrounded by fire. Burning, choking, that was all she could remember. Was she dead? Being dead felt too painful. It couldn't be that.

Emry winced as she absentmindedly leaned against her shoulder. Then she realized Damon was right there, sitting next to her bed, watching her.

"Emry," he breathed.

"Damon." Her voice came out hoarse. "The kids—"

"Are alright." He nodded reassuringly. "Each one of them is safe and sound. They were sent back to the base."

She took a deep breath. "Where are we?" She tried to sit up, and succeeded in leaning against the headboard.

"We're in a hospital not far from the shore. Both of us were injured pretty badly back there. Headley's still around, waiting for Jenna and the others to translate and solve the encryption from the letters. I don't know where the Intelligence crew is staying, but Headley's in touch with them. He wants the leaders around here until they're finished."

"Oh." It took her a few moments to organize her thoughts, and his eyes distracted her. They were grim. His eyes were *never* grim.

"I was supposed to die," she recalled.

He grimaced. "No, you weren't."

"How did I make it out of there?"

"Does it matter?"

"Yes." She tried not to get mad. Not with him, not right now. "Tell me what the hell happened."

He was exasperated. "I came back for you, got you out. Because somehow, you found yourself stuck between walls of fire. What were you thinking when you ran off alone?"

Her mouth felt dry. "You came back and got me out?" she asked, trying to wrap her mind around it. "But... how?"

There was no way he could've crossed the fire and come back with her alive. Yet here he was, right in front of her. She examined him and noticed the bandages around his body for the first time. He had red burns and scars over his tan skin. It was so cold, but he was shirtless, wearing only gauze.

"I just did." He looked away.

She bit her lower lip, fixated on the marks on his body. Her heart clenched painfully inside her chest. "You shouldn't have done that," she said quietly. "You should have left me there."

"To die?" He crossed his arms. "Would you like that?"

She frowned. "Are you angry with me?"

"Yes."

She felt bitter. "Well, I didn't ask for you to come back. The deal was that the kids are—"

"The kids are the first priority, as we agreed. But I also made a promise to you to keep *you* safe. And even if I didn't..." He looked down and ran his hand through his hair before he returned his gaze to her. "I would die before I let anything happen to you."

The words choked her. All Emry could do was stare at Damon as he reached out to cup her cheek.

"You scared the hell out of me," he whispered. "For a moment there, I thought I had lost everything."

She didn't want him to see her cry. No matter how many times he made it clear that she was important to him, the feeling of astonishment never ceased. She wiped her eyes quickly and felt him take her hand and bring it to his lips.

"Damon," she said quietly, "I'm not sorry. I had to do what I did. I'm a soldier, after all. This is what we do."

He nodded. She knew that he knew she was right. The reason why relationships between co-leaders were forbidden could not have been any clearer to her.

"It was stupid of you to go up the stairs alone," he repeated, despite it all.

"I didn't have a choice. If I'd tried to bring anyone's attention to me, the demons would have noticed the staircase was exposed and taken away the red book."

He huffed, clearly displeased. She gingerly laced their fingers together, and he turned his head so his amber eyes met hers. He was so beautiful, even now, even injured. Like a fallen angel, it hurt to even look at him, especially when he was looking at her like that.

"Do you need anything?" he finally asked. "Something to eat, drink? I should go get the doctors."

She shook her head, squeezing his hand. "I'm fine."

Of course, he never listened. He gave her hand one last kiss before he got up. He grinned before he opened the door. "By the way, congratulations. You're officially Headley's favorite."

Chapter 38

Faith

Emry

Come night, Emry couldn't sleep. Instead, she watched as the violent wind struck the trees outside her window. Branches and leaves were pushed and pulled, but continued to hold stubbornly to their hosts, even after hours had passed.

A single knock sounded at her door. In the dark, Emry could see Damon quietly enter, securing the door behind him. His eyes shone in the dim surroundings, brightening the room.

He plopped down next to her bed like he was on guard duty. She longed to reach for him, to caress his cheek. He looked disturbed just sitting there, not saying anything.

"You okay?" she eventually asked.

"Yes," he whispered, looking away. "Just wanted to see you."

"If Headley comes—"

"It's the middle of the night. Besides, if he does come, we're just co-leaders discussing our first mission. We're shaken and need to debrief. That's all he would interpret it as."

Maybe he was right, but he still looked like something was bothering him. "Tell me what's going on with you."

"When the night falls..." He hesitated. "My heart falls with it—most of the time."

She swallowed, but let him continue.

"It's the terror of the night..." He looked out her window. "It can make me feel like my gut is tied, like something is wrong. I've felt it for years, but when night falls and I know it's time to go to bed, all I can feel is dread. It's because I know how I'm going to feel when the nightmares come."

She took his hand and gave it a little squeeze.

He closed his eyes. "I never feel this way when I'm with you, when you're near me."

Emry's heartbeat quickened. "I've had so many sleepless nights that the darkness and I are practically friends," she joked. "I'll tell her not to hurt you."

A little smile lightened his face, and the longing to touch him increased. "Are you making a joke?"

She rolled her eyes. "Don't get too excited. It's dark and gloomy."

Damon laughed. "You need to spend a little more time with Jenna and me."

"She's not as easy-going as you."

"No," he admitted. "She's very sarcastic, but it counts. You could only pray to survive her sharp tongue."

"Yeah, right," Emry scoffed.

"What?"

"Like I would pray," she snorted. She would never pray for anything ever again.

"But you performed that ceremony in the woods when—"

"I told you, it was for the sake of tradition. I wouldn't bother if I wasn't worried about the culture disappearing."

"So you really don't believe in a higher power?" he asked quietly, cocking his head.

"No, Damon." She raised an eyebrow at him. "I'm surprised that you do."

She didn't believe in God. Miracles never happened to her, and she was quite certain that no divine providence was watching over her.

"You really believed in that?" she asked, annoyed that he still hadn't answered. She stood up to look into his eyes. "How?"

"I do." There was something secretive about the look on Damon's face, as if he were a child. "I want to believe there's a purpose to our existence."

"There isn't." She looked down so she wouldn't have to face his disappointment.

"But what if there is?" he countered. She raised her eyes to look at him. He seemed determined. "What if God exists?"

"Then what's taking him so long to find me?" Emry asked bitterly. "Why have I called out to him again and again, never getting an answer? All this time, I've been alone, trying to survive this prejudiced, cruel world he created."

They stayed quiet, lost in each other's thoughts.

"I want to hold you," he whispered. "But I know that it's risky."

She nodded, feeling numb and broken. Why did she have to bring up this conversation? Why had she been certain that Damon didn't believe in God? He was no ordinary soldier. He'd proven that from the first moment they met, when he won the finals and crashed her to pieces.

"Emry," he said, pulling her back to the moment. "What are you thinking about?"

She shook her head, trying to clear her mind. "Does your grandma believe in God too?"

He laughed. "No."

She felt instant relief.

"The look on your face." He snickered. "Are you *that* glad to hear that my grandma is a nonbeliever?" He rolled his eyes. "I wish *I* had that effect on you."

Emry blushed, averting her eyes. The effect he had on her went above and beyond anyone else's influence. "I'm just glad some of the people in your life *do* make sense."

"I'm not making any?" His eyes glinted in amusement. Trust Damon to find joy in being a minority. Beyond that amusement, she could see the patience and affection that appeared in his eyes only for her. How could he look at her like that, like she was something beautiful, even when she argued and scorned his right to believe in something she didn't?

She sighed. "You're right," she gently said. "The fact that you believe in God doesn't mean you don't make any sense. I'm sorry. It's just that for me, faith just makes everything even more painful."

"Emry—"

The door burst opened, and they instantly leaned away from each other. Headley marched inside, surrounded by Slayers in green uniforms. "You're not supposed to be here," he growled at Damon.

"We were—"

"I don't care," he spat. "Get up, both of you. Demons were spotted a mile from here. They're tracking us. I called more Slayers for backup, but right now I need you hidden. You're putting the hospital at risk."

"Where do you need us to go?" Emry threw the blanket off and got up from the bed.

"There's a car waiting for you outside the main gate. I need you to pack up quickly and get in. The driver will take you to the place where you'll lay low until we figure out our next move. I'm sending Al and Liz into hiding as well, and I will be guarding Intelligence from a third location."

"Yes, sir," they both replied, hurrying to gather medical supplies.

When they finished, they rushed out into the cruel wind. When they reached the car, the driver glanced at them before he started the engine and drove away. Emry realized that he was not a soldier, but an ordinary man.

"Emry, look," Damon said, pointing out the window.

Tiny, white flakes were falling from the sky. Despite everything they'd been through, it was beautiful.

After some time, they arrived at a mini cabin. The driver helped them bring their things to the door, despite the two assuring that they'd be fine.

"You're only kids." The driver shook his head, locking eyes with Damon. "Only kids in this war. It's such a shame. You could have been my son."

The young soldier put a hand on his shoulder, grinning. "We're Slayers, sir. We're the deadliest kids you'll ever meet."

"You're right," the man grumbled. He cast a look behind him at the dark night and the wind that was waiting for him. "I should head back before it gets too dangerous. There's supposed to be a blizzard coming."

Damon nodded. "Would you like to take some food and water with you?"

"No, thank you." The man shook his head, but took Damon's hands in his. "You youngsters stay safe. I'll pray for you."

"You too," Emry answered quietly from inside, and he left.

Damon watched until the man had driven out of sight before closing the door. It was dark, quiet, and they were all alone. He lit a match and pressed it to the lantern. "I should go collect some twigs to make a fire."

"I'll go." She moved past him, but he grabbed her hand.

"I'll come with you."

She stared up at him, at his determined ocher eyes. "Fine, let's do this together."

Chapter 39

Inside and Out

Damon

Damon cursed as they both stumbled back into the cabin, clusters of snowflakes clinging to their hair and clothes. The storm outside had grown wilder, and they barely made it back, but at least their trunk was stocked with wood for now.

Emry sighed as she knelt by the fireplace. "I wonder what's up with the kids now."

"It's weird not being with them, huh?"

"This man was right. You and I? We're kids too. Have you ever thought about how it all is so messed up? What's the point of all this? Of life?"

He took a few steps towards her and held her face, turning hers up to his. "I think about it, yes. But then it passes, because I want to keep on living. Because I see the good that there is in what we do."

"Yes," she mumbled, clutching his shirt. "I think, for the first time, I can see it. I can see it too, now. You help me do it."

"I can see you," he whispered, "for who you truly are. And I've never seen anything more beautiful."

"Damon—" She was breathless, and he used the opportunity to press his lips to hers.

He kissed her slowly, his lips exploring every seam of hers. His hand went to her lower back, and he let his palm press her body into his. She moaned at the contact, standing on her tiptoes, and he had to conceal his groan as he deepened the kiss.

When Damon slid his palm under her shirt at her lower back, there was no mistaking the shiver that ran through her body. He frowned as he realized her shirt was soaking wet.

He pulled away, both of them breathing hard. "You're freezing," he rasped, "and our clothes are drenched. We should... you should go change. I'll make the fire."

Her cheeks were rosy when she raised her hand to caress his cheek. "I'm sorry for being like that. It's just that... I'm still trying to figure everything out."

He sighed and put his hand on hers. "I know."

Her stare was so penetrating that he felt lost. "Damon, I choose you."

"What?"

She lowered her hand. "I'm tired of giving up on myself, of forbidding myself to live. If everything turns to ash, so be it. I want you."

His pulse jumped at the realization. She was choosing him, a relationship with him, and the risks that followed.

She painstakingly reached for his combat shirt. She undid the first button, her green eyes trained on his, then her pale fingers slid to the second. Desire coursed through his veins as her fingers went for the third. A gentle smile played on her lips as she exposed yet another layer to unwrap.

Damon swiftly pulled them both over his head, unable to withstand another second of measured undressing. Now there was nothing between her cold fingers and his skin. They caressed his skin slowly, from top to bottom. Her soft touch against the hard panels of his chest was painful. He was aching, ready. When she looked up to meet his eyes again, he saw the same feelings reflected in her eyes.

"Damon."

"I know, I know." He took a breath, fighting the urge to grab her. "Just let me make a fire real quick. I don't want you to get sick."

He rushed to the fireplace and knelt to light the fire. As he struck the first match, Damon felt a wet cloth land on his head, and then another.

He knew what it was before he removed it. It smelled like her. He turned around, a small snicker on his lips, but it died as he saw her standing there by the bed, wearing only her black undergarments.

The fact that she was standing scantily clad in front of him was all that he could focus on. Her body was covered in cuts and bruises, but she was the most beautiful thing he'd ever laid eyes on. It was more than lust, the feeling rising inside of him. It was holy. It was reverence.

He lit the fire, but kept his gaze fixed on her. The flames heated his already burning skin. He approached her until he was just a breath away. The flames were casting shadows on both of them, lighting the darkness. He touched her cheek. "You are so beautiful."

At that moment, there was nothing in the world but him and her. Emry looked at him with that determination that never failed to make his heart beat faster. The sound of their panting filled the silence, and they hadn't even touched each other yet.

She took the step that separated, pushing her body against him, and her arm snaked around his nape, keeping him close. The feel of her body sent fireworks through his mind, igniting everything. Reminding himself to be careful of her injuries, Damon's fingers caressed the back of her thighs. Turning his back to the bed, he pulled them into a soft fall onto the bed. Emry was on top of him, her fingers roaming his chest. His lips left hers and moved to her neck, collarbone, and chest, his tongue following their wake. She panted and flipped them. Her fingers danced in his hair. She was pulling him close, lips fused to his, sinking deeper into the mattress.

Damon pulled away to look at her. She was sprawled on the bed, her hair scattered around her face on the pillow. Emry was smiling at him, happy, so beautiful.

"Emry," he managed through labored breaths.

"Hmm?" she asked. Her face lightened up when she smiled.

"I need to know—"

"I'm sure. Are *you* sure?" she taunted, her delicate fingers caressing his face.

"There's nothing sexier than hearing you say that. I'm surer than I've ever been. It's just…" He looked at her, feeling dumbfounded. "I want to always see you like this."

"Like what?"

"Happy."

Her expression softened, and she reached for him. "Come here."

Damon leaned in, kissing her softly, and she wrapped her legs around him, tightening his torso to hers. She let out a moan, her chest heaving against his. His breath hitched as he felt her hand making its way to his belt.

Emry

It felt *right*.

She could see the shadows dancing around them in the dark, flickering at their bodies, melding together. Their uniforms were cast aside on the floor.

She trembled as Damon laid soft kisses on her body—her cheeks, her lips, her neck, her chest, her arms… then, finally, his hands slid to her bra, easily undoing the clasp. He was leaning on his forearms above her, looking into her eyes before he cast the fabric aside.

Emry bit her lip, resisting the urge to cover herself with her hands as he looked at her. The air between them, everything in that moment, felt sacred. She had no reason to hide. She could feel the blush across her cheeks, and he looked into her eyes as he traced that heat with his finger—moving down to her neck, then to her chest—making her breaths quicker and sharper.

Not tearing her eyes from his, she pushed down her underwear and tossed them away. Damon's eyes roamed down just once before coming back up. They were dark with lust, but full of frustration; frustration she knew derived from his feelings for her.

"You're beautiful, every single part of you, inside and out," he whispered.

He was the beautiful one; kind, generous, and devoted. But he was looking at her so reverently that she *felt* beautiful.

Emry stood on her tippy-toes, letting her lips meet his, as she fused their bodies together again. Damon groaned loudly; the sound was music to her ears. He tried to remove his trousers, and she helped by nudging them down his legs, earning another groan from him. His hands stroked up and down her thighs. The tension was almost unbearable.

"Damon, please." She tugged at his hair.

"Please what?"

She could feel his smile against her skin. The desire was rapidly building inside of her. She wanted him, *needed* him, and he knew it. His hands went up, caressing her hips, her waist, her breasts—and then he grabbed her arms and clasped her fingers to the carved wooden plank above the pillows.

"I *know*, Emry. Hold on to the headboard."

The look in his eyes didn't give her a choice. Curious and excited, she tightened her grip, feeling vulnerable. He gave her a brief kiss on the lips, then down to her neck, finally finding the soft skin of her breasts.

"*Ah*," she gasped, arching her body forwards, grasping the headboard as he was taking his time. What she needed from him was too much. *It* was too much. *"Damon."*

His lips went down to her stomach, trailing kisses down, down, then his hands gently spread her thighs, and he laid a feather-soft kiss on her center.

"Damon!"

He laughed, his voice husky. He looked up at her, his eyes dark, lustful. "Feels good?"

"Yes!"

"Tastes good, too," he murmured, diving in. Every move of his mouth, every glide his tongue made, every little groan pushed her closer and closer to the edge.

"Damon, I—" Emry gasped breathlessly, but then she screamed, pleasure overtaking her completely with a white blaze. He continued as she came undone, eventually slowing down to a stop. She was breathing hard, her head spinning. She felt like she was floating on air until she opened her eyes and saw him watching her.

And again, the need for him was back. She slowly rose, leaning in until she could grab his shoulders and drag him back over her, relishing the feel of his body pressed against hers.

"You're okay?" he murmured to her cheek.

"Yes," she breathed, letting her fingers stroke the bulge between his legs. He growled, and she laughed. "But I still want you." She raised her head to kiss him hard, before nudging him away, smiling at him. "I love you, Damon."

He smiled at her, so beautiful it hurt. Then, to her bewilderment, he got up from the bed. When she saw him search his bag and pull out a condom, she understood. In a matter of moments, he was ready, hovering over her, looking into her eyes. There was electricity between them, mixed with sharp desire and partnership. Emry brought her hand up to tug at his hair, just as he brought his to her lower back. She gasped at his touch, shifting her hips against his, wrapping her legs around him.

Slowly, Damon thrust into her. His eyes were focused on hers the entire time. The movement was slow, not enough. She desperately needed more.

"*Damon.*" She pulled at him impatiently, and he laughed, but she could feel his torture as he held himself back.

"You okay?"

She nodded, biting her lip in anticipation. Emry was *throbbing*, waiting. She could feel Damon's body straining as he slid out, then in again, torturously slow, stoking the fire inside of her. She drove her hips up against his, her legs pulling him closer. He groaned and let her lose control under him, urging him to move, and he obliged.

The sensation surprised her. They were so in rhythm together, and she couldn't do anything but be there with him. Her vision went blurry, and she was certain that the only intelligible thing that came out of her mouth was his name.

He hit a spot that rendered her stunned. When she blinked at him, she saw the satisfaction in his eyes. He was so wild, so glorious.

And he was hers.

When pleasure came, hot and unbridled, she let it.

Chapter 40

Dissociation

Emry

Emry only slept for a couple of hours after that. Damon's strong arm was wrapped around her body, his face buried in her hair. She could easily go back to sleep, but instead she gently removed his arm, stood up, and walked to the little window.

It was still dark outside, but she wasn't sure what time it was. The storm had ceased, leaving only the wind and the snow to adorn the world together.

She closed her eyes, shivering from the cold and the memories of hours before. The way Damon had touched her… the heat, the passion—some part of her wanted to wake him up and go again. She knew that she had to stay sharp and focused, but the images kept replaying in her head, and she could feel her body responding to them.

She didn't know if she was doing the right thing with Damon. If they got caught, it would be the end, and her family would have to find another source of income. The army was the only purpose she'd ever had, but deep down, she knew that she would take the chances, anyway. Damon was worth it, and for the first time, she actually felt peace. Maybe allowing herself to enjoy life and take risks was healing. It felt good. *She* felt good.

Emry felt a blanket being put on her shoulders from behind as he gently draped every bit of exposed skin. In a moment, she felt warmer.

Damon pressed a kiss to the top of her head, then lounged against the wall by the window so he could look at her. His hair was ruffled, and she blushed as she remembered why. Even if she *was* worried, one look at him could erase any doubts she had. He felt safe, like the home she'd never had.

"Did I wake you?" she asked quietly.

"No. How are you feeling?"

"Good... Exhausted." She shifted in place. "It was my first time, you know."

"Yeah, I figured." He tucked a lock of her hair behind her ear.

"It didn't hurt," she said after a pause.

"Wasn't supposed to. Not with someone who's taking care of you."

She cleared her throat, returning her gaze to the window, hating her blush. She just knew it would give away her insecurities.

"What are you thinking about?" Damon's voice was almost a whisper. His gaze was smoldering with curiosity.

Emry peered at him, fighting the urge to grumble. "I'm not—I just... Was it any good for you? You've done it before—"

He shook his head fondly. "Emry." His voice was gentle, yet decisive. "Before tonight, I've never done what we did. It was the first time it had *meaning.*"

She took a deep breath, affected by his words. "But did you... Damn it," she cursed and crossed her arms.

"What?" He smiled, amused.

"Did you... have fun?"

He cocked his head. "Couldn't you tell?"

"I don't know." She shrugged and looked away. She did know. Maybe the petty side of her needed reassurance.

He tore himself from the wall and slowly pulled her into his arms. "It meant everything. Did you?" His voice was teasing, but also curious. "Have fun?"

She leaned into him. "You know I did."

He laughed, stroking her hair. "Now I'm addicted to you in one more way."

It felt so reassuring, so soothing, to be engulfed in his embrace.

"How are we going to hide, Damon?"

"Hmm," he mused. "Maybe not by making out in front of Headley, even though it would be entertaining to see his reaction." He grinned.

"Do you think we can make it?"

"Absolutely." There was no doubt in his voice.

"Do you think Headley will send us on another mission soon?"

He ran his hands through his hair. "I hope not."

"It will be too much for the kids." She frowned and let out a sigh, but it died on her lips as she realized he was watching her.

The intensity of his gaze trapped Emry. She couldn't look away as she instinctively ran her fingers down his bare chest. Damon's hands slid up her thighs, and shivers ran through her in return. In one swift move, he bounced her up, and she wrapped her legs around his body.

Heat was blossoming in her core, pounding. Her hands were mapping out his back as he threw himself back on the bed with her on top. He had done that earlier. Did he do it because he didn't want her to be smacked by the mattress? He held her thighs to keep her in place as she sat up, and he leaned back against the headboard. Her legs were still around his body, her core painfully pulsing in reaction to the intimate touching. He caressed her legs and waist lazily as she panted and looked into his eyes. It wasn't enough. It could never be enough.

His fingers lowered to her waistband, and they dragged her underwear off as well. She was squirming, and from the dark, wild look in his eyes, she knew he felt it too.

Damon brought his upper body forwards abruptly, so their faces were only inches apart. She rested her cheek in the crook of his neck, shifting her hips against his, her arms wrapping around his broad back. Her eyes slammed shut and her nails dug into his upper back as he slowly pushed into her, and she instinctively pumped back into him. His hands caressed her thighs as they moved on her skin, up and down, with velvet touches. Her forehead fell to his shoulder as she moaned in pleasure, bouncing on top of him. When she pulled away to look at him, she caught him watching her with fascination. Her arms moved to stroke every inch of his abdomen, chest, and back as they moved, and gasps left her lips.

She heard him utter her name, and then his mouth swallowed her scream.

* * *

It was noon by the time Damon woke up. Emry remained twisted in the bedsheets, enjoying the fact that she could stay there and be lazy. She couldn't remember the last time she'd had that luxury. She couldn't remember the last time she'd felt... like this. Maybe never.

She turned when she heard Damon let out a quiet curse. She yawned and sat up to see what had frustrated him. Their supply of kindling was soaked. They had accidentally thrown their wet clothes at it, and now most of it was useless.

"I'm going out to collect some more," he said. He walked over and took her face in his hands, kissing her forehead.

"Do you want me to come?" Emry tried to blink the sleep away.

He grinned and shook his head. "Just rest for a change, will you?"

How was it possible that she wanted him again so soon? His mere presence was intoxicating. She wondered if that was what she was bound to think about every time he was near her again, forever.

His smile widened knowingly. "I'll be back soon," he assured her. His fingers dropped to the sides of her neck, massaging her.

"Okay, but don't do any stupid shit. Just collect some wood, and come back. Quickly."

Damon gave her a playful scowl. "There goes my plans to do some stupid shit."

He laughed as she smacked him.

Damon

Damon marched through the fresh snow, grinning from ear to ear.

Last night was the most erotic experience of his life.

Emry was the one. He was sure of it. He wouldn't tell her just yet—not when she'd just agreed to have some kind of relationship with him—but he knew it was true.

Maybe, if they were caught and thrown out of the army, he could convince her to move her family to Egma. It would be perfect. Damon knew that her parents weren't thriving in lost, empty Rows. He could take care of them. He could take care of everything.

He exhaled as a woeful thought crossed his mind. Emry would never let him do it. Not only that, but if he became the reason she was dishonorably discharged from the army, she may never forgive him. It wasn't easy for her to accept the risk of being in a relationship with him, and in a way, their connection felt solid, but also very fragile.

Thoughts swimming, he walked a little farther than he had intended. He stopped and bent down to collect some firewood, but then he saw it. A baby raccoon was lying against a tree trunk. A knife was stuck inside its body, and its blood was spread everywhere, dyeing the snow red.

Damon shook uncontrollably. He couldn't move. In his nightmares, a kid was sitting in a corner, just like that. Suddenly, he wasn't in the snow anymore. He was a crying child, shrinking into the corner, pain radiating in every bone of his body.

A taller youth was standing in front of him, face hidden, palms drenched in blood, knife in hand. Two bodies, a man and a woman, were strewn across the floor, covered in stab wounds. The sight was too painful. Damon knew that he was next. Then he heard a scream coming from the kitchen. The murderer turned towards the noise, and Damon cried, *"Please, stop!"*

As if just sensing Damon for the first time, the killer unexpectedly turned around, slowly facing him. The motion filled Damon with dread, but he couldn't do anything but watch his killer reveal themself.

Black hair, black eyes, sharp cheekbones, and tan skin. Then he smiled—a cruel, sinister leer—baring his teeth, and Damon screamed.

"Please…" Damon whimpered.

He fell to his knees, hitting the frigid ground. He was back to reality, back in the woods. Tears were streaming down his face, and he realized he was sobbing uncontrollably. The sorrow inside of him would never cease. He buried his face in the snow, muffling his cries. He couldn't bring himself to move.

In his first few years of elementary school in Egma, Damon would occasionally doze off, detached from reality. Those moments of dissociation were meant to protect him, but they were entirely beyond his control. He rarely had them now, and he made sure to never hear about what had happened to his family in order to keep it that way. Avoiding those reminders had been a constant effort. He'd made sure his consciousness was broken all along.

At last, after he raised his face and took a few deep breaths, easing his shaking frame. When he looked over, he saw that the raccoon was gone. His heart flipped. Damon's eyes frantically searched for the animal, but then the silhouette of a tall figure appeared before him. It was a man—a *demon*.

"Do you remember, little one?" the figure asked in a menacing tone. "Do you remember me? Do you remember what happened to your precious mommy and daddy?" The demon smiled. "Because I'm coming back for more."

Chapter 41

Hidden Memories

Emry

Where the hell is Damon? Emry had already sharpened their weapons, eaten, showered, and still, he hadn't returned.

Don't panic. Stay focused. She took a few steady breaths through her nose, then fastened her weapons to her belt. She went out into the snow, closed the door behind her, and leaned against it. She looked around, trying to see if he was coming from afar, but she saw nothing but pillars of white.

Emry walked to the woods, heart beating fast, trying to be alert and careful between the brown trunks, until she heard quiet, recurring breaths. She passed the tree, knife out, but stopped in her tracks when she saw a pool of blood pigmenting the snow.

Before she had any chance to gather her thoughts, she saw him. Right in front of her, Damon was sitting frozen to the forest ground. His bright eyes were wide open, shocked. His hair was wild, clumped with chunks of ice.

She called his name, and he flinched. He glanced at her, but his eyes still held the same terrified expression. "What happened?"

Emry hurried over and knelt next to him. She frantically searched his body for injuries. He closed his eyes, comforted by her touch. "Emry."

Her name on his lips felt like a blessing.

"What's wrong?" She fought the urge to shake him. "Tell me!"

He shook his head, and she realized with frustration that the loud noise was disturbing him.

"What are you doing here?" he asked, brow furrowed. He opened his eyes again, and they were distant. "We agreed you'd stay at the cabin."

"We also agreed you'd come back," she barked.

He stared into the distance. "I'm sorry."

"No, no." She tried to be gentler. "Are you okay?"

"No."

"Let's go back, okay? Can you do that for me?"

He looked at her again, and the wretched look on his face scared her. He let her help him to his feet, and they slowly started to make their way back. She was clutching his arm, making sure to mirror his steps.

Her fear was overshadowed by absolute determination. Whatever it was that struck him, they would overcome it together. It had to be something serious. They were in the middle of nowhere, but she didn't sense any demons around.

"Emry," he whispered. "I don't know if I can fix this."

"Let's get back. I'll make some tea, and we'll talk." She stopped and rotated him to face her. Her fingers caressed his face, and he silently leaned into her touch. "I'll make you warm."

Damon

When they finally made it to the cabin and were locked safely inside, he grew more still. Emry insisted he sit on one of the chairs while she whirled about. She came back holding the tea, bread, and canned ham. "Eat. Drink." She slumped in the chair next to him.

The food was tasteless in his mouth, but Damon felt some energy return to him as soon as it hit his stomach. He devoured the food, then drank the tea, relishing the heat that spread through his chest. It was very hot, but he didn't care.

Only on his second sip did he realize that Emry was watching him. Her eyes didn't move when he turned to look at her. Worry had long left her face, and instead, she looked like she was preparing herself for a battle. After all, she was his beautiful survivor.

"Are you feeling better?"

"Yes," he tried to say. Instead, the scolding-hot drink burned his throat.

Emry's hand went to his back. She slowly rubbed him, smoothing down his shirt. "What's going on?"

He didn't know if he could talk, but he had to try for her. "I'm... I'm sorry I didn't come back. I would have, but—"

"It's fine."

He closed his eyes to try to hide the tears forming in their corners. Her cold hands snuck into his, and she squeezed before she pulled him up. "Open your eyes and look at me."

He did. She stood before him, her eyes soft but decisive. "I'm not going to let anything happen to you," she declared.

Her presence, even her scent, was comforting to him. Damon's breathing stabilized as he continued to look at her, but the tears came out again.

She pulled him in close, letting him sob into her disheveled hair. His arms were tight around her, but she didn't seem to mind.

"Emry."

"Right here with you." Her voice was steady and strong.

Her smell washed over him and once again he felt himself relax. "I can't do it," he muttered. "I can't talk about it."

"Does it have something to do with your nightmares?"

"Yes."

She glanced down for a moment. "I'll take care of you, but I need you to talk to me."

"I can't." The panic churned inside of him.

"Damon, do you trust me?"

He stroked her hair, focusing on the green of her eyes. "Yes."

"Okay." She led him in front of the fireplace, found some usable broken twigs, and made a fire. Fondling his arm from the seat next to him, she said,

"We have all the time in the world, but we're doing this. Tell me what happened in the snow."

With firm hesitation, he told her how he found the dead raccoon. "Then…" He rubbed his nape. "I don't know how, but I lost it. I felt like I was in a vision. The same…" He stopped.

"Go on." She nudged his arm. Her face was only inches from his.

Damon regained control. "The same vision from my nightmares."

Emry bit her lip. She knew how he felt about his nightmares. He never talked about them, he couldn't. It always felt like it was going to trigger his memories that he'd struggled so long to hide.

"Tell me about the visions," she demanded. "What happens in them? What do you see?"

"I can't. It… It brings me back."

"I need you to," she whispered. Her face twisted, and he realized that it was painful for her to see him like this. "Please, Damon."

It was so ridiculous that he almost laughed. He was inflicting pain on her, when all he had ever wanted was to take it away from her. The only thing he could do to make up for his weakness was to cooperate with her, even if it was going to send him to Hell itself. It was going to be his undoing, but he finally understood that it was bound to happen. He'd always known there was going to be something that would rip him apart, force him to face his fears, and it seemed that the time had come.

Damon looked into her eyes, accepting his fate. "In my nightmares, I usually see a kid," he said quietly. "I don't see his face, but he's awfully familiar. He's crying, sitting against a wall. In front of him there's… someone with a knife. Usually… he stabs him to death."

The memories were burning him. He could vividly see the child, the knife, and the ruthless figure repeatedly slashing him, again, and again, and ag—

Emry took his hand before the scream escaped his mouth. With labored breathing, Damon tried to focus on her to calm down.

"Shhh. Breathe."

He felt terrorized, but he continued. "There's always blood everywhere. On the walls, the floor, on that kid. Sometimes it's..." He could feel the bile rise in his throat. "Emry, I can't do this. I'm going to be sick."

"Then throw up." She ran her hand over his back. "You're doing great. It's okay."

He took a few deep breaths through his nose. "Sometimes the blood is choking him..." He felt dizzy. "It's down his throat."

She nodded.

He had to take a few moments. He was not going to throw up. He wasn't.

But in the end, the memory of the sickeningly warm liquid sliding down his throat got the best of him, and he had to run to the toilet. He expected to see blood spew from his mouth. Damon's eyes blurred with tears and he could only see his yellow bile.

Then she was next to him, brushing back his short strands of black hair with her fingers. She helped him clean his mouth and supported him on the way back to the fireplace.

He sighed. "Today, I saw the same vision. The child was there, but there were also two bodies next to him, a man and a woman. There was also an older kid. He was the one holding the knife. Someone screamed, and then... he *smiled* at me. After that, the flashback was gone, but I couldn't find the dead raccoon."

"Was that all?" she asked, her voice soft.

He shook his head. "Someone—a *demon* appeared before me, after the vision ended. I couldn't see his face. He asked if I remembered what he did to me, because—" He swallowed. "Because he's coming back."

"Who was he?"

"I don't know."

"Was he familiar?"

"I don't remember him, but he seemed to know me."

She stayed quiet, and he could see from the way she frowned that she was deep in thought.

"I'm sorry," he said softly.

Emry turned to look at Damon, giving him a small smile. "For what? You did so well." She caressed his cheeks, his forehead, his lips. "I am so proud of you."

His heart had never felt so broken, but so whole before. She was here to tear him to pieces, but only so she could build him up again. "I'm sorry."

She shook her head. "Do you know who the people in your visions are?"

"No, none of them."

"It's okay. We're done, Damon. That's it."

He couldn't believe that he'd actually told her everything and survived to keep looking at her. She deserved so much better than this. "Emry, I promise I'll return to myself. I didn't see that coming, but I will get over it. Soon," he said.

"I know." She grinned, and his heart fluttered at the certainty in her eyes and her confidence in him. "You're the big, scary Slayer, after all."

He laughed softly, but then remembered the demon's words again. "I have a bad feeling," he told her quietly. "We're going into war, just like years ago. Perhaps even worse."

"Maybe. But war will have to wait. I think we should go see your grandma first."

Chapter 42

Dam Va' eish V' timrot Ashan

Headley

Headley's nerves were shot. He didn't know how much longer he could stand waiting.

His body ached, sore from the fight at the shore. His right leg was scarred from the ankle up. But then again, all of his body was scarred. Each mark told a different story from a different time in his life. He was proud of all of them, as a warrior should be.

For the last few days, he'd been staying with the Intelligence soldiers in a little safe house owned by the army. Those soldiers weren't Slayers, that was for sure. Two of them were insecure and didn't speak much. Whenever he approached them, they seemed intimidated.

The third one was different. When he approached her, she answered him head-on. She was impatient, but brilliant. He suspected she was the friend Primrose had told him about at the hospital.

One night, he was awoken by one of the other two running into his room, calling for him to go to the meeting room. "We've finished! Jenna stayed up all night and figured out the last letter."

Headley hurried through the halls. When he opened the door, he found the curly-haired soldier hunched over the letters, scribbling in a notebook.

"You took your time." She didn't even look up.

His nostrils flared. Definitely Primrose's friend.

"You better not speak to me like that if you don't want to get punished," he growled. "I was sleeping." He pulled out a chair and sat next to her. "Is it done?"

"Yes." She straightened up and stretched, looking down at her work. "We still need to go through it, but I managed to analyze it a tad."

"And what do you think?"

She flipped through the red book. "The good news is, I don't think there's a reason to stay here."

He was glad to hear it, but his fists clenched. "And the bad?"

Jenna locked eyes with Headley. "We don't have much time before trouble comes."

He let her words sink in. "Can you guide me through the letters?"

She nodded, flipping the pages until she made it to the first page. Her fingers touched the black ink. How she could understand those oddly shaped letters was beyond him. "The first sentence was not encrypted, sir."

"Read it to me," he ordered.

"*Dam va'eish v'timrot ashan.*"

He closed his eyes, taking in the foreign language. It did not sound good, and he had a bad feeling.

"What does it mean?"

Jenna abruptly closed the book, gripping it in her hand. "Blood, fire, and pillars of smoke."

Acknowledgments

I would like to thank MoonQuill for working with me on this novel. This has been one hell of a journey, and I was honored to do it with you guys. A special thanks to Terri and Madison for the incredible editing process.

I would also like to thank my beloved ones at home, who believed in me accomplishing my goals, becoming a psychologist and an author. Your consistent support and love are not taken for granted; I cherish each one of you. I couldn't have had a better team to go to war with.

A special thanks to Betty's cat, Nils. Thanks for purring on my lap whenever you felt like I needed it.

Last but not least, I would like to thank you—the reader! It means the world to me, to know someone could derive comfort, reading something I wrote. Thank you for giving me the opportunity to share a bit of fantasy with you.

About the Author

a

Gili Levy is the author of *To Slay a Demon*, a book she began writing while still a psychology student. Now psychologist, Gili never stops dreaming and writing, and wishes to combine fiction and mental health together.

Thank you for reading a MoonQuill original novel. More exciting stories can be found on our website, www.moonquill.com.

We would greatly appreciate it if you would take a moment to leave a review. Every review greatly helps the author and supports their ability to continue writing fantastic books for everyone to enjoy!

Additionally, we're looking for dedicated ARC reviewers and experienced readers to join our beta reader team. To learn more, drop us an email at info@moonquill.com or stop by our Discord.